Wall Of Doom

The Princess Maura Tales
Saga of the de Magela Family

Book One

Abigail Keam

Worker Bee Press

Worker Bee Press
P.O. Box 485
Nicholasville, KY 40340

Acknowledgements

Thanks to my editors,
Patti DeYoung and Layla Darnell

Artwork by Karin Claesson
www.karinclaessonart.com

Special thanks to
Peter Keam, Sarah Moore, Deborah Struve,
Phil Criswell, and Betsy Meredith

Book Jacket by Peter Keam
Author's photograph by Peter Keam

Also by Author

The Josiah Reynolds Mystery Series
Death By A HoneyBee I
Death By Drowning II
Death By Bridle III
Death By Bourbon IV
Death By Lotto V
Death By Chocolate VI
Death By Haunting VII
Death By Derby VIII
Death By Design IX
Death By Malice X

The Princess Maura Epic Fantasy Tales
Wall Of Doom I
Wall Of Peril II
Wall Of Glory III
Wall Of Conquest IV
Wall Of Victory V

Last Chance For Love Series
Last Chance Motel I
Gasping For Air II
The Siren's Call III
Hard Landing IV
The Mermaid's Carol V

Audio Books
Last Chance Motel I
Gasping For Air II

To my sixth-grade teacher, Mrs. Victor,
who loved a ripping good story.

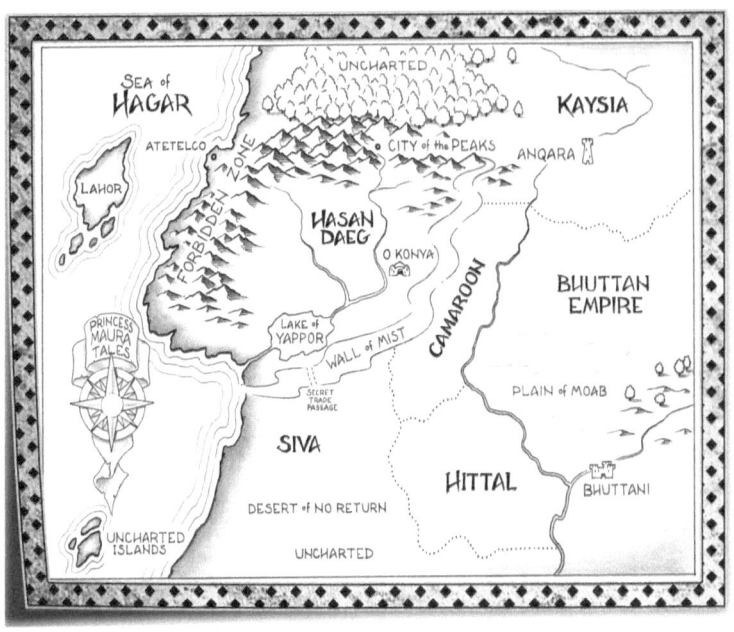

The Princess Maura Series Glossary

Abisola de Magela (character) – ninth queen of Hasan Daeg and mother of Princess Maura

Aga (character) – term for king of the Bhuttanians

Alexanee (character) – top Bhuttanian general, illegitimate older brother of Dorak

Anqara (place) – ancient cultural and banking city located in country of Kaysia

Atetelco (place) – former capital of the Dinii located in the Forbidden Zone

Beca (character) – Princess Maura's pony

Benzar (character) – gray male hawk from secret society that protects Maura

Bes Amon Ptah (character) – Moab prince hiding under the name of Timon Ben Ibin Moab

Bhutta (character) – female deity of Bhuttanians, wife of Bhuttu

Bhuttan (place) – country ruled by Zoar and his son, Dorak

Bhuttani (place) – capital of Bhuttan

Bhuttanians (characters) – nomadic people who rose to world domination under the leadership of Zoar

Bhuttu (character) – male deity of Bhuttanians whose worship calls for the sacrifice of one's life

Bilboa (characters) – race of people with red eyes who see in the dark

Bird People (characters) – the Dinii who were Overlords of Kaseri

Black Cacodemon (character) – evil wizard of Bhuttu

Blue and gold – royal colors of the Hasan Daegians

Blue Queen (character) – nickname for Maura

Boaeps – small domesticated hopping animals

Borax (both plural and singular) – bison-like animals with sharp blades down their spines

Camaroon (place) – borders Hasan Daeg, absorbed by Bhuttanian Empire

Cappet (character) – petty thief, controls eastern part of Bhuttani

Caromate plant – provides hypnotic mist when leaves are pressed

Chaun Maaun (character) – prince of the Dinii and son of the Dinii Empress Gitar

City of the Peaks (place) – city on top of highest peak in Hasan Daeg where the Dinii live

Colla – nuts from the colla tree, brewed for teas

de Magela (characters) – name of ruling family in Hasan Daeg

Dini (character) – singular of Dinii

Dinii (characters) – ancient rulers of Kaseri, formerly called Overlords, human-like beings covered with feathers who fly

Divigi (character) – spiritual leader of the Dinii and uncle to Empress Gitar

Dorak (character) – son of Zoar, aga of the Bhuttanians

Duchy of Enos (place) – estate passed down through the family of Iasos, husband of Queen Abisola

Duke Enos (character) – father of Iasos

Dyanna (character) – princess born to Maura and Dorak

Everlynd (character) – duchess of Enos and sister of Prince Consort Iasos

Forbidden Zone (place) – former home of the Dinii, cursed by both the Dinii and Hasan Daegians

Gitar (character) – empress of the Dinii and Hasan Daegians

Gootee – duck-like animal

Great Death – name given to the practice of Hasan Daegian queens willing themselves to die

Great Mother – title of respect for older women or those in power, including queens of Hasan Daeg

Hasan Daeg (place) – peaceful agricultural country ruled by the Dinii and the de Magela family

Hasan Daegian betrothal (custom) – woman asks man permission to court by kissing man's hand; if man wishes to engage, he returns the kiss; woman gives man flowers

Hasan Daegians (characters) – peaceful agricultural people who were former slaves of the Dinii

Hetmaan (character) – Bhuttanian term for Spymaster KiKu

Hittal (place) – country conquered by Zoar, land of KiKu the Hetmaan

House of Magi (place) – ancient residence of scholars in Anqara

Iasos (character) – consort of Queen Abisola and father of Princess Maura

Iegani (character) – uncle to Empress Gitar, spiritual advisor to the Dinii, and founder of secret society that protects Princess Maura

Jezra (character) – first wife to Dorak, mother of his first child

Jon (character) – minister to Governor Petenptope of the northern Hasan Daegian state of Kinton

Kaseri (place) – name of the planet

Kaysia (place) – land in which Anqara was located

KiKu (character) – Zoar's Hetmaan, former prince of Hittal who becomes a double spy

KiKusan (character) – daughter of Kiku and concubine of Zoar

Kimtimee (character) – Queen Abisola's highest-ranking general

Kinton (place) – northern region of Hasan Daeg

Kittum (place) – country to the east of Hasan Daeg which has a treaty with Bhuttan

Knoxel (character) – magician who was mentor to Zedek

Land of the Setting Sun (place) – romantic name given to Hasan Daeg by the Bhuttanians

Lahor (place) – former island home of the Lahorians

Lahorians (characters) – originally from Lahor and ancient enemies of the Dinii

Mamora (character) – first wife of Zoar and sister of KiKu

Maura (character) – tenth ruler of Hasan Daeg, daughter of Queen Abisola and Consort Iasos

Meagan of Skujpor (character) – healer to the royal house of de Magela and member of the House of Magi

Mehmet (character) – high priestess of the House of Magi

Mekonia (character) – nature goddess of the Hasan Daegians

MeNe (character) – Yesemek's first lieutenant

Mikkotto (character) – Hasan Daegian baroness who becomes a traitor and joins with Zoar

Mingo tree – tree with large, flat limbs that is treasured for its endurance, beauty, and strength

Mother Bogazkoy/Royal Bogazkoy – intelligent, self-aware plants that have a special relationship with Hasan Daegian rulers

Nani (character) – adopted granddaughter of Lady Sari

Noabini (character) – Mehmet's assistant who becomes high priestess of the House of Magi

O Konya (place) – capital of Hasan Daeg

Onxor (character) – priest of Bhuttu

Petenptope (character) – governor of the northern Hasan Daegian province of Kinton

Plain of Moab (place) – traditional home of nomadic people

Prosperot (character) – one of two top Bhuttanian generals, along with Alexanee

Qatou (place) – Hasan Daegian city

Rakel (character) – Lahorian woman who helps Princess Maura

Red – royal color of the Bhuttanians

Renna (character) – daughter of Riza

Riza (character) – scion from oldest noble family in Hasan Daeg

Rooshars – rare marsh flower

Rosalind (character) – first queen of Hasan Daeg

Royal Bogazkoy – plant offspring of the Mother Bogazkoy

Rubank (character) – consul to Queen Abisola and then to Queen Maura

Sari (character) – Hasan Daegian nurse to Queen Maura/Queen Abisola and grandmother of Mikkotto and Nani

Shaybar – Bhuttanian drink of boiled water or milk mixed with an equal portion of borax blood

Sinjo – rare berry made into wine that stimulates feelings of pleasure

Siva (place) – desert country south of Hasan Daeg

Sivans (characters) – merchant desert people

Sumsumitoyo (character) – family name of Mikkotto and Sari

Tarsus (character) – gray male hawk Dini who belongs to secret society that protects Maura

Tnpothar (character) – Zoar's father

Toppo (character) – red female hawk Dini, belongs to the secret society that protects Maura

Tsnsuni – ritualistic national prayer for the Hasan Daegian queen

Uultepes – mythical animals that are the symbol of Hasan Daegian royalty

Water Orbs – Lahorian mechanical devices constructed for transportation

Wise Ones (character) – title for the Lahorians

Yagomba tree – largest hardwood tree on Kaseri, has mystical powers

Yappor (place) – sacred lake of the Hasan Daegians and thought to be home of their goddess, Mekonia; home to the Lahorians

Yesemek (character) – commander-in-chief of the Dinii and wife to Iegani

Yeti (character) – red female hawk Dini, belongs to secret society that protects Maura

Yubuto (character) – sacrificed son of Mikkotto

Zedek (character) – Black Cacodemon's given name

Zoar (character) – aga (king) of the Bhuttanians

Wall Of Doom

Prologue

Queen Abisola sat numbly by the fire.

The shadow of the flames danced on Abisola's troubled face, eerily reflecting in her worried eyes. She was dressed in a foot soldier's battle attire, her long dark hair braided and tucked down the back of her tunic. The queen wore no insignias of any kind to note her rank. She waited deep in thought and wondered how her life could have come to such a pass. She waited and waited, this being the fourth day and night of waiting.

Iasos, her consort, gently rocked the baby he held, cooing if the child stirred. This was the child he had sired with his queen—Princess Maura. As Iasos gazed at his child, he did not wonder at the events he knew were to come, but his luck of having been chosen the Royal Consort. It was more than luck. The stars had decreed it to be his fate, for he truly loved his lady and had since the day he first met her.

Iasos had been sent by his father, Duke Enos, to further his education at the university in O Konya, the royal city. As he was of noble blood and his older sister was soon to inherit the Duchy of Enos, the boy was entitled to live at court during his stay in the city.

Duke Enos wanted his only son to make a grand impression at the royal court. Knowing the queen was fond of beautiful clothes, he gave Iasos shimmering cloth made by the nimble hands of the desert men from Siva as a gift to the monarch.

A nervous Iasos presented bolts of turquoise and iridescent white with river pearls for fringe. They had cost his father a year's profit from the duchy, so rare were they.

"These are from my father, Duke Enos," boasted young Iasos, waving his hand over the expensive bolts, "but this is from me." The handsome boy took a slim volume from his breast pocket.

The queen's personal guards quickly surrounded him.

"Oh, dear," he piped as he handed Rubank, the Royal Consul, his book.

After inspecting the volume, the Royal Consul placed it on a gold platter and handed it to the amused but wary Queen Abisola.

"I composed these poems myself in honor of our

most beautiful and illustrious queen."

"You honor me," responded Queen Abisola. "I will certainly entertain your poems before I retire tonight. I hope I do them justice."

"You are most kind, Your Majesty," answered Iasos, blushing. He bowed very low, and the royal consul waved him back into the court audience.

Queen Abisola spent the rest of the afternoon meeting with impatient ambassadors, fawning nobility, wealthy merchants seeking charters, anxious artists needing a patron, and weary messengers from the far-off corners of her vast country. As she listened to the speeches and announcements drone on, she occasionally glanced at Iasos who stared sheepishly up at her. Something about him pleased her very much.

She gestured to Rubank. "I want Duke Enos and his family investigated. Find out everything there is to know, but do it discreetly."

Rubank nodded in reply, such was the custom as he could not speak. His tongue had been cut out voluntarily when he became consul to the queen.

The queen stood and left the throne room without glancing back, but she was smiling. She was still smiling when she entered her private quarters. Handing her crown, jewelry, and official robes to her maids, she quickly stripped and lay down on a table for her massage.

A woman in her late autumn years entered the room with a basket of herbs and oils. After selecting perfumed oil, she heated it by rubbing it between her hands and began massaging Abisola's shoulders. "You seem pleased tonight, Your Majesty. The cats seem almost at rest."

The masseuse was referring to the two tattooed jungle cats facing each other on either side of the queen's back, starting at her shoulders and extending down the back to the buttocks. They looked as though they were springing in mid-flight with their extended paws crisscrossing each other. Inside the figures of the cats were ancient symbols and words.

The cats, called uultepes, were the personal mascots of the Hasan Daegian royalty. However, by modern times, the majestic cats had been hunted to extinction. Many believed the cats existed in myth only, but the images of two springing uultepes were tattooed on every Hasan Daegian queen or king as dictated by tradition, the meaning of which no one could fathom any longer.

Abisola murmured, "Sari, do you believe in love at first sight?"

"No, Great Mother, can't say that I do."

"Then do you believe in lust at first sight?"

"Aye, that I can attest to. I fell under the spell of a

fat cook with a nightmare of a wife and three grubby babes. But, oh, how that man could cook and make love after stuffing me with roasted eggs in a spinach base and hackleberry wine. No man has fed me so well since." Sari paused massaging, remembering.

"What happened to him?"

Sari poured more oil into her hands and stood thoughtfully. "His wife found out about us and kept whacking him on the head, so he told me I had to go."

"Hmm, by the Goddess, that feels good. Lower. Are you talking about Grebbe, the cook who died about forty years ago? He was found face down in a yoko root pudding."

"The very one."

"Sari, you didn't kill him?" gasped the queen, hiding her mirth.

"It was his heart. All that weight."

Abisola patted Sari's arm. "I'm just teasing, Sari."

"Oh."

"You're right. He was a wonderful cook. Too bad he died. Hmm, that feels wonderful," murmured Abisola, drifting off. "Sari, you are such a liar. What would a relative of mine be doing with a mere cook?" she mumbled sleepily.

"Your Majesty, has someone caught your eye?"

Queen Abisola didn't respond, for she was fast

asleep.

Sari smiled to herself. "I will answer you now that you cannot hear me. He loved me truly even though I was royalty. Such is a rare commodity in life."

IT WAS ANOTHER three weeks before Abisola sent for Iasos. In her small private audience chamber, she told Iasos that she desired him and asked permission to court him if he so wished.

Iasos sighed with relief, for now he knew why he was being watched all the time. He stammered, "Ah, yes."

Abisola reached over and kissed his hand.

Iasos returned the hand kiss.

The queen handed him a flower, and the courtship officially began. He was a lad of twenty, and she had been the ruling monarch for over three hundred years.

THAT HAD BEEN three years ago. Now, Iasos looked down at his child. She was the color of a dark blue sea from the top of her royal crown to the bottom of her chubby royal heels. A dark indigo baby! She even cried blue tears. All royal Hasan Daegian babies were born blue and lightened to a bluish-white cast as they grew older.

As old as Abisola was, she still retained a bluish cast

to her nails, the outlines of her eyes, and her sex. Their blue blood was a sign of the royal family's predestination to rule Hasan Daeg.

Iasos nuzzled the baby's cheek. The tension of waiting was beginning to strain his nerves. He was alone with his queen, having dismissed the servants. The guards were positioned down the mountain and ordered not to intrude no matter what they heard until the queen descended. The royal couple realized if anything went wrong, there would be no one to help them.

"Do you think she will come tonight?" asked Iasos impatiently.

There was no reply from his downcast wife.

"Abisola," he insisted.

Abisola jerked her head up. "Shh, listen!" She jumped up and strained to hear sounds in the night.

Iasos strained too, turning his head. There was a faint whooshing sound coming from the west. He dreaded the moment that would soon be at hand.

"She comes!" cried Abisola, jumping in front of Iasos and her child.

Their tent quivered in the loud and fearsome wake. Sticks and twigs, as well as their food and gear, scattered about the ground. A great cloud of dust flooded the air, making it hard for the royal couple to see.

A sharp cry pierced the sky. It was the cry of the

great eagle as she snares her prey.

Both mother and father of the babe stood rooted, seemingly unable to move.

"Queen Abisola and Consort Iasos, come forth!" cried a loud and unnatural voice. A series of loud clicks followed.

Abisola looked questioningly at Iasos.

He nodded.

She tucked a dagger inside her tunic. Looking about, Abisola motioned for her husband to join her.

On a small knob not far from their camp, three figures stood silhouetted against the starry sky with their wings occasionally fluttering. Large these creatures were, just as the old stories stated.

Iasos shuddered to think he was going to hand his daughter over to the Dinii, Overlords of Kaseri, a race which had become a myth to his people.

The largest of the figures beckoned impatiently. "Hurry, there's not much time!"

Abisola and Iasos trudged silently to the hill, grateful that the baby had been given a mild sedative so she would not cry during the transfer. Abisola wished she had taken some of it herself.

Iasos could not feel his limbs move as he followed Abisola. He wondered how his wife could be so calm. Thinking he would explode at any moment, Iasos wished he had learned how to fight, but it was too late.

They stood before the mighty avian emissaries.

"Empress Gitar," addressed Abisola as she bowed.

Iasos bowed as low as he could with the baby.

"Queen Abisola and Consort Iasos," replied Empress Gitar, her wings expanding in acknowledgment and honor. "I wish we could meet on a more joyful occasion." She pointed to her two companions. "This is my Commander, Yesemek."

Yesemek pulled off her plumed leather helmet and made obeisance to Queen Abisola.

Queen Abisola nodded.

"And this is my uncle, Divigi Iegani," announced Empress Gitar.

Iegani stepped away from his empress and the commander, expanding his wings to their full breadth and bowed as low as his old bones would allow.

Queen Abisola heard him in her mind, "Salutations, Queen Abisola, Great Mother and Protector of Hasan Daeg."

The Hasan Daegian queen glanced at Iasos. She could tell from his wide-eyed expression that his mind had heard the Divigi too. She nodded to Iegani and turned her attention to Empress Gitar.

Gitar was an astounding presence. She stood over eight feet tall with a wingspan of fifteen. She was taller than her subjects by a head. Downy black feathers covered her body, which resembled a Hasan Daegian's. The feathers on her head were white with the tips dyed purple while the rest of her black feathers sparkled with diamond dust. Her nails were purple too, and this same shade was used on her lips as well. She wore no clothes except for a V-shaped crown studded with multi-colored gems.

Abisola could see six nipples protruding from the feathers on her torso. She realized that Gitar must have recently given birth herself. That's why the Overlords had kept them waiting four days.

Iasos must have realized this too. "Empress," he said, stepping forward with the baby.

Abisola pulled him back and turned angrily to Gitar. "How do we know what you say is true?" she hissed.

Gitar held out her hands in supplication, understanding Abisola's indecision and anxiety.

Iegani spoke aloud. "My good queen, our spies tell us the same as yours. The enemy to the east makes ready to move on us. Not today, not tomorrow, not next year even, but they will come as sure as it rains upon the land. They will come before our deaths, before yours. Unless we move now and plan for the future, we will never be able to defeat them. Their armies will become too powerful, their magic makers too knowledgeable. You know this to be true. You've been getting reports for years."

Abisola blinked in confusion.

Yesemek clicked a message with her teeth to her ruler.

Gitar nodded.

Dropping her weapons on the ground, Yesemek bowed and stepped closer to Queen Abisola. "Your Majesty, if this were not true, why have you been sending out parties searching for the Mother Bogazkoy? It is because the Royal Bogazkoy, her offspring, is dying. It will cease to exist within forty years. Even now, you grow old as it can no longer sustain the Hasan Daegian queens as it once did."

Rattled, Abisola asked, "You know about the Royal Bogazkoy?"

"We gave the offshoot of the Mother Bogazkoy to the first queen of Hasan Daeg to bind our pact," replied Iegani.

"Do you know where the Mother resides?" asked Abisola.

Iegani shook his head. "That secret was not handed down. I'm sorry."

It was true that the Royal Bogazkoy was slowly dying, almost imperceptibly, but dying still. Abisola's grandmother had first discovered the awful truth when she plucked out her first gray hair at the age of two hundred. No ruler of Hasan Daeg had ever aged until released from ruling and from the Bogazkoy's powers.

"What can my child do about an unnamed enemy or the death of the Royal Bogazkoy? She's only a babe. Not even weaned," cried the desperate queen.

Empress Gitar spoke to her. "She will not be a babe always. We plan to teach her the way of the warrior. Our military is more modern. Your countrymen have not fought a battle in over six hundred years. We need her to fight and motivate others to pick up the sword, or we shall all perish!

"Over two thousand years ago, our ancestors allowed your people to settle in our kingdom. We needed beings to manage the land so it would attract the game needed to sustain us. In return, you would recognize our sovereignty. We are creatures of the air, not of terra firma. We are warriors, not farmers. As we hunt at night, your people rarely see us. Most do not even believe we exist." Gitar sighed. She wanted to sit down as she was fatigued. She clicked at Yesemek who spoke for her.

Yesemek affirmed, "We fly outside these borders and have seen first hand the destruction of the enemy. Their leader moves at random with no other purpose but to plunder and burn, terrorizing the population into submission. He is gathering a confederation of states controlled by his men that has become the bulwark for an empire. He is unstoppable, a great military mind who rarely shows mercy."

"This enemy which plagues us, what does he want?" asked Iasos.

"He is from the country of Bhuttan, thousands of miles to the east. He is called the aga and his name is Zoar. His followers believe him to have a religious destiny to rule. They worship him as the incarnation of Bhuttu, their god of destruction.

"We have only the basic facts about him and his people's beliefs. We do know they believe in a myth in which Bhuttu destroys the present world and joins with his wife Bhutta, giving birth to a new Kaseri. Zoar's people believe that he is the physical reincarnation of Bhuttu."

"What has this Bhuttu to do with us?" inquired Iasos.

Iegani straightened his shoulders, tired from the weight of his ponderous wings. "The Hasan Daegian culture has all the qualities of the Bhuttanian's goddess, Bhutta, who is the Great Mother who rejuvenates and restores the world. Like Bhutta, your culture stresses rejuvenation and health with the plants you cultivate. You rarely eat meat. There is little death, except from extreme age. Your bloodlines are through the female. Hasan Daegian queens are long-lived. They have the power to restore and heal. They are referred to as Great Mother and Protector. Even though the Royal Bogazkoy is dying, it is still potent. You are the living proof as you have lived many years. You have a secret the aga will want one day . . . longevity. Zoar will seek to possess the tree."

Iegani looked at Princess Maura. "And he will come for her, because through the princess, Zoar will aim to control the Royal Bogazkoy. I have just enough years left to teach her the way of the mystic. She will need many mental disciplines to accomplish what she has to do."

Iasos shuddered and clutched his baby closer.

"What *is* she to do?" asked Queen Abisola, quaking with dread.

Iegani looked into the queen's tearful eyes. "She must destroy the aga."

"Oh, Great Divigi, tell me. Can you foresee whether she succeeds?"

"She may and then she may not."

Iasos asked, "If she succeeds, will she know peace then?"

The owl-like man shrugged. "Upheaval is what she will know." He paused. "I'm sorry, but I do not write the future. I merely interpret it."

Iasos sobbed.

Abisola, able to stand it no more, took the baby from Iasos, gently kissed the baby's forehead, and gave her to Yesemek.

Both Yesemek and Iegani placed the baby securely in a pouch wrapped around Empress Gitar's neck and torso.

Without saying adieu, the empress of the Dinii and her companions spread their mighty wings and sped upward into the night sky, each crying its particular totem cry—those of the eagle, the hawk, and the owl.

Queen Abisola fell into her consort's arms and collapsed upon the ground from the great rush of wind pushing them down. As Abisola cried, she knew it was the end of peace for Hasan Daeg.

1

Aga Zoar awoke with a terrible thirst.

He rolled over onto his current wife, who was nursing their latest child. She cursed him for his clumsiness as she pushed him away. Looking about for some wine or even water and finding none, he rolled back to his wife, took her free breast in his mouth and began to suckle.

His wife slapped his face and kicked him, ranting at Zoar in a language he had never bothered to learn. She made gestures usually not demonstrated by a highborn woman before leaving in a huff with the baby.

Zoar rubbed his stinging face, wondering what she said to him. He did not doubt for one moment that it was not polite. Still, it would be nice to know what she uttered occasionally. He was just too lazy to learn her language, and she hated him enough not to learn his.

After killing his wife's family and torching her small mountain village, he gathered her upon his horse while she kicked and screamed as they rode away . . . and she hadn't stopped screaming at him since.

Zoar thought perhaps he should be kinder to her.

His wife had given him three children, including his heir, Prince Dorak, who was beautiful like his mother and intelligent.

Zoar was pleased with his first-born, legitimate son. He pondered on his pretty young wife again. He was sorry that her family had been killed, but that was the way of war. It was nothing personal. It was business.

He climbed off the bed and pulled on his pants and woven tunic. At the clapping of his hands, a servant girl entered with a tray that held a bowl of warm water and hand towels. He washed his face and hands before sitting back in a high leather chair for a young girl to braid his black hair, trim his beard, and clean his nails. Her hands trembled a bit.

Other servants entered carrying food and drink. After placing the trays near Zoar, they went off to the side, kowtowing and awaiting further instructions.

Standing silently behind the leather chair was KiKu, Zoar's advisor and spymaster. He was a tall, dark man with black eyes that missed nothing. KiKu waited patiently.

Zoar was suspicious that KiKu thought himself to be better than Zoar as his country had a more advanced culture. This irritated Zoar more than just a little.

Tired of waiting, KiKu coughed softly.

"What is it?" asked Zoar, gruffly.

"Great Aga, I bring reports of a fog barrier to the west of us." KiKu's eyes gleamed with excitement.

"And?"

"I believe there is land beyond this gray mist. It is not the end of the world as we thought. The fog is not a natural phenomenon. I believe it to be a defensive screen."

Zoar pulled at his beard. "How is it made? With magic?"

"We're not sure. Information is still coming in." KiKu stepped forward. His bald head gleamed in the smoking torchlight. "Great Aga, I have studied various reports over several months now, and I find them to be of great interest." KiKu shifted his weight. He wondered how to make this barbaric king understand there may be something astonishing to be discovered beyond the mist. How did one give another the gift of imagination?

"Do they concern gold?"

KiKu's heart sank. "Eh, no, Great Aga."

"Humph," groused Zoar before sucking on a peach.

KiKu quickly added, "Something better than gold. I've had all the ancient records and maps studied. Prior to six hundred years ago, there are records of a country called Hasan Daeg at war with the Cameroons. They lost the war and receded within their borders for good. After that, this fog appeared, and no one has seen anyone from Hasan Daeg again. The country was just forgotten and became the stuff of myths."

"How can you forget about a country's existence?"

"This fog or mist produces a hypnotic effect as one tries to penetrate it. It makes one forget why he wanted to go into the fog. I have gathered many reports of travelers, vagabonds, and merchants entering the fog only to wake up several days later with a terrible headache, but they have food and water beside them. For whatever reason, they never try to enter the fog again. They are not afraid. They simply don't want to."

Zoar thought hard. A fog which makes one lose heart. "I can see you are excited. There must be more, and I love a good story. You will make this a good story, won't you, KiKu?" purred Zoar. He watched KiKu blink.

KiKu blinked only when he was nervous. Otherwise, his eyes never closed but remained large black pupils, forever watching. Even when he killed, he never blinked.

Zoar had once watched him rip out a man's throat with two fingers. It had only taken a second. That's because Kiku had liked the man. If KiKu didn't like someone, he could make that person suffer a long time—very long time.

"Aga, Hasan Daeg is a culture older than two thousand years, according to the oldest records."

"What of it? I've conquered countries older than that."

KiKu's guts twitched. How very well he knew. His country had been one of them. "But this is a two-thousand-year-old state rumored to still exist, and it has had only seven queens and two kings."

"You mean they have lived in anarchy much of the time?"

"No, Great Aga."

"The place is run by priests?" Zoar loved baiting KiKu. He enjoyed the spylord's humiliation. It tasted sweet.

"No, Great Aga."

"I grow weary with your impudence," growled Zoar, throwing his peach pit at KiKu. "Be quick with your tongue or I'll feed it to a borax!"

KiKu sighed inwardly. "The people of this land have been ruled by the same family for over two thousand years, each ruler succeeding by right of ascendance from the last in an orderly and calm fashion. From my accounts, which are from both written and oral sources, the rulers of Hasan Daeg live to be an average of 370 years old, ascending the throne when they are about forty. They abdicate around the age of 330, and then they travel to the woods to meditate and wait for their impending death." KiKu stopped. He wanted his words to leave a strong impression.

Zoar stared at him for a long time. Finally, he murmured, "Let me understand. You are telling me there is a country to the west of us, which no one has seen in the last six hundred years, where the rulers live to be almost four hundred years old, and in two thousand years, they have had only nine rulers."

"Yes, Aga, it is a great mystery."

"If it is a mystery, how do you know your sources to be true?"

"Because one of my men penetrated the mist barrier."

The Aga leaned forward. KiKu now held his interest. "How did he manage that?"

"A year ago, I sent twelve men to explore this region. Eleven returned with strange tales, but none of them had been inside Hasan Daeg. Only one man returned, having been in this land several weeks ago. He had traveled the outskirts of the mist, always going southwest. At the southernmost region of the country, there is a corridor in the mist where one can enter freely as long as one is a Sivan. My man dressed as a Sivan merchant. He brought back not only wondrous tales but plant specimens and water samples."

"What is so important about plants and the water?"

"The plants sing. I know it sounds impossible, but I've heard them myself."

"Bring me such a plant. I wish to hear such a plant sing."

KiKu dropped his head. "Alas, Great Aga, I cannot. We did not know the proper way to care for the plants and they died."

"How unfortunate for the plants and perhaps for you," rasped Zoar. He grabbed a knife off a tray and began peeling a fruit. "What else?"

"The Hasan Daegians do not venture outside their borders. Their economy is an agricultural one. They make items such as hemp ropes, perfumes, oils, salt, and teas, but they are most famous for their herbal medicines, especially those used by women. They even make medicine from a fungus that stops infections within the body."

Zoar carefully cut the pear-like fruit into even slices. "I have never heard of this Hasan Daeg, even as a myth."

KiKu looked defeated as he now regretted mentioning this report. He could have escaped and made his way to Hasan Daeg, and Zoar would have never been able to find him. KiKu now realized how foolish he was to reveal these treasured secrets.

Only a great mind could fathom Hasan Daeg and what it could mean to the world. A great mind like his own and not this buffoon lounging before him, but KiKu plunged on.

"Aga, the desert men of Siva front for Hasan Daeg. For six hundred years, the Sivans have acted as middlemen for them, taking their goods at the southern border and trading in the Sivan name."

KiKu could see Zoar's face was starting to turn red. This was not a good sign.

"You said there had been seven queens and only two kings."

"Their society is a matriarchal one. The bloodline runs through the women."

Zoar looked truly baffled. "But that goes against nature. Who has heard of such a thing?"

KiKu did not remind Zoar that his own society had been matriarchal before Zoar had scattered the Hittal nobility to the four corners of Kaseri. KiKu shrugged.

"How do you explain the rulers' longevity?"

"My spies cannot answer this question, but there is

an ancient tale that the first of the Hasan Daegian queens made a pact with a plant that needed a host in which to live." KiKu felt strained.

Couldn't Zoar see that he was handing him something more important than metal or land for conquest? KiKu was talking about life extremely long-lived. If they could get their hands on the secret, they could live four hundred years or more. Perhaps forever! This was information worth granting a slave his freedom. His heart raced at the thought of being free.

Zoar was enraged. KiKu was feeding him horse dung. A plant singing indeed! "I need to pay my soldiers. I need land to give my governors. A populace to govern. Slaves, minerals, grain. I don't need a bunch of old ladies growing pretty flowers. Does this country have anything else to offer?"

"No, Great Aga, nothing but health and long life." KiKu would not get his freedom now. He realized belatedly that a sneer was in his voice.

Zoar jumped up, grabbing KiKu's embroidered silver robe and pulling KiKu effortlessly toward him. "Take care. You try my patience. I've got a world to conquer, and I don't need silly fools like you daydreaming about singing plants and old hags who rule an imaginary kingdom."

KiKu knew it would be futile to attempt killing

Zoar. He would be dead before he could raise his arm. Zoar's guards stood attentively around them, and since they regarded KiKu and the rest of his spies as not worthy of spit, they would have been only too glad to put a spear through KiKu's neck.

"I need facts," Zoar spat. "Hard facts. Just the plain truth like how many troops, the nature of the terrain, the climate, important details like that." He pushed KiKu to the floor. "What do you give me?" Zoar roared. "Fairy tales. Nothing but little children's bedtime stories!"

KiKu kowtowed. "Master, Master, forgive me. I thought you would be interested. All of your subjects adore you. We want you to live forever!"

Zoar gave him a vicious kick. "All of my subjects fear and hate me, you piece of borax feces. I am the Great Aga. I am a god-king. I have subjugated many peoples to do my bidding. And with all those millions, I have an addled-brained ninny like you in charge of my spy network. Get out of here! Go before I cut your liver out myself!" screamed Zoar, kicking KiKu.

KiKu, a once-proud prince now a slave, crawled out of the tent while grunting with each blow.

Zoar, working himself into a lather, paced his tent. He pounded his chest. "Idiots! Idiots! I am surrounded by fools." He flopped on a stool. "All my subjects fear and hate me," he muttered. The Aga winced at the enormity of his statement. Fear and hate were all he had ever known, even from his mother, and he barely remembered her.

It was all he would ever know. That's what power did to a man. So, why did he lust for it? Had he ever loved? Yes, he loved his son Dorak, and he loved his first wife for a brief time. They had been young but not careful. She died during a hunt when a borax charged, and her horse went down. He couldn't get to her in time.

Zoar saddened at the memory. He cried at his wife's funeral while placing zuni petals on her pyre. It had been her favorite flower. He stood until the fire burned itself out, and with it, a part of him died too. But, oddly, he felt relieved. He was free from the cares of love and would never have to give of himself again. Zoar had walked away from the smoldering pyre never to look back.

Now, he loved only power. A great empire was being born under his leadership. He scoffed at the notion of Hasan Daeg. Two thousand years be damned. He was building for ten thousand years and more!

Even after his death, his son Dorak would honor his father by constructing grand temples and monuments to the legend that was Zoar. He may never live to see the completion of his dream, but Dorak would. The Great Aga! Ruler of Kaseri!

2

This was a mistake!

Not only did Empress Gitar have her own chicks to nurture, but now she had a screaming Hasan Daegian baby to contend with and an ugly Hasan Daegian baby at that. She covered her ears with her taloned hands and spread her wings around her torso, covering her face. Gitar didn't think she could bear it much longer, worried she might be moved to throw the child over the precipice.

Iegani entered her room and asked permission to come forward.

The weary empress peeked out through her sparkly wings and nodded. There was no need for strict protocol. She didn't feel like a monarch, just a weary mother who was overwhelmed at the moment.

"Have you found out what is wrong?"

"Yes, the child is colicky. She will cry until the colic runs its course, and then she will stop of her own accord."

"It is nothing we have done?"

"No, Empress, sometimes Hasan Daegian babies get it for no reason. Queen Abisola said she had been the same way, crying for six weeks and then just stopped. The royal healer has prepared some herbs."

"For the princess?"

"Err, no, they are for you. Herbs to relax and soothe until the crying is over."

Empress Gitar did not look happy.

Iegani continued, "Also, I have brought a wet nurse for Princess Maura. Maybe your milk is too rich for her."

Gitar sat up straighter, looking brighter. "This means no more nightly feeding."

Iegani smiled. "Yes. You can now rest peacefully."

"Why didn't we think of a wet nurse before?"

Iegani smiled weakly. "We've never been in this situation before."

The Dinii did not have wet nurses in their culture as they breast-fed only in the early weeks following their chick's birth. Later, they regurgitated food into the chick's mouth until it was old enough to eat on its own.

Nodding, Gitar stretched and came down from her

nest. "I can hunt again. Oh, how I've missed it."

"Your nights will be your own now."

Gitar looked thoughtful. "Do you think we can do this? I mean," she faltered for a moment, "the consequences are so far-reaching if we fail. Everything will be different. Everything will be changed. We will have no place to go if we fail."

"We have done all that we were instructed to do by the Lahorians," replied Iegani softly. "Even I do not understand the ultimate goals of what we are attempting. There have always been kings and queens who want total dominance over others." Iegani spread open his hands. "But this is the first time the Wise Ones of Lahor have interfered in my lifetime or many lifetimes. Zoar must be terrible indeed."

Gitar lowered her voice. She did not want anyone to overhear of the secret meeting with the Lahorians months ago. She did not even like thinking about the Wise Ones of Lahor. "I thought they were just the stuff of legends until I saw them." Gitar shuddered. "Abisola must never know."

"Yes, I agree. We have told too much already," Iegani asserted, leaning his head closer to his niece's.

Gitar looked away from her uncle. "We are sacrificing this child for a purpose we don't even understand." Guilt shone from Gitar's eyes.

Iegani took Gitar's hands in his. "We don't know if she will be sacrificed. We don't know the end, but we cannot defy the Wise Ones in this. They are too powerful."

Feeling tears spring to her eyes, Gitar lowered her head. "Why during my rule? Why do I have to bear this?"

Iegani put his arms around his niece. "Because they were waiting for you and Abisola. You two are the right ones. In what way, I don't know, but your fates are intertwined. You were both born to prepare the way for Princess Maura. You both will be the key to her success."

"Or failure."

"Perhaps there will be success in failure."

Gitar looked at him in disbelief. "Don't talk to me in riddles. No, no, you are wrong. She must succeed or the world will live in darkness." She pulled away from him. "Yes, yes, this is what I believe with all my heart."

Quivering with fear, Gitar would not be consoled.

3

Iegani seared Gitar's words in his mind.

He left to meditate at the top of the highest peak overlooking the valley. Perched on a craggy rock, he could see only clouds drifting below in the sky. Not even the sister vulture flew this high.

The cold felt good to him and helped him drift into the *seeing state*. After a lifetime of practice, it took him only minutes to reach an ultra-aware level. He tapped into his memory and relived the day the Wise Ones of Lahor materialized before him.

Empress Gitar and Iegani had been hunting when shimmering beings appeared suddenly on either side of Gitar.

Iegani flew to Gitar's defense but could not penetrate the transparent shield erected around his niece. Then, another being appeared beside Iegani and told him he could follow or not. It did not matter, but it was conveyed that Gitar had no choice. She would not be allowed to resist. Iegani followed Gitar and her captors, trying desperately to keep up.

Gitar's eyes were wide with panic. He saw her struggling in vain to change her course but to no avail. They were trapped by the legendary Wise Ones, their ancient enemies.

When Iegani thought he could fly no further, Gitar began descending. Slowly. Cautiously.

Even though Gitar was not the most courageous of rulers, she would still die well. She was an empress from one of the oldest ruling families still in existence and a Dinii. Iegani was determined that Gitar would die with honor and readied himself to die too.

Gitar finally came to rest on the bank of the Sacred Lake of Yappor.

Iegani settled on a tree branch behind her.

Exhausted, they both panted a long time while swiveling their heads, looking for the Lahorians. The Wise Ones were not to be seen.

When Gitar had rested, she edged toward the lake. Carefully, she scooped up water in her hand and sniffed. It looked clean. In fact, it was the clearest lake water Gitar had ever seen. She could see to the very bottom, which was made of fine sand, and see fish darting in and out of vegetation. She tasted the water. The water had a refreshing quality to it. She drank cautiously at first and then more until her thirst was quenched. Feeling dizzy, Gitar thought she had made a terrible mistake until her head suddenly cleared, and she experienced a serenity that she had never felt before.

Anxious, Iegani called out, "Niece, are you all right?"

She laughed, waving to him. "I've never felt better! Come join me."

Iegani shook his head and moved higher up in the tree.

Gitar stood up with her hands on her hips, surveying the sacred lake. "What do we do now, uncle?"

"I guess we wait unless you can leave."

Gitar bowed her head and thought for a moment. "No, I don't think I can, but you can go. They want only me."

Iegani bristled at the suggestion.

"I have no fear now. I don't think they will hurt me. They want to parley."

"Humph," snorted Iegani. "If the Wise Ones wanted to talk to you, why didn't they ask for an audience at court?"

Gitar shrugged. "I don't think they do things in such a fashion. We must wait, that's all." Not one to be idle,

Gitar gathered reeds and made a bed, being too tired to perch. She was spent after her long flight. Her uncle would stand watch until she awakened, and then she would guard while he slept. She closed her wings over her face, wondering if search parties were looking for her. Gitar pushed such thoughts from her mind and fell into a deep sleep.

It was nearly dusk when she awoke. Gitar had slept the entire night and most of the next day. Looking for Iegani, she could not find him and became alarmed. Stumbling to the lake's edge, she took a drink of the pristine water and immediately became calm. She began thinking of ways to escape and look for her uncle but soon gave up.

Gitar knew intuitively that she would not be allowed to leave until the Wise Ones of Lahor spoke to her. Still, she was not angry, just thirsty. She drank more water, feeling very relaxed. Gitar stood her full eight feet, flapping her wings. With long talons, she preened her delicate feathers and washed her face. Her face felt tingly at the touch of the water just as her hands had felt each time she dipped them into the water.

"Empress."

Gitar heard Iegani speak to her mind. "Where are you?" called out Gitar, spinning around.

"Turn again. I'm in the yagomba tree."

Squinting, Gitar found her uncle. "Where did you go?"

"I was thirsty, so I went to find water."

"What? With all this water here?"

"I do not trust that water. I've watched you when you drink it. You seem as though under a spell," Iegani answered telepathically.

"You can leave at any time. I must stay."

"What do they want of you? We have not had contact with them for thousands of years. Our kind didn't even know they still existed," said Iegani, raising his voice in her mind.

Gitar shook her head, flapping her wings. "Quit yelling," she commanded.

Ignoring her order, Iegani continued. "You act as though kidnapping the ruler of the Dinii happens every day. This is madness. Fly off, I tell you! Fly off!"

"I cannot. Something keeps me here, and here I will stay until they are finished with me."

The old owl-man shook cumbersome branches in frustration.

Gitar called to him, "The Wise Ones will speak when they are ready. They are just waiting for something."

"What, what, what?" shouted Iegani at the heavens.

Without warning, a deafening clap of thunder

sounded, although there were no clouds in the darkening night sky.

Iegani immediately flew down to Gitar and extended his talons, pushing her behind him. In his younger days, he had been a fierce warrior, and now with his special powers, he hoped he could stall the Lahorians long enough for Gitar to get away. She was the future of their people. He was the past.

Gitar clasped her hands over her ears at the continuing roar of thunder, and then remembering who she was, she extended her talons. If she was going to die, she was going to die as a Dini warrior. She would not dishonor her people. Gitar was ready for battle.

The sky turned an eerie black. The light from the stars and moons died from view.

Gitar could see nothing, even with her excellent vision.

An unearthly light shone from beneath the lake, rising and spreading from shore to shore.

Iegani strained his eyes, but he could not make out the source of the light.

Gitar glanced at Iegani. "Do you know of such power?"

"No, Empress," answered Iegani with his mind.

"Not even from our legends?"

He shook his head.

Gitar gaped at the lake as it filled with a yellow glow of shining light from beneath its surface.

Without warning, the thunder stopped. All was quiet for several minutes until the water in the middle of the lake began to roil as if boiling.

Huge bubbles popped up to the surface. Some floated into the sky and drifted off. Some dissipated. Other orbs rolled toward them as if with purpose.

Suddenly, one of the orbs burst, and there stood a woman who proceeded to walk calmly on the water toward them. She was clothed only by her long, dark hair. When she was ten feet from them, she stopped. Slowly lifting her hair, the woman turned, showing she carried no weapons.

Though the woman was seemingly middle-aged, her skin exhibited no signs of wrinkles, but was translucent, faintly showing her innards and blood rushing through her veins.

The woman held up her hands. In each palm was an open eye which blinked at them.

"May I approach?" she asked. Her voice echoed off the lakeshore.

Gitar nodded but stood with her talons extending.

The woman came to the lake's edge but did not leave the water. "We are called the Wise Ones of Lahor." She gestured to other beings appearing suddenly on the water. "We wish to speak with Empress Gitar."

"Just you," replied Gitar, pointing.

"We speak as one. We cannot separate ourselves from the other. We speak as one. We will come no closer."

"What do you want with me?" demanded Gitar.

"We have a mission."

"What mission?"

"Queen Abisola this night has borne a child. A female child. We want you to raise her as one of your own."

"For what purpose?"

The Lahorian woman closed her eyes for a moment. She reopened them. "We see no need to tell you. You are to do as you are told."

Iegani gasped at the strange woman's rudeness.

"I give orders, not accept them," barked Gitar. "Who are you to tell me what to do?"

"We are guardians. We watch and are disturbed by what we see. We have gazed into the future and saw Zoar. If we do not stop him, there will be no tomorrow. You must help."

"What's he to do with us?" roared Iegani.

"For centuries, the rulers of Hasan Daeg have depended upon the Royal Bogazkoy to be long-lived.

We've allowed this, for the royal family has ruled wisely, and the secret was kept hidden from the rest of the world. Now, the secret is in jeopardy. It is only a matter of time before Aga Zoar discovers the secret, and this cannot be. The aga is the descendant of the god Bhuttu mating with mortal woman. He will covet long life if he discovers the Royal Bogazkoy. He must not have it."

"How do they know of the Bogazkoy?" demanded Gitar, glaring at Iegani.

Iegani shook his head.

The woman of the lake took no notice of Iegani, though he was sure she was scanning his thoughts. She continued speaking to Gitar.

"The kindred of the aga is of immortal and mortal blood. They tend to grow more immoral with each passing generation, so their evil grows. Now, Zoar seeks to become ruler of the known world. He is extremely talented, ambitious, and ruthless. He must be stopped before he discovers the Royal Bogazkoy."

"If you want him stopped, then kill him," retorted Gitar. "You seem to have great power."

The woman jerked. Both the eyes on her face and hands closed tightly as she stood quivering. After composing herself, all the eyes opened again slowly.

"We cannot kill, even for a just cause. Death of any kind is against our nature. To kill would destroy us."

"My good lady," sputtered Iegani, "we all must kill in order to survive. It is the way of nature."

"We do not. For one of us to commit an evil deed would condemn all of us. We are interconnected. We are one."

"So you want us to do your dirty work for you!" spat Gitar angrily.

"There is only one person in the foreseeable future who will be able to stop Zoar, and that is the daughter of Queen Abisola, but she will need training and guidance. You cannot refuse us. If you do not help, you will be condemning your race."

Gitar hissed, "You lie."

The woman seemed unperturbed. "We cannot lie."

Gitar turned to Iegani. "Discern if she is telling the truth."

"Permit me," said Iegani. He closed his eyes and searched the heart and mind of the Wise One. To his surprise, it was as she alleged. There were many hearts and minds intertwined with hers and there was no deception. He bowed his head before the Wise Woman of Lahor.

The Wise Woman extended her hand. "Look and see the future."

Both Gitar and Iegani stared at the hand with the open eye in its palm until they felt themselves being engulfed in the center of an unyielding force. In their minds, they saw scenes of great destruction. Foreign cities across the sea razed. Peoples they did not know existed were chained and sold into slavery. They witnessed mass starvation as the agricultural cycles were disturbed by war and mayhem. All freedoms were systematically stripped away. Places of worship were destroyed as holy leaders and their followers were hunted down.

Gitar gasped when she saw herself much older, fleeing with only a few of her race. A male she knew to be her son was wounded and dropped out of the sky onto the burning ground. She felt the emotions of the older Gitar, and she knew how despair felt. Gitar heard herself cry out, "No more, no more! Please!"

The visions stopped immediately.

Empress Gitar fell to her knees, sobbing. Feeling Iegani's arms around her, she realized he was weeping as well.

"We are sorry for the pain," said the Wise Woman, "but how else could we reach your hearts and minds? What you have witnessed are events that are to be in the future if the daughter of Queen Abisola does not succeed in her quest, but they are events that can be changed. You must help!"

"What must we do?" asked Empress Gitar.

"The princess must be raised as a warrior. She must train to kill, hunt, track, and live in the forest without benefit of civilization. That is the first step. For the rest of her training, we have others in mind. They will be contacted when the time is right."

"What makes you think Queen Abisola will hand over her only child to me?"

"Because you are her sovereign, and she is living on your land in accordance with ancient treaties and tradition. To defy you means war. This she will not abide.

"She is an intelligent and caring monarch. Queen Abisola will put personal feelings aside and do what is best for her people, regardless of her distaste for the task or you for that matter."

Empress Gitar looked at Iegani. He nodded and spoke to her telepathically. "It seems we have no choice if our way of life is to continue."

"That is correct," spoke the Wise Woman to Gitar.

Iegani realized the Wise Ones had been monitoring their thoughts throughout the entire interview. They must know Gitar was pregnant.

The Wise One continued, "You will communicate with Queen Abisola through special messenger according to protocol arranged by your ancestors. Since Queen Abisola has never been contacted by you, much less seen a Dini, she will probably ignore the initial message, but you must persist. Sooner or later, she will make the connection. Then you will take the child."

"How will I know what to do once I have the child?"

"We will send messages. You will know."

"What if I fail?" asked Empress Gitar, feeling overwhelmed.

"You will not as we will guide you," said the Wise Woman as a radiant orb began to envelope her, slowly sinking into the illuminated water. "We will always be with you. You will never be alone." And with that, she and the others were gone. The lake dimmed until it was as dark as the surrounding night.

Iegani looked up and noticed the stars. "It is over," he announced.

Empress Gitar stroked her belly while scanning the sky. "I feel strong. Let's fly home now. We could be there by morning."

"Yes, by morning," agreed Iegani, unfurling his wings to follow his empress into the night sky.

4

Princess Maura was a sickly baby.

It was discovered she did not have the colic but was allergic to feathers ... all kinds of feathers! Chicken feathers, hawk feathers, eagle feathers, pigeon feathers, finch feathers, duck feathers ... the list went on and on. Of course, this information sent both Queen Abisola and Empress Gitar into a tailspin.

Queen Abisola and Consort Iasos came to stay with their child until the danger passed. Since there was no way to the City of the Peaks but through the air, a special litter was devised for the royal couple. Queen Abisola insisted that she and Iasos be flown up separately in case their litter was dropped, allowing at least one ruler to survive until Princess Maura became of age.

Empress Gitar ignored the implied insult and cheerfully bade her warriors to do as requested. She understood Abisola's anxiety. She was anxious herself, for she did not want a royal princess of another civilization to die in her care. She had bonded, albeit reluctantly, with the squalling, indigo-faced infant.

Gitar would coo to the female non-Dini as affectionately as she cooed to her chicks now molting their baby down.

This strange baby had bonded with her and her nursery mates as well. She would look at Gitar with wondering eyes and hold her mouth open as the other chicks did when it was feeding time.

There had been four chicks at birth. Now there were only three since a chick had died. Of Empress Gitar's hatchlings, there were two females and one male left. Still grieving for her dead baby, Gitar accepted the Hasan Daegian newborn with her blue-black hair, blue eyes, and even blue toes taking the place of her beloved blonde chick. If she felt pain over one chick with three still living, how could she ignore the sufferings of one woman with one child. She understood completely. Pain from a mother's heart was universal.

Once Queen Abisola settled into the nursery, she clasped her hands and stood over the nest. "Oh my goodness, look how big she is!" she exclaimed.

Iegani stood silently by the door, appreciating the enchanting sight of a mother claiming her child. He watched intently for a few minutes, and then his thoughts drifted.

Sitting on a stool, Queen Abisola picked up her daughter and held her tight, kissing her face and hands.

Prince Iasos stood by beaming.

Queen Abisola counted her daughter's toes and fingers. The baby happily gurgled while Abisola removed the baby's clothing, inspecting for rashes or bruises.

Iegani straightened up.

On the baby's back was a tattoo of two large cats with all sorts of symbols and numbers. Since he had never been around when the baby was changed or bathed, he had not seen the tattoo. He sensed the tattoo was something significant. A piece of the riddle. Knowing he could not approach the queen now, he would wait until the dinner honoring her presence in the City of the Peaks.

Tables and chairs were available for the Hasan Daegians to dine on. The Bird People liked to perch while eating raw meat but sat at the tables while Queen Abisola and her husband stayed with them. Cooked boaeps with fresh greens were brought in on a large ceremonial platter. Queen Abisola eyed it gratefully. She was glad she was not expected to eat bloody meat. Her people seldom ate meat, but at least it was thoroughly cooked when they did.

Iegani sat uncomfortably on his chair while noticing the younger Dinii had no trouble at all sitting. "Old bones," he muttered.

"What's that?" asked Queen Abisola.

"Your Majesty, I was wondering about the tattoo on the back of Princess Maura," he asked innocently. "I did not know your people tattooed their young."

"We do not as a rule, just the monarchs. We prefer jewelry and flowers as adornment," Queen Abisola answered graciously.

"I might add you look stunning tonight. We are not accustomed to bright stones in necklaces such as you are wearing, but as you can see we like to color our feathers."

"Yes, such intricate and unusual designs," she answered, glancing around the room.

"Only our empress wears the bright stones. Our empress likes to grind stones such as you are wearing and sprinkle the dust on her. It gives her such a glittering effect, don't you think?"

"She looks lovely."

Iegani bowed his head to hide his smile. He knew the compliment had cost the Hasan Daegian queen.

"You say that only the queens have this tattoo?" he asked while pouring Sivan wine for Queen Abisola.

"Only the ruling monarch. The uultepes are the mascot of the Hasan Daegian royalty."

"And all of the Hasan Daegian rulers have had these same markings?"

"Yes, why do you ask?"

"As you know, our people do not read or write but commit our knowledge to memory. I find it very interesting that your rulers have a tattoo with very ancient-looking symbols. Can you tell me the meaning of the tattoo, that is, if I am not impertinent?"

"I don't know the meaning. I've always considered it just a mark of our station. As for the symbols, many of them are in our old way of writing from before we accepted the Sivan script for everyday use."

"And the other symbols?"

"I don't know to what they refer."

"Do you think there is anyone who can translate it?"

Abisola looked thoughtful. "I would guess the priestesses from the House of Magi could translate the symbols as they still read from texts in old languages, but I know of no one else. Why? Do you think it really means something?" She laughed. "Oh, believe me, it was some old crone who wanted to create some mystique for the royalty. I wouldn't think it would go beyond that."

Iegani lifted his goblet. "To your health and continued prosperity, Your Majesty."

Queen Abisola nodded and studied the old owl when he looked away. She would have to look into the matter of her tattoo. If this wise owl-man was asking questions, there was a reason beyond idle curiosity on his part. She turned and smiled at her husband. This would be a good project for him when they got home.

AFTER FIVE DAYS of negotiation, it was decided that Princess Maura would spend winter and spring under the loving protection of her parents and summer and fall with the Dinii who would train the princess as a huntress and warrior, but only in the presence of a Hasan Daegian nurse, nanny, and guard selected by Queen Abisola.

Consort Iasos taught Empress Gitar how to write her name. The empress practiced writing with a stick in the dirt for hours as she was excited to write her name on the written agreement concerning Princess Maura.

Finally, the Hasan Daegian queen with her consort and entourage, went back to O Konya, much to the relief of the Dinii.

The nurse, nanny, and guard did their best to fit in as best they could around seven-foot-tall birds that left the city every night to go hunting. The Dinii, not accustomed to the smells, sounds, and customs of

Hasan Daegians in their midst, did their best to ignore and then gradually accept these beings who had no feathers. The three Hasan Daegians, in return, hid their alarm when the bird warriors would take Princess Maura high into the sky and then drop her hundreds of feet into the arms of a waiting hawk.

"It teaches our chicks not to fear heights," Empress Gitar explained patiently to the sweating and furious Hasan Daegian guard. She was perplexed. "Doesn't everyone do this?" It went without saying that no one reported this to the overprotective and quick-tempered Queen Abisola.

It was a struggle for everyone to get along, except for the princess, who thought all the attention was lovely, especially the rides in the sky. The baby laughed and grabbed the nose of her hawk rescuer who shed feathers at the thought she might miss catching the future ruler of Hasan Daeg.

Maura was a child who wanted to eat, sleep, and, most of all, be loved. What could she know of the harsh wind of evil preparing to blow into her country and destroy everything she would grow to cherish? She was just a babe, after all.

5

Iegani was anxious.

He left the City of the Peaks early one morning with several warriors.

They flew in a V formation with Iegani at the head. His mission was of the utmost importance. Only Iegani knew where they were going, and he was not telling. "Just follow me," he ordered.

Iegani wouldn't even tell Gitar where they were going or why. She didn't pursue the matter with Iegani, for she knew he acted for the good of their people. She also knew from her secret spies that Iegani had sent teams to search Hasan Daeg's cities for ancient scrolls. Gitar even knew that Iegani studied the tattoo on Princess Maura intensely.

He had burned wood for charcoal to copy the tattoo onto bark and hidden the copy in his nest house. But she didn't know why.

It wasn't that Gitar didn't trust her uncle. She did, but not so completely that she wouldn't embed a spy among one of the warriors accompanying him. She didn't trust anyone that much.

After Iegani flew away, Empress Gitar went to the nursery and picked up Princess Maura to study the tattoo. She held the baby upright and then dangled her by her foot, inspecting the tattoo. "I can't make heads nor tails of it," she sighed, handing the gurgling baby back to a distraught nanny. Bored, Gitar made her way back to the audience room. Bad times were coming soon enough. She did not need to go looking for trouble.

That was Iegani's department.

For now, she just wanted to hunt, raise her chicks, and make love with whom she desired . . . and they were many.

6

They flew all day.

After the initial day, Iegani and his bird warriors changed their routine. They traveled only at night, sleeping by day in mountain peaks or deep within forest treetops. They were careful not to be seen and left no trace of their presence. All debris and food carcasses were buried, as was any bodily waste.

While the Hasan Daegians were peaceful, the Dinii were not and often fought those who encroached on their hunting territory outside Hasan Daeg. They were skilled killers.

Iegani chose his warriors from the Hawk clan with care—two female and two male warriors who were not related to each other by marriage or kinship and possessed different skills, having shown valor in military operations.

The female red hawks, Yeti and Toppo, were larger than the male hawks, possessing endurance and strength. The male hawks, Benzar and Tarsus, were better at stealth and had more patience than their female counterparts.

Iegani paired them male and female. The females were in charge of hunting food and water while the males covered up their trail and conducted reconnaissance work. Since they ate their food raw, they did not worry about fires. If the night was chilly, they perched together to keep warm while one remained on watch.

For many nights they flew.

Iegani kept quiet with his thoughts. The others noticed that he carried a pouch from which he would pull a piece of bark covered with writing from time to time.

When they gathered close to see the writing, he would cluck a warning at them. After that, they kept their distance but secretly speculated on what their mission was and where they were going. They wondered if Iegani could read.

Each night before they began their flight, Iegani would scan their thoughts. As the hawks were young, they were eager to try their mettle, wishing for something thrilling to happen. He often chuckled to himself after reading their minds. *Was I ever this full of hubris?* Iegani thought. He was surprised to find that they were in awe and a little frightened of him. It gave him pause.

Soon they reached the eastern border of Hasan Daeg. The wall of mist caused no harm as they flew high above it. For two of the hawks, it was their first time they had gone beyond the borders of Hasan Daeg. They shivered with excitement.

For several more nights, they traveled toward a destination that only Iegani knew. One night they began to smell smoke in the air. They could see refugees clogging the main roads below. If the refugees kept traveling west, they would hit the mist wall but would be unable to penetrate it. They would have to travel north and finally come to the ocean or go south where they would be greeted by unsympathetic Sivan merchants and their hired mercenaries. To keep their whereabouts unnoticed, the Dinii turned northward and flew over less populated areas.

Everywhere they flew, they saw signs of war. And not the kind of skirmishes they were used to, but a new kind of warfare that not only killed large portions of the population but devastated the land as well. Food became increasingly scarce for the Bird People. They resorted to hunting and eating berries and nuts as did refugees fleeing from war-torn areas.

Due to their seclusion, the Dinii had enjoyed a mostly prosperous history. Not many peoples knew of their existence and the ones who did respected them as god-like creatures that swooped in deadly silence from the sky. They could slice the throat of a victim in a split second just as the poor wretch heard only a slight whoosh of wings. The Dinii didn't make a habit of killing people, especially Hasan Daegians. However, poachers were fair game, and their flesh was tasty indeed.

Iegani loved the taste of raw, bloody meat, although several times he had tried to become a vegetarian as he believed it was a higher step on the moral ladder. Each time he had failed, only to consume his fellow creatures with a relish topped with guilt, until one day he decided that each creature must be what she or he was. Nothing more. Nothing less. Who was he to fight the inexplicable web of nature? Only nature herself understood the great workings and interconnections of Kaseri. He may not have believed in a supreme being, but he did believe in harmony. And to step out of one's nature was disharmony. This philosophy set his mind at ease.

But Iegani did not wish to eat the suffering refugees roaming below him. Still, they might suffice in a pinch as berries were becoming monotonous.

Iegani shook these thoughts out of his head. He realized that if he was thinking unclean thoughts with the little privation he suffered, what were the refugees themselves enduring? He would not add to their misery. He prayed that the mist would withstand the onslaught of these poor wanderers. If not, Hasan Daeg would be overrun in a matter of weeks. Their peaceful society could not cope with the demands of these angry, hateful outsiders who would, through sheer madness looking for food, trample the fields and destroy the crops. They would drink from the sacred black streams and cause harm through the insanity that would follow.

Yes. Yes, thought Iegani. *The world is being turned upside down because of an ambitious fool.*

Iegani felt rage at all the suffering. Righteous anger radiated from his being. He called his warriors to him. Perching on the limbs of a tall mingo tree, they looked at him with expectation.

"Warriors from the City of the Peaks, have you seen the suffering?"

The hawks nodded. They too were sickened by the evil they saw. They knew death. They were pledged to it. It was expected. But the destruction they saw had no honor. It seemed to be without purpose. Total destruction did not make sense. To them, war was simple. You had an enemy. You struck this enemy. You either lost or won. That was the end of it. You did not set the world on fire. What did the field mice, borax calves, or trees have to do with one's enemy? Why destroy their homes?

What sense was there in making all creatures and plants feel one's hate?

"Never before have the Dinii seen such destruction."

They murmured in agreement with him.

Iegani continued, "I have a great tale to tell you. Listen carefully, my children, for what I tell you is true. We were once like the nomads of Bhuttan. Angry. Greedy. We were the Overlords of Kaseri, lords of the entire planet, but we were without code or honor. We took because it was in our power to do so. We enslaved smaller and weaker beings to do our bidding. We killed without discretion. We were lords of the most high. Very little could stop us until we encountered the Wise Ones of Lahor. They are no fable, my young ones. I have seen them with my own eyes."

The warriors gasped, staring at Iegani in astonishment.

"We all know the mythical story of Lahor, a great island of learning across the water, known for its art and science, immense libraries, and institutions of knowledge. Architecture such as the world has never seen before or since.

"But a great storm arose after a blazing star fell from the sky and engulfed the island. What you don't know is that many survived the great flood that ensued and crossed the water in quickly constructed rafts and makeshift boats. Many died at sea, but some landed near our old homeland, which extended to the sea, now in the Forbidden Zone.

"Our ancestors found these creatures and tried to enslave them as was our custom with inferior beings. But this ancient people resisted slavery, causing us great harm by their thoughts. These thoughts caused immense pain as if we were exploding from within.

"We had never encountered such an enemy. We were enraged and sought their destruction. We hunted them relentlessly. We knew their powers were limited and thought we would just wear them down by our sheer numbers. We did not. We did not understand their desire to be free was dearer than their fear of death. We killed hundreds of them, ripping their hearts out and eating the sometimes still-beating heart. Female, male, babe . . . it made no difference to us.

"But something started to happen. We began to think differently. We did not understand that eating the Lahorians' flesh would evoke subtle emotional changes within us. As we absorbed their flesh, their blood, we were absorbing their thoughts and values. Many of our ancestors committed suicide because they could not stand the internal conflict. Those who survived lost the taste for hunting the Wise Ones of Lahor.

"Because we were so ashamed of our barbarism, we resisted everything the Lahorians stood for and wished to erase them from our memory. We destroyed our centers for learning. We tossed our scrolls into the ocean, eventually forgetting how to read and write. No longer able to be humbled by our defeat, we fled our ancient homeland by the sea. We transported our remaining slaves over the mountains into Hasan Daeg, a land which had been used primarily for hunting. We set them free to work the land.

"Our ancestors cultivated the wall of mist to protect our freed slaves from raiders out of the east. With time, we gradually forgot about the danger of the Lahorians. We were convinced they were a people tied to the water and would remain near the sea if any of them were still alive. We had met our superiors, and they left us scarred. We withdrew to the City of the Peaks, letting the world do as it wished.

"Our former slaves grew into an intelligent and industrious people. Their specialty was plants. They had an understanding of nature that we did not foresee. We found that their agricultural methods and husbandry increased the animal population from which we fed. In return, we protected them but generally left them to their own devices.

"Once they established their own royalty, we made a

formal treaty. They could live in our territory as long as they kept the land in good condition. Our former slaves grew fat and prosperous. We noticed that they had taken many of our customs and adopted them as their own.

"Time passed and they forgot about us as we were rarely seen, clinging to myths that they had been created by winged gods. The Wise Ones of Lahor became clouded in time for us too, until our empress and I discovered their existence again in the middle of the Sacred Lake of Yappor."

"How long have they been here?" asked Yeti, the largest of the red hawks.

"It seems for many centuries. They have established a colony. Their mental powers have increased to such an extent that it would be folly for us to resist," said Iegani.

Yeti gasped, "Do they mean to enslave us?"

Iegani shook his head. "It is hard to discern their true purpose. But I do not think they wish to harm us. It is not in their culture to enslave."

"Then they can stop Zoar," said Tarsus.

"They will not. The Wise Ones claim they cannot kill. They will help us destroy Zoar but will not directly cause his downfall," affirmed Iegani. "From what I can discern, they can only leave the water for short periods of time, and that's why they need our help to implement their plan."

"How is that?" asked Yeti.

"They are going to stop Zoar through Princess Maura."

Yeti laughed out loud while the others twittered. She quickly covered her mouth when Iegani sternly glared at her.

"You must understand," Iegani explained. "The Wise Ones of Lahor have mental powers of which we only can dream. They can look into the future and thus plan for the outcome they wish. Don't you think that a rather opportune skill, Yeti?"

"Oh, Great Divigi, I meant no disrespect," she replied awkwardly. "It's just that Princess Maura is a mere babe."

Iegani spread his wings for effect. "Babies sometimes have the bad manners to grow up."

The hawks were suitably impressed. Their eyes gleamed with excitement. While Princess Maura was still a riddle, their mission had now become clearer to them. They were attempting to solve the mystery of the Hasan Daegian baby.

Iegani pulled the bark scroll from his pouch and unrolled it.

The hawks moved closer to peer at it. He held it up

for them. "On this scroll is an exact copy of the tattoo on Princess Maura. Even its dimensions are comparable."

"Yes, yes, this looks very much like it!" exclaimed Benzar, who had been assigned to take Princess Maura on flying assignments to accustom her to great heights.

"Did you never wonder about this tattoo?" asked Iegani, peering over the scroll.

"Yes, Great Divigi, but it is not my place to question."

"Good enough. Still, tell me what you think."

Benzar paused.

"Come, come now, don't be shy," encouraged Iegani.

"Well, I think," ventured Benzar, "that the tattoo is not merely for decoration."

"Why is that?" asked Iegani.

Benzar cast a glance at his comrades. He was afraid of making a fool out of himself.

Yeti nodded, giving him confidence.

"Well, Great Divigi, if the tattoo was for decoration or even for announcing the status of the wearer, it would not be placed on the back. It would be on the face or hands where it could be seen at all times, and there are numbers in a specific order. This tattoo is a message or code."

"Go on," encouraged Iegani.

"Also, the symbols seem to be in a pattern," blurted out Yeti, "like other writings we have seen. Oh, I'm sorry," she said, realizing she had spoken without waiting to be called.

Iegani was pleased with her reply, although he did not show it. He made a mental note to himself that he would have to curb Yeti's impulsive nature. Iegani pressed, "Why on the back?"

Benzar continued. "It makes perfect sense. If it's a message, it would be placed on an area that would be less vulnerable to scarring or damage, not on hands, feet, or even a face. As the wearer matures into adulthood, the writing on the back becomes larger, more discernible to the viewer."

Toppo looked questioningly at Iegani.

He nodded.

She gingerly reached out and touched the scroll, then jerked her hand back.

Iegani looked at her, waiting for a reply. Since the Dinii had forgotten reading and writing, they still needed a way to communicate with written symbols— those who had the ability developed powers for interpreting messages. They could not decipher the writing, but could read the intent and emotions from the vibrations in the message left by the writer.

"What do you feel, my young fledgling?" Iegani asked.

"Great Divigi, I feel nothing from the messenger, but strong vibrations from the scroll. No, that's not right. From the tattoo. It feels very powerful, like it has a beat to it."

"Like a heartbeat."

"Yes, you can say that. It feels very unnatural."

"I wrote that scroll myself, but only after I had emptied my mind of all thoughts and emotions. And still, it is as you say . . . strong." Iegani stared at the sky. "But not anything as powerful as when I touched the princess myself with both hands."

"What did you feel?" questioned Yeti.

Benzar nudged her.

"Was it evil?" asked Toppo, a wave of empathy spreading over her.

"I've never felt anything evil when touching her," said Yeti.

Toppo snapped back. "Some hawks do not possess the power to feel."

Iegani carefully rolled up the scroll and placed it in the pouch. "That's why you are here, my children. We must solve this riddle."

He slowly related the events at the Sacred Lake of Yappor when the Lahorians had captured Empress

Gitar. Iegani spoke of the trust regarding Princess Maura and her future as seen by the Lahorians.

No one spoke when he finished.

He waited until Yeti asked, "What is our mission?"

Iegani knew they had accepted the facts and were willing to do as he requested. "I chose the four of you because each of you possesses a specific skill which will be needed in the future. Toppo, you are a seeress. Be my protégé, and I will teach you secrets that you cannot even suspect exist yet."

Toppo looked astonished. "I have only a little talent," she whispered.

"For now, that is true," replied Iegani, "but you have much potential."

Looking very pleased, Toppo bowed. "Thank you. Thank you, Great Divigi." She reached for his hand and kissed it.

Iegani patted her on the head. "My child, I don't think you will be thanking me in the dark days to come. I will ask of you sacrifices that will make you want to tear your heart out."

Each of the warriors looked alarmed.

"I see no other way," Iegani continued. He sighed. "You will form with me a secret society pledged to protect Princess Maura until she can finish her mission. In return, I will teach each of you the magical path that you may pass down to your children. I will give you power unknown to you."

He paused, closed his eyes, and whispered, "Are you with me?"

The warriors felt Iegani in their minds, moving among their secret thoughts. It was unnerving. They knew they could not hide their fears from him, the Great Divigi. There was no place to run, to hide. "Yes, we will follow you," their minds echoed back to him.

"Then you each pledge your heart, soul, and mind to me. Bind them with mine. Let us do what we must to save our land, our freedom, our people's existence. Let us not be tempted by the darkness that pervades Kaseri. Let us be strong, seeking to remove the hand of evil that attempts to strangle us."

"Yes, yes," answered the warriors, swaying with the hypnotic rhythm of Iegani's voice.

"Do you swear to me?" Iegani cried, stretching out his iridescent, white wings to their impressive size.

"Yes, we swear with our hearts and minds . . . our very souls." They shuddered upon speaking the vow. They knew their lives would never again be their own.

Iegani held out his hand. "Pledge your honor to me."

Each warrior placed her or his hand on Iegani's opened palm. "We pledge with our honor, Great

Divigi!"

Iegani placed his other hand on top of theirs.

Each warrior shook with currents of power emanating from Iegani.

Iegani's eyes flew open and rolled back into his sockets. "It is done," he croaked. "It is done."

The warriors murmured in unison, "It is done."

Iegani broke his hands from theirs.

The hawks stumbled away.

Toppo wept.

Benzar held Toppo's hand, too dazed to do much else.

Yeti and Tarsus looked at each other with pride. They felt they had been given a great honor.

"Why are you crying?" snapped Tarsus, surprised at his vehemence since he seldom spoke.

"Because we came very close to death," answered Toppo. She stole a look at Iegani.

He nodded.

"If even one of us had not accepted the vow, Iegani would have slain us all," she asserted.

The rest of the warriors snapped their eyes to Iegani.

"It is true," Iegani confirmed. "I must have loyalty from all four, otherwise my plans would be at risk. I would have simply destroyed each of you and started over again."

The hawks exchanged stunned looks.

"I told you this would require sacrifices that might tear your hearts out." Iegani spread his wings to fly. "Next time, pay more attention to exactly what I say. I'm not one to speak in riddles." He looked about him. "It looks like it's going to be a beautiful evening. A good night for flying." He took off without looking behind him.

The others followed without a word.

7

The city of Anqara stank.

Its odor could be detected long before it came into view. Raw sewage was dumped into the river. Everyone knew not to eat fish unless it was imported. Only the rich could afford indoor plumbing. The poor threw their bodily waste, along with the kitchen scraps, into the streets.

Anqara, besides smelling like an old boot, was not pretty. It had no expansive boulevards. No grand fountains. It never entered anyone's mind to plant public gardens. Smoke from cooking fires blotted out the sky. People went for days without ever seeing the sun.

Crime was a constant nuisance. At least, everyone thought it was a nuisance rather than a problem. The criminals of Anqara were a good-natured lot and, although they threatened one's life with dull, rusty daggers, no one was ever injured. The well-to-do employed bodyguards, not because they feared for their safety, but because they disliked muggers pulling their hats over their heads, hiding their house keys, or tugging their whiskers.

Women especially disliked being held up for a token of their private undergarments only to see their garters worn on the sleeve of some ruffian weeks later in the bazaar. It seemed people were more concerned with their dignity rather than their purses.

Narrow streets meandered without rhyme or reason. During the summer, people lived on the roofs of their houses as the first floors were unbearable with the heat and fleas, which were always hopping on one's legs or in food.

Though Anqara was a smelly, rather unattractive city with swarms of common pickpockets and "kissing" bandits, it could boast of being one of the most populated and exciting cities.

It was the largest cultural center on Kaseri. Anqara was a city of more mildewed volumes of wisdom and drunken scholars than anywhere else. Hundreds of spectacled, hunched over, gnarled sages took to the streets every dawn, hurrying to their small cubicles where they pondered, reflected, and speculated on the wonders of the universe. And if not that, they drank a nice cup of hot tea with a little extra something added from their hip flasks. These old women were the guardians of the world's knowledge.

But none of this interested Zoar. It was the banking district of Anqara with its hundreds of secret deposits hidden in catacombs underground that took his fancy. He couldn't risk taking the city and allowing the banking houses to destroy or hide their entrusted wealth. Zoar knew that the scions of the banking world would never divulge their treasures' location even if the aga began cutting off their children's heads. They would just spit on Zoar's shoes in defiance. No, he would have to bide his time, trusting that his spies would find the hidden treasures before he entered the city.

This gave Anqara a respite and the bankers time to fund resistance groups throughout the country.

Iegani was not interested in any of this, although he was aware of Zoar's army surrounding Anqara. The divigi and his warriors hid in the woods outside Anqara and rested for several days.

At night, Benzar stole inside the city, scouting its convoluted passages.

Yeti would visit local butcher shops, taking provisions after leaving coins on the counter. Once she encountered an angry butcher working late. Yeti had to knock him in the head. She then threw distilled spirits on the unconscious merchant so no one would believe his story about a person of great height covered in feathers taking his best roast.

Iegani was unconcerned with the tales of encounters that Yeti and Benzar brought back. He only concentrated on a lighted window at the top of the highest tower in the city—the House of Magi!

The House of Magi was considered by the rest of the world to be a law unto itself. Remote, majestic, and cloaked in mystery, it stood as the tallest building in Anqara. Crumbling stairways, a block wide, stood below the marble-columned portico.

Only one magnificent doorway granted entrance with its doors that never shut. On either side of the portal stood colossal braziers in which yellow flames continually burned. No one ever saw a servant tending to them, nor was one tempted to cross the threshold—not even the most desperate thief. At night, windows threw misshapen shadows of priestesses as they paced back and forth in their studies in front of oil lamps.

It was said that every twenty years, the High Priestess of the House of Magi would consent to entertain application—those who sought the solitude of the House of Magi to contemplate and study. Once granted admission, they could pursue any project that would be funded for any length of time.

Scientists, scholars, and philosophers would go before the grand door, calling into the darkness their proposal of study. Most applicants waited years, sometimes decades, before a response was given. No matter where they were or what they were doing, an acceptance or rejection letter with the seal of the House of Magi appeared silently on their doorway or tent flap.

No one knew the origin of the House of Magi or the source of its wealth. The oldest city records mention the House of Magi standing quiet and forbidding by the river inside the first city walls with its open door and the huge fire sentinels guarding, guarding, guarding.

It was to the House of Magi that Iegani flew one smoke-filled night. To the highest window he flew. With beating wings, he hovered outside the window and tried the sash. The window was shut fast. Seeing no other way, he burst through the glass with great clamor and fury.

On the far side of the room behind a massive desk sat an old woman peering over some manuscripts. She looked up in surprise and gasped. Blinking hard, she waved her hand in front of her as if to ward Iegani away.

Iegani quickly folded his wings. "High Priestess of the House of Magi. I come in peace on a quest. I seek no lies, only truth to which you may possess the key!" He bowed very low in abject supplication, peering up at her from under his massive feather eyebrows.

"What damnation is this?" the priestess sputtered. "What foul evil is this that has a giant bird speaking?" She peered hard at Iegani. "A male bird, at that. Good gracious man, cover yourself. Who wants to look at your withering male tool?"

"Madam, you cannot see anything. My splendid feathers cover all."

The old woman laughed. "You are wrong. Breaking windows must excite you."

"Great Priestess, I did not come all this way to talk about my male anatomy."

"Have you come to kill me?" asked the old woman, eying Iegani with curiosity.

"Absolutely not."

"You're not some foul thing Zoar has conjured up to do away with the High Priestess of Magi?"

"I assure you that I have never met the aga and do not wish to."

"Mmm." The woman wet her lips with her tongue. "I need a drink. A little spirit to clear my head and steady my heart." She poured ale out of a pitcher and into a glass. "Did you not worry that you would cause me heart failure with your dramatic entrance?"

Iegani was disturbed. "To tell the truth, I never thought of it. My species does not suffer from the heart."

"Health of the heart or having one?" The woman got up and walked from around the desk toward him.

Iegani noticed she limped slightly.

She touched the feathers on Iegani's torso. "Are these glued on?"

"No, High Priestess, they are real. Go on. Feel them down to the quill. See how they grow out of my skin."

"Amazing." The woman stroked the feathers and pried them apart to investigate. "Come over here by the light so I can see better." She pulled at Iegani's feathers.

He obliged and followed her over to a lamp.

"They seem iridescent, almost glowing. Is that to reflect light? I have a hundred questions. Now, let's see, I must get paper and pen to write down your answers. Let me call for a scribe."

Iegani stopped her as she reached for the bell. He gently pushed her down into a soft chair near her desk. "There must be no witness to my visit. I'm sorry."

"Why is one of the Dinii here?"

Iegani looked surprised. "You know our name?"

"Yes, I thought I would never see an Overlord." The High Priestess stretched out her bad leg. "I know all about Hasan Daeg and its secret wall of mist."

Iegani felt truly humbled. "High Priestess, you are wise."

"Pshaw," she snorted, "One should gather some information when reading for over forty years, and quit calling me High Priestess. We worship no god here. We are devoted to the study of knowledge. I don't know why everyone keeps thinking we are some kind of a cult." She fussed with the pillows in her chair.

"What shall I call you?"

"Madam if you're the formal kind or Mehmet since that is my name." Mehmet beamed a smile at him. It was a lovely, dimpled smile.

"Mehmet suits you. I am Iegani, Great Divigi to the Empress Gitar."

"And why have you crashed into my chamber, Iegani, Great Divigi to Empress Gitar?"

Iegani gathered a stool and sat beside Mehmet. "I am here seeking information, Great Lady." He turned his head and whistled.

Toppo glided into the room with the leather pouch. She landed lightly on her feet, dodging the glass on the floor. Toppo smiled weakly at Mehmet and bowed. Handing the pouch to Iegani, she retreated to a far corner of the room and tried to look inconspicuous.

Mehmet seemed delighted with the arrival of Toppo and craned her neck to get a good look at the other

Dini. "A female of your species!" Mehmet exclaimed. "Tell me, dear, all about your kind. I want to know about your mating rituals, how you raise your young?"

Toppo spread her wings about her, hiding her face and torso.

"Oh, goodness," pouted Mehmet, staring at Iegani. "She's awfully shy."

Iegani pulled the bark scroll out of the pouch and waited for Mehmet's attention.

Mehmet's eyes finally landed on the scroll. Curious, she reached for it.

The Great Divigi gently presented it to her.

The scholar studied the writing on the bark for a very long time.

Iegani watched her expression, but whatever Mehmet thought, she kept to herself.

"Where did you get this?" she asked, still holding the scroll tightly.

"I'm sorry, but I cannot tell you."

"Why do you want to know what it means?"

"I believe my kind are in danger, and this writing may help save us."

"The whole world is in danger. Did you not see the troops outside Anqara's walls?"

"True, but I am only concerned with my people," said Iegani. "It is selfish, I admit."

"But honest," declared Mehmet. "In this day and age, I appreciate your words." Mehmet raised her glass and swallowed. She rested the empty glass on the desk. "So, you are not noble."

"I care nothing about Zoar and his minions, except that they stop at my doorstep. He can tear the rest of the world apart as long as he leaves my homeland alone."

Mehmet clapped her hands. "Spoken like a true cynic, or so you try to appear. I will take your words at face value." She smiled. "For now, at least." Mehmet changed the subject. "Where did you get this?"

"The place where I found this writing is strange in itself. It is the same message handed down from one generation to the next."

"Yes, but where?"

"I cannot tell you."

Mehmet studied Iegani for a time. "It could just be gibberish," said Mehmet.

"I think not. I think this writing is a code," answered Iegani, pointing to the bark.

"Maybe so, but why bring it to me?"

"I could think of no place else to find someone who would be able to tell me what it means."

Mehmet sighed loudly. "Many of the world's intellectuals are either dead or in prison. But why do you think I will tell you the truth of what it is?"

"The House of Magi is honorable."

Mehmet looked pleased. "We do try," she said vainly. "But I cannot tell you what it means. It does seem to be a code, but its symbols are so ancient no one remains who would know what they mean. I know of no language that looks similar. It almost looks not of this world. See here," she said, pointing to a star symbol divided into four sections with a cross. "This symbol looks like ancient Lahorian writing when they were still using pictographs. It refers to long life."

"Lahorian!" exclaimed Iegani. "They are just the stuff of old wives' tales."

Mehmet gave Iegani a grave look. "Stop lying. You and I both know that the Lahorians exist. Being disingenuous with me will not make me help you." She turned her attention to the bark. "Oh, yes, I'd say about twelve thousand years old. But the rest of it, I don't know."

"Can you decipher it?"

"I think so. It will take time, of course. We have a very good linguist here."

Iegani held up his hand. "No one else may know of this."

"You expect me to decipher this alone? To drop all of my projects just because you want to know what this bit of wood says?" Mehmet drew herself up. "You must be mad."

Iegani nodded. "I think this bit of bark is so important that the High Priestess herself must decode it. I think the world depends on it."

"You said you didn't care about the world."

"Yes, Great Lady, but you do."

Mehmet laughed. "What a flatterer you are. Great Lady, indeed. So important it needs only my attention," she mimicked. "I suppose if I refuse, you will kill me."

Iegani said nothing.

Mehmet shrugged. "I guess I'm bored with studying the habits of the Kawanda giant beetle."

He handed her the pouch.

"I don't suppose you have a copy in case I lose this?"

Iegani pointed to his head. "It's up here."

"Birdman, you intrigue me. If I were younger, I might be interested in you."

The Great Divigi grinned. "I don't see what your age has to do with it. I like a bit of mature meat myself."

"Well, this venture may prove to be most interesting. Most interesting indeed."

Iegani plucked one of the beautiful white feathers from above his heart and presented it to Mehmet.

Mehmet eagerly took it. Looking at it closely, she

murmured, "I've never seen anything like this. It changes color in the light like a prism."

Hearing a sudden whooshing sound, Mehmet looked up.

The Dinii were gone.

Alone in the room, she sat composing her erratic thoughts. Finally, Mehmet walked over to a portrait of herself and took it off the wall. A hidden door in the wall slid open, exposing a small antechamber. She quickly placed the scroll and pouch in the room and then replaced the portrait. The door to the room closed. Then she went to bed, holding the feather as she fell asleep.

Across from the House of Magi in a dark alley, a beggar made note of the exact time he saw two large birds fly out of the room of the High Priestess.

I have certainly earned my pay tonight, he chuckled to himself. Still playing the part of a beggar, the spy shuffled off into the darkness. He had much to report. He would make sure that he would report this to Zoar himself.

There might be a reward.

8

*Z*oar rested comfortably.

He lay on soft pillows and carpets as he watched a dance troop. Zoar had seen many dancing girls, but this group was particularly good. They combined acrobatics with dancing. Zoar loved acrobatics, and he especially liked watching well-toned and muscular girls dancing in skimpy attire. *Simple pleasures of life*, he thought to himself. He looked toward his son lying beside him quietly eating some fruit. Zoar tousled his hair.

The boy looked up at him questioningly.

Why doesn't he smile at me? thought Zoar. *It must be his mother's influence. I'll soon take care of that.* Zoar reached over and picked some other delicious tidbits and offered them to his son.

Shaking his head, his son continued to eat his fruit.

This refusal angered Zoar, but he didn't show it. He

wanted his son to love him. Zoar would do anything for him. Reaching over, he stroked Dorak's cheek while watching the dancing girls, his heart a little wearier.

Out of the corner of his eye, he saw several of his commanders talking amongst themselves. *There is news, but they are deciding who will tell me. It must be bad. And whom shall I punish if it is bad?*

Finally, the youngest of the commanders approached the aga, asking permission to speak.

"What is it?" demanded Zoar gruffly. "Can't you see I'm spending time with my son? What do you want?"

The young commander glanced back at the other officers.

This pleased Zoar. He wanted his soldiers to be afraid. Men fearing for their lives were easy to control.

"Well, speak up! Speak up!"

"Great Aga. One of our spies in Anqara has reported something that we think would interest you."

Zoar sat up. A servant immediately straightened the pillows behind his back. "You have found the secret hiding place of the banks?"

The young man, knowing better than to answer with a negative reply, simply dodged the question. Zoar asked so many questions he sometimes forgot. "One of our spies in Anqara reported that several nights ago two large beings of an unknown origin burst into the room of the High Priestess in the House of Magi."

"Continue." Zoar leaned forward, showing his interest.

"These beings were dressed as birds and flew into the High Priestess' room which sits at the very apex of the building."

Zoar laughed.

The commander did not smile.

"You really don't expect me to believe your fairy tale, do you?" asked Zoar.

"This particular spy has been extremely competent in the past and swears with his life this is true."

"Two men, dressed up as birds, flew into the room of one of the most revered persons in the world. Is this what you are telling me?"

"Great Aga, we have other reports of people seeing these strange birdlike creatures in the past several weeks. There is a butcher in Anqara who swears he was attacked by one."

Zoar waved the dancing girls away as the music died. He slowly sipped some shaybar—a boiled drink of borax blood and milk. "You know, this story reminds me of something." He placed his finger to his mouth, thinking, "But I can't think what."

He held out his hand. A servant wiped Zoar's hand with a warm cloth and then dried it. The aga held out the other hand. She wiped it clean.

"I would like to speak to this spy."

Smiling, the commander replied, "Great Aga, our man thought this so important he has traveled here to speak to you personally."

"Good. Bring him in."

The commander waved to the guards standing by the large tent flaps. They opened them carefully. Outside, a dust storm was raging.

A small, meager man stepped inside. He stood by the aga's favorite horses near the edge of the tent and shook the dust off his new clothes. Adjusting his eyes to the light, he soon saw the commander beckoning. He approached the young officer timidly. When he reached him, he spoke to the commander in a language unknown to Zoar.

The aga watched the spy carefully.

The little man realized he was standing before the Great Aga and kowtowed.

"Tell this little baggage to get up!"

The commander spoke in low tones. The little man shook his head and mumbled a reply.

"He says he is not worthy to look upon your greatness."

Zoar was pleased but did not respond. He called for more oil lamps so he could see better.

Servants with lamps and torches immediately stood beside the commander and the spy.

The commander spoke again to the little man.

The kneeling man responded at length, making various hand gestures.

Nodding from time to time, the officer kept encouraging the man to keep talking until the spy was through telling his story.

"Great Aga," said the commander, turning toward Zoar. "This man is Kaysian from the northern region of Kaysia. He has been in your service for over two years now. Several months ago, he was assigned to Anqara where he dresses as a beggar. His orders were to watch the House of Magi for any unusual activity. For the time he has been watching the House of Magi, nothing out of the ordinary had occurred until three nights ago."

The commander paused as if for effect and glanced around him, studying his comrades' faces. "Three nights ago, this man swears he saw two persons fly to the chamber of the High Priestess, hover in the sky without benefit of ropes or wires, and burst through the glass to the room."

The beggar spy remained kneeling with his forehead on the carpet.

Zoar interrupted, "Were they male or female?"

The commander turned to the spy and asked him,

giving him a little kick.

The little man sat up and shrugged as he replied.

"He says he does not know for sure. He thinks male because they were so large."

"How large?" queried Zoar.

When asked, the diminutive man pointed toward the horses.

"As large as my warhorses!" exclaimed Zoar.

Frightened, the little man pressed his forehead into the carpet again.

Zoar ignored him. "What else did he say?"

"He says they stayed for half an hour and then left via the same window, flying due west," answered the commander.

The spy looked up questioningly.

"What happened to the High Priestess?"

"Nothing, as far as we know. He said he stayed until he was sure there was no death call."

"She could have been murdered, and the rest of those witches are covering it up," said Zoar.

The commander spoke again to the spy.

The spy shook his head, replying quickly while stealing looks at Zoar.

"He says there would be no reason to do that as the House of Magi has no known political or religious affiliations. The House of Magi is a house of study and intellectual pursuits. There is no reason to hide the death of the High Priestess."

"Why is she called the High Priestess if she is only a reader of dusty scrolls?" questioned Zoar.

The commander looked sheepish. "My lord, it is a type of joke. The scholars are given to whimsy."

Zoar mulled this over for a moment.

"Great Aga, women with the best minds from all over the world come to the House of Magi to study and contemplate."

"Just women?"

"Yes, sire. Mostly women. There are a few men."

"Do we have any contact with them?"

The commander consulted his comrades. "Great Aga, I am sorry to report that we have made attempts, but all of our applicants have been rejected."

"What about servants?"

"They use none."

"Slaves?"

The commander shook his head.

Zoar gave an astonished look to his son, who was listening carefully. "Who cooks? Who cleans? Who serves?"

"Um, they do. They apparently take turns."

"I understand that there is only one door and it's open all the time. Just have one of our people enter it."

Zoar was growing agitated. He disliked the thought of smelly, old women getting the best of him.

"Several of our men disguised as scholars have entered just as you suggested. The doorway leads into a stone room where the only doorway is the one they've entered. We have not been able to discover an entryway into the main part of the building. Also, our men have reported that while searching, even in the dead of night, the priestesses appear out of nowhere and assault our men, chasing them from the building."

"Chase our men away? How did they manage that?"

The commander blushed. "They were hit on the head with brooms and pots, Great Aga."

"Brooms?" questioned Zoar. "Our men are chased away by gray-haired women swinging brooms?"

"Most of the women are young and quite strong."

"Brooms!" shouted Zoar. "My soldiers, my best spies, men in the prime of their lives, run off by straw and wood! Little man, have you been inside the House of Magi?"

The commander translated as the spy spoke rapidly. "He says that was never his assignment, Great Aga. But if you will give him the opportunity, he will find a way in."

"Who gives him his assignments?"

"He does not know. He finds written instructions

inside his bread basket and burns the instructions as soon as he finds them."

"Someone is leaving written instructions in a bread basket so anyone can read them. I don't believe the imbecility of my network!" Zoar shouted.

Both the commander and the spy bowed low, moving out of Zoar's reach.

Zoar kicked over a fruit tray.

When a servant bent over to pick up the fruit, Zoar kicked him as well.

"Little man," said Zoar to the beggar spy. "I will make a deal with you. Find the way into the House of Magi and find out the secret of your flying birds, and I will give you your freedom and ten more of these." Zoar threw a bag of gold at him as the commander was rapidly translating.

The spy's face lit up at the sight of the gold. He greedily grabbed it, almost slobbering.

The man's lack of control disgusted Zoar. He turned his head and waved the commander and the spy away.

The commander grabbed the arm of the spy and dragged him from the room as the beggar spy continued speaking gibberish and bowing his head.

Wishing to calm himself, Zoar called for refreshments.

The musicians began to softly play again as the

dancing girls floated in. They swirled in their colorful costumes while flirting with Zoar's men.

Zoar paid them little attention. He was thinking about what the little spy had said.

He was not alone.

In the dark shadows of the tent, KiKu was seething with rage. He slowly pacified himself with controlled, short breaths, a technique he had learned on his journeys. That man was *his* spy with orders to report only to KiKu personally. The little traitor would have to pay for his disloyalty, but not here, not now. He must bide his time. KiKu knew who the birds were. They were the Dinii, an almost mythical species told about in fairy tales to children. How strange Zoar did not see the connection. But he might soon enough. KiKu studied Zoar's face. He knew Zoar was deep in thought. It would be only a matter of time before Zoar realized who the Bird People were and determined their connection to the land beyond the mist.

KiKu must stall him until his own plans could be placed into effect. That must be done first. Then, KiKu had a little surprise for the beggar spy who would meet his death in a dark alley, but not before the cat played with the tiny mouse for a long time.

9

Iegani returned to Mehmet.

He visited when the moons were the weakest and
the night was the darkest. At first, it was to check on the
deciphering of the code. At least that's what he told
himself even though Toppo was keeping watch on the
priestess. However, as the passage of time lengthened,
Iegani found himself growing very fond of Mehmet.

Months grew into changing seasons and seasons
grew into years. A strong friendship developed between
the two of them, which later blossomed into a romance.
It was not easy for Iegani to make love to a fragile
creature such as Mehmet, but they went very slowly, and
he did his utmost to be gentle.

It was very different from mating with a Dini. Dinii
females tended to be a passionate lot with strong, fierce
emotions. Since the females were stronger, the males

had to be careful. And Dinii mated while flying in the air, which is what Iegani preferred, but Mehmet had other qualities, which gave him just as much pleasure.

Mehmet had a quick wit, making Iegani laugh. She suited Iegani at his advanced age. He was glad she was not Dinii, although he strongly suspected what really interested Mehmet was that he was. This caused him to smile. She was incorrigible in her thirst for knowledge.

Over the years, Iegani regaled Mehmet with stories of Hasan Daeg and its people who were geniuses with plants, but he spoke very little of his own city and people.

Iegani's visits were more frequent lately as groups of Dinii, under the cover of night, smuggled in supplies to the House of Magi.

Zoar, frustrated that his spy network had been unable to ferret out the bankers' strongholds, finally laid siege to the city with the intent of starving the Anqarians into submission.

That had been seven years ago.

Anqara had resisted with splendid courage. The people of Anqara had spat from the tops of the city walls upon the heads of Zoar's soldiers as they tried unsuccessfully to storm the great stone barriers.

No outside enemy had ever taken Anqara in her five-thousand-year history. Even if the city's walls were breached, the enemy would be confused by the winding narrow streets. Not being able to march more than two men abreast would markedly slow the enemy's advance into the heart of the city.

But the citizens of Anqara had never encountered an enemy like Zoar. He was indomitable.

The underground of their city was honeycombed with secret exits into the countryside. Special agents were given the task of searching outside and bringing back foodstuffs.

Zoar discovered the secret exits, and the Anqarian military had no choice but to destroy them to keep his men from entering the underground passages.

Rebels from neighboring villages catapulted supplies over the city walls. They were quickly sought out and killed by Zoar's men.

Still, the people of Anqara were stout and resolute. During the spring months when the river ran high and wild, they cheerfully threw buckets over the walls into the moats surrounding the city and drew up water heavy with silt. Every available patch of yard, street, or alleyway was converted into a garden. Vegetables of all varieties were growing on balconies, rooftops, porches, wagons, troughs, and window boxes. Seeds became more precious than gold.

Carpenters made a small fortune constructing water-tight rain barrels. The city's garbage was taken to the House of Magi where many of the reclusive scholars came out and showed the Anqarians how to make compost, recycle, and handle their own waste without contamination.

In response, Zoar constructed a great dam across the river and diverted its flow out of the city's reach.

Zoar personally admired the Anqarians' tenacity, even though his generals cursed them. They wanted to return to Bhuttan.

The Anqarians were a very intelligent people, by far his most worthy opponents to date, but Zoar would not be deterred. It was only a matter of time. After seven years, the city had exhausted its resources. The huge compost heaps surrounding the great portico of the House of Magi existed no more. Every scrap of available wood had long since been made into a water barrel or an arrow. Zoar constantly harassed the city with flaming coals shot over the walls. Over the years, anything not made of stone had burned to the ground. The people were reduced to wearing rags. Still, they resisted.

The plague broke out in Zoar's camp. He rejoiced. Special catapults were constructed so that plague-ridden corpses could be heaved over Anqara's walls. Sickness soon spread throughout the city.

The women from the House of Magi knew how to combat the plague, but they had no way of making the medicine they needed. They could only make the ill comfortable until they died. Mehmet sent word for the Dinii to stay away. Nothing could help them now as there were not enough soldiers to stand guard. Zoar would storm the walls soon. Yet Mehmet kept her window open just in case.

The next dark night Iegani appeared.

"Didn't I tell you not to come!" snapped Mehmet, although she was relieved to see him.

"The Dinii are not affected by your little illness," growled Iegani. "Is the code deciphered?"

"Code, code, that's all I hear from you. The world is burning, and you care for nothing but your little piece of bark."

"That's right. Have you discovered the meaning?"

Mehmet gave him a disgusted look.

Iegani suddenly felt ashamed and held Mehmet in his winged arms, enveloping her.

She loved the woodsy smell of him. Mehmet sighed as she laid her head against his feathered chest and listened to his steady heartbeat.

"I'm sorry, Mehmet. You are struggling to survive here, and I pester you month after month about the code. Look, I have brought food."

"Give it to the children outside," she chided, pulling away.

"No, you are more important."

"Will I be as important when I have finished deciphering the code?"

"You're speaking gibberish."

"Am I?"

"Sit down, Mehmet. I have something to discuss with you. For the past several weeks, I have been having secret talks with Queen Abisola. She has agreed to absorb fifteen hundred refugees from Anqara."

"What do you mean?" asked Mehmet, clutching Iegani's arm in hope.

"Tomorrow night, two thousand Dinii will fly into Anqara and fly out fifteen hundred persons. It is a one-time operation. I dare not risk it again. Zoar never makes the same mistake twice. We think that, with careful maneuvering, most of us will make it. It will be raining, and we are hoping the thunder will cover the sound of our wings."

"But there are more than four thousand children in Anqara!"

Iegani paused. "We will take those we can, but not all. We are going to evacuate all of the scholars from the House of Magi. We will also be taking with us the bankers and their families. Whatever soldiers are left we will fly out, and finally the children."

"Monstrous!" cried Mehmet. "I will not be a party to this!"

Iegani grabbed her by the shoulders and shook her.

Mehmet looked at him with fear.

"Listen to me," he commanded. "We must rescue the most important resources. I know it sounds cruel, but that is how it must be. Your women must be the first flown out of here. Your minds, your knowledge, your logic must be preserved to fight Zoar. Do you really think Anqara would have withstood Zoar for seven years without you and your disciples? Anqara would have been starved out in two years at the most."

Mehmet turned her head away.

"You know it's true," said Iegani.

"Why the bankers?"

"Because of the money. In return for their lives, they will hand over to us the treasure of Anqara." Iegani searched for words. "Don't you see? Queen Abisola can use this money to trade with the Sivans to make a last stand against Zoar? It makes sense to take it. Why let it fall into Zoar's possession?"

"You are not taking this money for yourself?"

"Take a good look at me, Mehmet. We used to be the lords of this planet. We used to be great teachers and knowledge gatherers like yourselves. We were powerful like Zoar until we met the Lahorians. Our minds never recovered from the encounter. We now shun knowledge for intuition.

"Instead of great houses, we live on the tallest mountain in a city built of sticks plastered with mud. We have almost refashioned our beings into a true animal state. Our needs are simple. What would the Dinii want of the Anqarian treasure?

"It is for Queen Abisola so she may buy weapons. It will be she who makes the last stand. Your work is done here, Mehmet," he said, stroking her hair. "You gave us the time we needed."

"And what of the code?"

"If you cannot decipher the code, I will find another way to fight Zoar. I truly thought it was a riddle to the future. What matters is that you be ready with your women tomorrow night. You must wait for us on top of the roof."

Mehmet began weeping. "Oh, these terrible choices. What will become of those not taken?"

"If they are lucky, they will die quickly." Iegani kissed her forehead, sighing. "I know, I know," he whispered. "It is terrible." His eyes grew moist.

"Iegani."

"Yes, loved one."

"I know what the code says."

"What!" exclaimed Iegani.

"I have known for years."

"Why didn't you tell me?"

"Because we needed the Dinii's help. I thought that if I told you the truth, you would go away with the secret, and the medical and food supplies would stop being flown in. We needed them so desperately."

Mehmet went to the window and looked out. "I am an evil woman, I know. I realize the end is soon. Even with the plague medicine from Hasan Daeg, most of us will not survive. We are simply too weak. That's why I sent word not to come." Mehmet chanced a look at Iegani. "There was no reason to risk your life anymore. Please forgive me. I was trying to save my people, my city." She held out her hands in supplication.

Iegani fell on his knees and kissed the palms of her worn hands. "Mehmet, it is I who should beg for your forgiveness. I should have taken you away years ago."

"You tried," she laughed, "but I always stopped you. It would be the death of me. I would rather meet Zoar face-to-face than touch the clouds. Oh no, I am a land-bound creature. You are the one that wings to the sky." She laughed again. Hastening to her desk, she spread a scroll across the desk.

Iegani bent over to look.

"The writing you gave me is very ancient. I had to

scour for many months in our library before I could find a comparison. I was correct about one thing. It had its basis in Lahorian. But I was looking for words. The code is not a message but a formula. These symbols are not words but numbers and chemical compounds."

"But what does it mean?" asked Iegani, quivering with excitement.

"What you see before you is an equation for extreme longevity. Perhaps even immortality. Just think of what this means."

"I am. Zoar must never have this."

"You don't think this equation could really work, do you?"

"I do. I got this code from a tattoo on the back of Princess Maura. Only the rulers have this tattoo, and all Hasan Daeg rulers are extremely long-lived." Iegani thought for a moment. "What are the chemical compounds?"

"Very rare protein compounds found in very evolved plant life. These compounds interact with natural hormones in a donor's body. Mutates them. If we were to take a sample of Queen Abisola's blood, I think we would find her blood altered from that of her countrymen. How do the rulers die?"

"They voluntarily die. They wait until their only child is forty years of age, and if the child is not defective, the ruling monarch abdicates and retires to a special compound in the forest. There, they meditate until they simply will themselves to death."

"If the child is unsuitable for the throne or simply dies, can the parent reproduce again?"

"Yes, but it has only happened once before."

"You have told me that the Hasan Daegian rulers are blue. Do you know of any plant that only they use and not the rest of the population?"

"There are ancient myths that the Hasan Daegian rulers once made a treaty with a plant that was self-aware. Complete rubbish."

"And this plant does not exist?"

"Never did. It is just a story," Iegani lied.

Mehmet rubbed her chin. "But we have seen evidence that the Hasan Daegians are gifted with understanding the uses of plants. Were they like this before they were relocated to Hasan Daeg?"

"We have no memory of it. They were slaves. Maybe under servitude they were not able to act out their natural tendencies and had to compensate."

"What are their origins?"

"They were of different stocks collected from all over the world."

"But the Hasan Daegians are not like the rest of the world. You tell me the females are on average two to three inches taller than the males and almost twice as strong. They are naturals with plants, which seem to respond to them in a positive manner. Plants grow very fast in Hasan Daeg and produce much more food than the same plant, for example, in Anqara. Right?"

"I have observed this to be true."

"And you don't think this is strange?"

"The Dinii females are larger than the males and stronger."

"But you are a bird. These are people!"

Iegani acted insulted.

Mehmet tried another avenue. "Don't you think it is a wondrous thing the Hasan Daegians claim their plants can talk to them?"

Iegani shook his head. "I don't think they mean the plants have an actual language. They mean to say that from intuitive thinking and observation, they understand the biological nature of plants. It is just the same way a Dini can read nature by observing natural phenomena."

"Oh, Iegani, open your eyes!" exclaimed Mehmet, frustrated with her lover. "Your race has had this mystery under its nose for centuries and never investigated. If you didn't know Lahorians were living in your territory for almost two thousand years, what else was going on that you didn't know? Maybe the Dinii should start hunting in the day instead of the night."

"There is truth to your words. We were negligent. As long as there was plenty of game to eat, we did not look too hard."

Mehmet sat in her chair and lit her pipe, smoking quietly until she remarked, "There is so much to do. I must rest awhile now."

Iegani knelt down beside her and held her hand gently.

Mehmet caressed Iegani's leathery cheek. "A plant could provide the compounds listed in this equation. Do you think such a plant exists, dear one? I believe such a plant exists, probably right under your nose, Iegani, Great Divigi from the House of Gitar. Take the scroll and go now."

"Everything is explained in this scroll?"

"Yes, all the compounds, the amounts needed, and how they should be introduced into the body are written on the scroll."

"Is there another copy?"

"No," lied Mehmet, eyeing Iegani suspiciously.

He handed her back the scroll. "You bring this with you. Have your women ready on the roof. They must dress warmly." Iegani turned to go. He turned back again. "How did you keep me from knowing? I scanned your mind periodically."

Mehmet took a long puff on her pipe and smiled. "Why do you think this is called the House of Magi? You're not the only one who can read minds, you know, or hide from scanning." She glanced out the window. "You must go now. It will be dawn soon."

"Be ready on the roof tonight. We will wait for no one. Understand?"

"Understood."

Iegani flew out the window and, with every beat of his wings, regretted leaving Mehmet and the scroll behind. He believed the rescue of her scholars would cause Mehmet to act with prudence and care. Iegani hoped nothing would befall Anqara before tonight's evacuation.

10

Zoar strode out of his tent.

He looked up and caught a glimpse of Iegani streaking across the orange sky. He watched until Iegani was out of sight. Whatever he thought of the huge bird winging through the sky, he kept to himself. Turning to his First General, he asked, "Is everything ready?"

The general snapped to attention. "Yes, Great Aga."

"Then we attack soon."

"Yes, Great Aga!" The general turned and strode off, screaming orders.

Zoar looked at the sky again, and turning, went back inside his tent.

By the day's end, Anqara would be his.

11

Most Anqarians were asleep.

They awoke to the sound of drums and ran to their rooftops or the city's parapet in their bedclothes to see what was happening. Many unashamedly groaned out loud, but mostly there was a deathly quiet amongst the Anqarians when they saw thousands of enemy soldiers in full combat armor standing like statues under the growing day sky.

Rows and rows of soldiers as far as the eye could see. Silent. Watchful. Deadly. An arrow was shot into the air. At its signal, all of the soldiers began beating their shields with their swords and shouting out war cries.

Many Anqarians covered their ears.

The sound was deafening.

Another arrow was shot into the air.

The soldiers in the front moved aside to let a massive platform emerge from the sea of men. Forty grunting slaves, twenty on each of the front axles, pulled the litter. On top of the platform sat Zoar on a golden throne encrusted with precious gems. He wore costly silk robes embroidered with the symbol of the dragon, his personal emblem. On Zoar's head was a wreath of flowers.

Beside him sat Dorak wearing a similar outfit.

Behind Zoar stood his two senior generals. Bright yellow plumes on their helmets danced gaily in the light morning breeze.

Musicians with drums stood on either side and followed the litter onto the plain.

At Zoar's signal, the procession came to a halt, as did all noise.

Zoar slowly stood. His gestures were exaggerated. "People of Anqara," he shouted. "I come in a last effort for peace. You must be tired and hungry. Open your gates to us. My men will bring food to your markets the likes of which you have not seen for years. Open your hearts to me. My healers will attend the sick and wounded. Let us put aside our differences. I am offering peace and prosperity. Join with me to build a great empire. Put your names alongside mine on the roster of glory."

Rude laughter erupted from a parapet. The mayor of Anqara, still dressed in his nightshirt, stood on a box so he could be seen by all. "Go to hell, you unnatural spawn of a demon's womb," the mayor shouted. "We'll not surrender on our knees. We'll die fighting like free men and women."

Zoar furiously threw off his flower wreath. "So be it, you cur. Their deaths," screamed Zoar, waving at the Anqarian people, "are on your head!"

"A pox upon you, Zoar. You would have slaughtered us anyway." The mayor spat in Zoar's direction and left the wall. He ran home to gather his armor and weapons, but he did not get far.

His wife met him at the parapet's steps with his gear. There was no use telling her to go home. He knew she would not leave his side. They smiled at each other, knowing they would be dead before sunset.

Meanwhile, Zoar threw off his robes. Steps appeared at the litter, and his armor and sword were brought to him.

The drums sounded again as his men marched into fighting formation.

Zoar kissed Dorak on the cheek. He turned toward his First Commander. "Place my son on the highest hill. I want him to witness the destruction of Anqara."

"Yes, Great Aga!" answered the commander, saluting.

Zoar turned to a waiting general. "We will begin as soon as Dorak is out of danger."

"Yes, Great Aga!"

Zoar started down the steps. He stopped and turned. "What is a hell?"

The general shrugged. "These people believe in only one god who will send them to a bad place if they do evil."

Zoar smiled. "And so he has." He jumped on his giant warhorse and rode back to his command post, his long black cape with the dragon's emblem flapping in the wind.

12

The battle raged for many hours.

Yeti and Benzar flew high over the city and landed on a hill to the south of Anqara. The sky was already darkening with the coming storm. They quickly assessed the situation and flew back to Yesemek and Iegani, who were waiting impatiently for them.

"Well?" snapped Iegani.

"Zoar has committed his troops in earnest. He has brought in reinforcements from Bhuttan. He will either take Anqara today or he will die trying," confirmed Yeti.

"He is in full uniform. I think Zoar will lead his men into the city himself," Benzar reported.

"No one ever accused Zoar of being a coward," claimed Yesemek. She looked at Iegani. "Now what?"

Iegani shook his head. "We will have to keep to our plan."

"But, Iegani, they could all be dead by nightfall," asserted Yesemek, Empress Gitar's First Commander and Iegani's wife.

"I realize that, Yesemek, but if we go in now, we expose ourselves to Zoar. If Zoar doesn't pick us out of the sky one by one, the Anqarians will kill us thinking we are Zoar's minions abducting their prize citizens. No, we will have to wait for night and hope the sky is very dark." He muttered to himself, "And pray the Anqarians are very good fighters. They must hold on until dark."

Yesemek nodded in agreement. She turned toward Lieutenant MeNe. "Tell the others to rest quietly for now. We move out as soon as it is dark."

Iegani asked, "Yeti, did you see Toppo?"

"No, she must be hiding in the city until nightfall."

Iegani nodded and wandered off by himself. Finding an empty branch, he perched, going into a trance. Hoping that Mehmet was really telepathic, he sent her word to hold her position and wait. All through the morning, he sent his message until, exhausted, he fell asleep.

13

The fighting was fierce.

Zoar rained the city with treated arrows that exploded on contact.

The citizens found it hard to breathe with all the smoke within their city walls. Every Anqarian man and woman who could fight, carry water buckets, or care for the wounded was doing so.

Many of the children were rounded up and hidden in the tunnels underneath the city. A group of women were digging the rubble out of a previously blown-up tunnel with the hopes of getting the children out of the city. Sweat poured off their bodies. Many tore off their shirts, tying strips of material around their foreheads to catch the sweat and their hands to stop the bleeding. The older children helped by carrying baskets of rock and dirt to the tops of the tunnels.

One of the women stopped digging long enough to form the children into a line, each handing the next a basket filled with debris. None of the children cried, not even the smallest.

The Anqarian military fought bravely. Unexploded arrows were recycled to fit Anqarian bows and shot back at Zoar's men. The Anqarians could hear the enemy scream as the arrows exploded on contact.

Zoar countered with two huge scaffolds dragged by hundreds of his men. One was set against the northeastern wall and the other against the southwestern wall, thus splitting the Anqarian defenses.

The Anqarians tried desperately to set the scaffolds on fire, but Zoar had installed roofs of brass, which deflected anything the Anqarians tried. Once installed, Zoar's men swarmed up the scaffolds and stood in position. The roofs were pulled off by a system of pulleys exposing hundreds of soldiers. They held their shields over their heads to protect them from rocks thrown by the Anqarians.

Moving as a single beast, Zoar's army swarmed over the walls, climbing blindly until they were safely on the parapets. Immediately, they set their shields upright and began hand-to-hand fighting.

The Anqarians, weakened by years of deprivation, were no match for the battle-hardened Bhuttanian soldiers and soon fell back into the city.

There was hard fighting on both sides.

Zoar's generals soon found that any map they possessed of Anqara was false. They were fighting blindly as to their position inside the city. Much to their dismay, each street had to be taken one at a time. No more than two soldiers could march abreast in the tiny, winding streets. They were met with resistance everywhere.

Anything the Anqarians could set on fire, they threw at the enemy. They struck from balconies and windows, using the house rooftops as their main corridors, moving up and down at will.

Zoar, furious that his men were taking such a beating, ordered his soldiers up, only to find the stairwells booby-trapped. Soon the stairs were impassable with the corpses of his men.

Ropes were ordered so his men could scale the walls of houses. Once on the rooftops, the sheer number of Zoar's men overwhelmed the Anqarians. Many roofs collapsed from the weight.

This slowed Zoar even more. Without the roofs to use as passages into the heart of the city, he had to stop and begin digging the streets clear again. To make matters worse, it began to rain and continued raining the rest of the afternoon with the storm intensifying as night approached. He did not even hear the Dinii arrive from the western sky and land on still-standing roof-tops.

The Dinii, in groups of twenty, flew in their regular V formation until landing was imminent. The V straightened to a single line, and they hovered in the air until the signal to land was given.

Iegani was the first to land on the rooftop of the House of Magi.

Mehmet ran and embraced him. The rain was pouring so hard she could barely see his face. Behind him, ten Dinii landed, forming two lines on the roof. Iegani shouted at Mehmet, "Are you ready?"

"Everyone was told to come here at dusk. If they are not here, they have died fighting."

The women behind Mehmet looked frightened. They knew of the existence of the Dinii, but only the High Priestess had ever had contact with them. They had never seen them. Many were silently praying. Everyone could hear the fighting had made its way to the street below.

"Tell your women they will be blindfolded and placed in a harness. They will go through this line." He pointed to the waiting Dinii. "My hawks will place them on the edge of the wall where my flyers will swoop down and snatch them up by the harness. My people are strong enough to attach the harness in flight. This will allow them to fly with their hands free. If your women struggle, my warriors have instructions to drop them. I will not endanger my race any more than I have to. Do you understand?"

Mehmet nodded. She had her women form a single file. She told the first woman, "Close your eyes. Don't open them no matter what. Don't move unless they move you." She kissed the woman on the cheek. "Good luck."

The scholar looked at Mehmet apprehensively. The din of fighting and dying men groaning increased in the streets below. She took a deep breath and walked toward the waiting Dinii. She closed her eyes. The first two Dinii in line straightened her arms perpendicular to her body and pushed her forward. The second two Dinii roughly put her in a harness. The third pair of Dinii buckled the harness. The fourth pair blindfolded her. The last duo checked the harness and placed the woman on the edge of the rooftop. Within seconds, a hawk swooped from the sky, gathered her up, and was gone into the dark night. The remaining women heard their colleague scream as she was lifted up.

Iegani did not give the women time to think. "Move, move!" he yelled, pushing them forward. "Keep it going!"

Mehmet helped by repeating over and over again,

"The blindfolds are so that you will not be frightened high up in the air. Don't struggle or they will drop you. Do as they say. It is your only salvation. Hurry! Hurry, my children! We must not fall into Zoar's hands!"

The scholars obeyed. After the first scholar, no one screamed. Any small sounds they made were muffled by the constant beating of the rain and roar of the thunder. During flashes of lightning, they could see Dinii on other rooftops doing the same. They wondered how many were going to get out that night. How many of them were going to die?

14

Zoar heard strange sounds.

He wiped the blood and dirt off his visor to scan the sky. He could see nothing, but he felt something was happening.

General Alexanee came up behind him. "The House of Magi is surrounded."

"Good," said Zoar. "Bring the ladders. What about the rest of the city?"

"The entire city has been surrounded. No one can get in or out without our knowing about it."

"And if they try?"

"They are being cut down on the spot."

Zoar grunted, "Take a platoon of men and search the catacombs. The treasure has to be somewhere near here."

"The catacombs are already being searched, Great

Aga."

"Report to me immediately if anything is found."

Soldiers bearing ladders ran past Zoar.

He followed them.

The House of Magi had no windows save those on the top floors and only on one side of the building.

Since the Bhuttanians couldn't penetrate the building, they would have to start at the top and work their way down. The soldiers put the ladders up and waited. No resistance. A special team assembled at the ladders and ascended. Reaching the top of the ladders, they began climbing the walls as if they were rock cliffs. They slowly made their way up until they reached the first set of windows. They jumped inside the building.

Zoar waited until his men poked their heads out and let down ropes. "No one here," they cried.

Other soldiers began a system of pulleys to easily lift men into the building. Zoar wrapped his hands and feet around a stiff rope, holding on as he was lifted up. His men pulled him inside a window. "Search each room. Don't kill any of the women. I want to interrogate them. Leave things undisturbed," he ordered. He began searching each room himself.

His men split into two groups, one group searching downstairs and the other up.

Zoar went up.

15

The women had been evacuated.

Iegani turned toward Mehmet. "You go next."

Mehmet pulled the scroll out of her robes and handed it to Iegani.

Iegani's eyes lit up. He put it carefully in a pouch and handed it to a courier. "Give this personally to Empress Gitar. She will know what to do."

The courier bowed and flew off, heading directly into the storm.

Mehmet backed away from Iegani. "I'm sorry, but I can't go with you, Iegani."

"What do you mean?"

"I'm terrified of flying. If you force me, I will die of heart failure. I cannot go."

"I can't leave you here."

"I don't want to die, but I can't go. Not that way."

Iegani started to panic. He scanned her mind.

Indeed, Mehmet did not bother to hide her thoughts from him. It was true. She was almost beyond reason with fear.

"Mehmet, listen to me," he yelled through the beating rain. "You can't stay here. You're being irrational. Let me blindfold you. You won't be able to see anything."

She shook her head and continued to back away from him. "Zoar will not know who I am. I'll pretend I'm a cleaning servant."

Iegani took several steps toward her. "I can't leave you behind. You're too dangerous alive if you get caught by Zoar."

"I'll be careful."

"Is this your last word?"

"Yes. Go now before we're caught." Mehmet turned to run only to find Benzar standing behind her. She looked up at him with her eyes pleading.

Without any expression, he quickly broke her neck and gently laid her down on the stone roof. He waited for Iegani.

The old owl went over to Mehmet and knelt down. "Oh, Mehmet, Mehmet. Why did you have to be so stubborn? You could have flown with me. I would never have dropped you."

"Great Divigi, Zoar is in the building. We must go!"

"Retreat then. I will follow in a moment."

Benzar flew off.

Iegani patted Mehmet's hand in the rain. He could feel her heat already dissipating. He heard Zoar cursing loudly down below.

Reluctantly, Iegani flew around the House of Magi to Mehmet's window. Entering her room, he pulled her portrait off the wall, causing the door to the secret chamber to open. Iegani was stunned at the material in the secret chamber. How could Mehmet have hidden this room from him?

To make matters worse, Mehmet had not destroyed her valuable papers and correspondence. Had it been Mehmet's intention to betray him and make a deal with Zoar? Iegani didn't have time to ponder this.

He could not take the chance her notes would be deciphered. Like a mad man, he pulled all books and scrolls into the middle of the secret room, forming a huge pile. Seizing an oil lamp, he started to throw it just as Zoar burst into the room, his sword drawn.

Zoar and Iegani stood frozen, staring at each other.

Even in old age, Iegani was fast. He threw the oil lamp into the secret chamber, setting it on fire. Grabbing Mehmet's portrait, he jumped on the windowsill, ready to take flight.

Zoar roared, "What are you?"

Iegani grinned. "Your nightmare!"

Before Zoar could draw another breath, Iegani disappeared into the rain.

16

D espair.

It's what Queen Abisola felt as she stood on her private balcony watching with the rest of O Konya as the Dinii ferried in the last of the survivors of Anqara.

This was the first time many of her people had seen a Dini, let alone scores of them dropping terrified and screaming Anqarians from the sky into nets woven to catch them.

After the initial sweep of Anqara, many Dinii had volunteered to go back to the burning city, saving whom they could. Starved children, bleeding warriors, terrified adults were plucked from the streets and rooftops of the dying city only to be unceremoniously dropped into a refugee camp on the southern side of O Konya, closed off from the rest of the city.

Injured, angry, confused, hungry, and just ready for

a good fight, the rescued Anqarians were anything but grateful.

They rioted.

Hasan Daeg's newly trained soldiers had to be called into the camp until the situation could be controlled.

Women from the House of Magi finally calmed down the frightened refugees by helping to ladle out bowls of hot soup. But bedlam broke out again as exhausted Dinii flew into the camp to receive medical treatment, eat, and sleep.

Several hostile Anqarians brandished large wooden spoons at the resting Dinii. An Anqarian soldier got too close to one of the Dinii hawks, who merely picked up the young lad with her taloned foot and threw him back into the antagonistic crowd. If the looks on the Anqarians' faces hadn't been so wild with terror, it would have been amusing.

The women from the House of Magi formed a barrier so the hungry Dinii could rest on constructed perches in peace while eating raw meat.

The Anqarians calmed down when they realized that *they* were not going to be the Dinii's dinner.

From her window, Abisola watched it all. She shook her head and wondered how they were going to assimilate the more combative Anqarians into the passive Hasan Daegian culture.

She received word from Iegani that all of Anqara had fallen. The intellectual center of the world had fought until she could no more. Abisola prayed for those who had gone to their graves bravely. She also prayed for herself. Abisola grieved over the eventual loss of the world as she knew it. She grieved over the loss of her child to the Dinii. She grieved over the hardships that were to come.

Abisola hated the changes that needed to be made if her people were to survive. But most of all, she grieved for herself and her husband. Queen Abisola had been contemplating suicide for several weeks. She even procured the powder needed to put herself and Iasos to death. She would not leave her faithful consort behind. She would give the powder to him in his nightly colla tea, holding him until he fell into sleep and then into death. After dressing him in his ceremonial robes, she would robe herself and, lying beside him, take her own life.

That had all changed. Several nights ago, an apparition appeared to Abisola and begged her not to take her life.

"We know what you are contemplating," declared the phantom. "This you must not do! It is imperative that you live."

"I have no faith left," answered Queen Abisola.

"There is no spirit in this body. I am bones and nothing more."

"You must find courage!"

"My mind is in constant turmoil. I am a selfish woman. I want the peace only death can bring."

"This is not about what you nor I want."

Abisola waved her hand in front of her face. "Go away, spirit. Leave me!"

A gaseous form drew together into a vision of a woman gliding across the room as though riding a wave. Abisola, so despondent, did not even become alarmed at the sight.

"Look at me," commanded the spirit. "I am not as I once was." The spirit turned around. "Look in earnest at me. What do you see?"

Abisola observed the spirit carefully. "You are with child!" exclaimed Abisola. "How can a spirit, not of flesh, be with child?"

"I am not a spirit, although my species is evolving. I am still flesh and will give birth. Without your help, my child will never see his own children, nor will your daughter see hers."

The queen searched the specter's face for answers. "What are you?" she asked imploringly. "Who are you?"

The visitor now floated inside an orb made of moving water bouncing slightly off the floor. "Who or what

I am is not important. What is important, Your Majesty, is that you take your place in history."

Abisola laughed.

The woman quickly held up a hand, in the middle of which was a closed eye. The eye opened at once and scanned the room.

Startled, Abisola fell back against her chair. She repressed a shiver.

"I will not lie to you," continued the woman. "I cannot. You will die before your time. It will be an ugly death, but only after you have seen all you love destroyed. It is not pretty what I see in the future. But neither is my future. My people will suffer as will yours. I will also die before old age takes me. But I will live until my child can carry on in my place and so must you!"

"My daughter is safe with the Dinii. They can fly from danger, taking my daughter with them."

The woman shook her head sadly. She winced as if in pain and then straightened her shoulders and clapped her hands over her belly. "This conversation is upsetting my offspring. I must hurry." Water inside the phantom's orb began glowing as its sides quivered. "Anqara will fall. Zoar will rip the city apart brick by brick, stone by stone, looking for the treasure of Anqara and the women from the House of Magi."

"I know this," spat out Abisola. "It was I who offered sanctuary. These women will be safe within my city as will be the treasure. Be gone, spirit. I am not afraid."

"Yes, you are, Queen Abisola. You are most afraid that you will not be able to make the sacrifices necessary to win this war. You are afraid of failure, afraid you lack heart. You want to run away and die a coward's death."

Abisola placed her face in her hands and wept. "It is true."

The specter continued. "Princess Maura is not safe. You and she hold the secret Zoar will one day lust after. You must see she completes her quest before he finds her or all will be lost."

"What secret?" implored Abisola. "I don't know what you are talking about." She pounded on the sides of the bubble. Water splashed on the floor. "What is it?"

"The secret is in Iegani's hands and yours," responded the phantom. The orb began to hum loudly and fade. "Seek out Iegani!"

Abisola ran after the bubble. "No, stop, don't go! I need more information. Stop!"

The phantom waved farewell as the bubble disappeared from view.

Falling to the floor, Abisola rolled on her side. Like

a baby, she clutched herself and drew her knees up to her chest. Rocking back and forth, she softly sang lullabies to herself and did not notice when Iasos found her on the cold stone floor.

Alarmed, he picked her up, carrying her to his bedchamber. Once he had her in his bed, he called for help. While waiting for a healer to arrive, he called her name.

Abisola did not respond to him but continued rocking and murmuring.

A servant brought warm, wet cloths that Iasos applied to his queen's forehead and arms. He wiped the perspiration from her torso.

Iasos drew himself up, hearing the commotion of the guards searching for a possible intruder. Iasos suspected whatever had transpired with the queen was in Abisola's mind and not in the palace.

A healer, still dressed in her nightclothes, rushed into the bedchamber. The healer bowed and hurried over to Abisola.

Iasos related how he had found the queen and stood back.

The royal healer threw back the covers with the help of Lady Sari, the queen's old nurse and companion, and stripped off the queen's clothes.

She searched for any kind of marks, even examining under the nails of her hands and feet. She felt for the pulse and examined the eyes and mouth. The healer smelled the queen's breath and sex. After an exhausting examination, she turned to Iasos. "I am sorry, my lord, but I cannot help our queen. She has had a profound shock to her mind. There is nothing wrong with her body."

"What do you mean?"

The healer wearily put away her instruments. "I mean, sire, she is not right in her mind. I can give her sedatives to calm her and herbs to bring her out of the stupor," the healer paused, "but look at her. The queen has regressed to an infantile state. She will come out of it only when she has healed here," said the healer, pointing to her head, "and here," pointing to her heart. "There is nothing more anyone can do." She bowed to Iasos and departed with Sari, giving her instructions about the medicine she was leaving.

"Abisola," Iasos gently whispered. "What trouble have you gotten yourself into? You are so like a child. You want everything to be perfect, to be lovely. You live for beauty and when you see beauty will not last, you want to hide. As if that will make evil go away." Iasos held her hand. "When will you learn I love you for you. You are one of the bravest and truest persons I have ever met. Wherever you have gone, come back to me. I need you."

Iasos stroked her hair. Finding a gray hair, he plucked it out. "I don't think you can stand a gray hair and all this mess too," he teased. He climbed into bed with his queen and held Abisola until he finally fell asleep with exhaustion.

17

Queen Abisola did not rise.

She would not communicate with Iasos nor take the morsels offered by his hand. She just rocked, singing softly.

Iasos would not leave her side, falling asleep in a chair with his arms flung over the bed only to awaken in the morning and finding Abisola not there. In panic, he rushed to her chambers and found her dressed, eating breakfast.

"Good morning, darling," she purred. "We have a good many things to do. Will you help me?" Abisola asked, reaching out to him.

Iasos clasped her hand and sat beside her. "Are you well now?" he asked.

Abisola stroked his cheek gently. "I felt as though I was straddling a high wall, and no matter which side I fell upon, there was doom for all. I will never be well again, dearest, but you and I must act as though I am. I must do things now I don't think you will understand, but we need to move forward if our people are to be preserved. You must help me. Give me strength, I beg of you."

"I will always love you," declared Iasos. "I will help you wherever I can, I promise."

"You are such a comfort to me. You will never know how much." She looked away. "I start in motion a way of life that will not be undone."

"I trust you, Abisola," said Iasos, looking at her with an understanding she had not realized he possessed. "Whatever you think best, I will stand beside you and support you."

Abisola wept. "You are so good to me!"

"You are my queen and wife. I would die for you."

She hugged him closely and kissed his cheek, neck, and then his lips. "I want you to know no matter what happens, I will never leave you behind." She looked deep into Iasos's eyes. "Do you understand?"

Iasos did not look away. "I understand. My destiny is yours. Where you go, I will follow."

More tears gathered in Abisola's eyes. "Who would have thought of such devotion from one so young."

Iasos wiped her tears away. "Will you ever stop

thinking of me as a mere boy?"

Abisola shook her head and laughed, throwing her arms around her husband. "To work now. Enough of this maudlin talk. I will assemble my advisors today. We must start as soon as possible."

"Finish your breakfast first," laughed Iasos. "Our people cannot have a half-starved crone sitting upon the throne."

The queen and her consort gazed at each other with tenderness.

Abisola smiled, pinching his cheek. "You are such a hen," she teased, stuffing her mouth full with a muffin.

Iasos returned his wife's smile, wondering if this happy breakfast might be their last.

18

Queen Abisola waited.

She had earlier sent word to all her ministers, governors, and nobles that there was to be a royal audience.

It had taken many weeks for all of them to arrive from various parts of the country. With great fanfare, they entered into the audience hall wearing billowing gowns, priceless adornments of precious gems, and rare flowers in their hair while holding large fans painted with their crests and stations.

They chatted politely with each other, each trying to glean information from the other since this was no ordinary summit. A royal decree had summoned them, stating they were to bring only five attendants with them and not their regular retinue. They were told to travel only on the north road and not announce their entrance into O Konya. Displaying their banners and flags was forbidden. Also, the southern parts of the city were denied to them.

O Konya, usually bright and cheerful, was quiet with its citizens rushing home by nightfall. The streets were dark and silent save for strange cries heard from the south side.

Many were sure the queen was going to announce an outbreak of the plague, but others had heard rumors of ghostly birds and war outside the wall of mist. All thoughts were put aside when trumpets blew, announcing the arrival of the queen.

Queen Abisola entered with Consort Iasos and Royal Consul Rubank. Wearing the royal colors of blue and gold, Abisola was resplendent as she proceeded to the marble dais to the accompaniment of drums and horns. Behind her large throne was a massive, stained glass window depicting the first Hasan Daegian queen, Rosalind. Shafts of light through the colored window fell on Abisola, giving her an ethereal quality. As she took her seat, Abisola gave Rubank the signal.

He nodded, and soldiers marched into the audience room. Never had soldiers entered the royal audience room in six hundred years. Once in position along the walls, the soldiers stood at attention, holding out their massive lances. Those soldiers near entrances shut and bolted the doors.

"What is this? How dare you! Open at once!" cried the court.

Queen Abisola sat upon her two-thousand-year-old throne as she waved her fan of royal authority with quiet dignity.

One by one, the crowd quieted down until falling silent and looking expectantly up at their sovereign.

"That is the last time you will be allowed to act with such impudence," announced the queen with resolve, her voice clear and strong.

The nobles and governors looked about at each other in confusion and glancing at the soldiers, determined the queen was going to enforce her wishes with violence if needed. It seemed the days of noisy protests and casual interaction with their Abisola were over. New rules were being put into play.

"Yesterday, we lived free from fear of want or tyranny. We knew such evil existed far away from us, but we were safe behind our veil of mist. But not now. Today, the world is a different place. The fear of war that we have not faced in six hundred years is now upon us and a wall of hypnotic fog is not going to save us. We must save ourselves. The unthinkable has happened. Anqara has fallen to Aga Zoar!"

The royal audience anxiously murmured to each other.

When the queen waved her fan, they quickly fell silent again, but an occasional sob could be heard. Many began sorrowfully wiping their eyes. While most of the court had never left Hasan Daeg, everyone knew that Anqara was the largest and grandest city on Kaseri. This was bad news. Very bad indeed.

"It is only a matter of time until the conqueror of Anqara turns his eyes west to us. Our current defenses will not keep this aga and his warriors out of Hasan Daeg. As he found a way to conquer Anqara, Zoar will find a way into Hasan Daeg, either through the fog or through the secret corridor in Siva. All it will take for our world to be destroyed is one rogue Sivan merchant with a loose tongue and a lust for gold.

"We must be ready. We must prepare. We must change and embrace this change or perish. And we have already begun.

"You all were ordered to enter the city by the north gate, because of sickness in the south side of the city. There is sickness on the south side of O Konya, but not as you were informed. On the south side of the city are refugee camps filled with survivors of Anqara. We endeavored to save as many of them as we could with the hope that they would share their knowledge and, in return for a new home, fight when the time came. We are currently caring for their needs while negotiating a treaty through the House of Magi."

The crowd gasped. Saving the women from the House of Magi and bringing them to Hasan Daeg was impressive. Many, who questioned Hasan Daeg's isolationist policy, were thrilled at having contact with outsiders. The hearts of others overflowed with loathing at the thought of foreigners tainting their "pure" society.

"If strangers are allowed in Hasan Daeg to fight, who else is expected to serve in this capacity?" challenged a high-ranking noble who forgot protocol in the shock of the news.

The nobles, afraid their pampered lives would be threatened, glanced anxiously at each other.

Stunned, the governors stood, wondering how they could implement changes in the general population.

Here was the one question to disrupt Hasan Daegian society more than anything else, but Queen Abisola could not avoid it and she must make her people accept it now.

"We have allies who must be bound tightly to us, but in the end, all of us, even our men, must learn to fight until this dreadful ordeal is over."

Pandemonium broke out. Everyone balked. Some had to sit down even in the royal presence.

"Great Mother," addressed one senior minister,

pointing to the soldiers in the audience room. "You have increased the army five-fold and are now using it to support your policies, but the inclusion of males in our military will cause a great moral collapse. They simply will cause too much confusion."

Another one added, "They are not strong enough to handle our bows."

"Then make smaller ones they can use," rebutted Abisola patiently. "Just as long as they can kill something."

"They have no endurance. Our men cannot handle long marches."

"I don't think they will have to travel to meet the enemy. I believe the enemy will come to us." Abisola raised an eyebrow and scanned the waiting faces below her. She waved the guards into view.

In full body armor, they stood menacingly between the crowd and the doors. They lowered their lances.

"I will tell you what is to happen, and you must accept," demanded Abisola. "You will recognize my royal authority or die."

Iasos was shocked at this implied violence, but showed no change in his expression. He stood unflinching near Abisola in her carved throne on the dais.

There were gasps from the ministers and governors. The nobles glowered.

Abisola leaned forward. "I tell you this once. I am trying to save our people from being wiped off the face of this planet. You stand before me, whining like curs when they don't get their regular bones to gnaw on. You have become soft. Well, Zoar is not soft and soon he will know where we are. Do you think he will come in expensive clothes with fancy manners and flowers in his hair?

"No, he will come with thousands of battle-hardened soldiers swinging weapons we have never seen, much less know how to use. They will break through our defensive wall, and then they will slaughter every living being they can find. Those who are young will be sold as slaves or worse.

"If you love your sons at all, teach them to fight. Dying in battle will be much better than being raped and beaten to death. Maybe, just maybe, we can salvage something of our culture when the time comes, but allow someone else to convince you." Abisola motioned to her consul, who went to a side door and admitted a robed figure.

The Hasan Daegians gasped as the robed person bent over to enter through the tall doorway and then stood in front of Queen Abisola, a full seven feet in height.

"Behold, a Dini!" cried Abisola.

The figure threw off his robe and stood before the crowd in all his feathered glory. To illustrate what he was, he stretched out his ponderous wings and hovered just slightly off the floor. With graceful movements, he retracted his wings and sat on a chair placed on the same level as the queen's on the dais.

The crowd murmured angrily at this breach of protocol.

Queen Abisola held up her hand. "May I introduce Prince Iegani—Great Divigi and uncle to Empress Gitar, fourth in line to the throne of Hasan Daeg, first husband to Yesemek, First Commander to Empress Gitar. Ladies. Nobles. This is your true prince and ruler."

"What lie is this?" cried out one noblewoman.

The crowd hissed and booed, shaking their fists. "Who is this Empress Gitar?"

Queen Abisola stood angrily. "Quiet! Prince Iegani is our guest and will be treated with all Hasan Daegian hospitality!"

The angry crowd fell silent.

The guards, relieved, lowered their lances a tiny fraction.

"Prince Iegani, please speak to my people."

Iegani stood. Facing the crowd, he scanned their minds. He felt hate and great fear, and quickly decided how to appeal to them. "I know my presence must shock you, but now is the time for truth, not myths or rumors. As you must realize now, I am of the Dinii, the winged creatures who brought you here to safety two thousand years ago just as in your creation myths. However, we are not messengers of your goddess, Mekonia. We are creatures like yourselves.

"We are made of blood and bones. Underneath this," he pointed to his feathers, "we have skin like you. And like you now, we have a common enemy—the Great Aga, Zoar. He is coming this way and will be here before your youngest children grow up. The choice you need to make today is whether you want your children to live as free citizens or to live as slaves."

"Zoar won't be able to penetrate the mist!" one woman called out.

"Why not?" Iegani countered. "I penetrate the mist all the time. I simply fly over it. What if Zoar finds a way to fly or he spreads a pollutant in the air and the plants die? The plants could get a fungus or there could be a drought. Oh, a clever man can think of many ways to beat the mist if he is expecting it. Let me assure you, Zoar is a very clever man, and he does know about the mist. He doesn't know yet what is beyond the mist."

"What would he want with us? We are a simple people."

Iegani paused, clenching his teeth, before continuing. "Resources. As simple as that. Hasan Daeg is a breadbasket for one thing. The land is so fertile here that food easily could be produced to feed a population of twelve million. There are, of course, the virgin timberlands in the northern mountains and untapped minerals, such as copper, just waiting for someone to mine them. Shall I go on?

"Hasan Daeg is a country rich in natural resources. Fertile land, plenty of rain, timber, minerals, and a pacifist population thrown in for good measure. You can rest assured that if Zoar knew what is behind the wall of mist, he would sacrifice thousands of his men just to conquer a little part of Hasan Daeg. He would drool at the thought of it."

"Why do you care?" someone cried out.

"Because Hasan Daeg is my country, too. You are here under special treaty signed by your first ruler, Queen Rosalind." He turned and pointed to the figure portrayed in the window. "In Article Seven of the treaty, any population living in Hasan Daeg will declare war on any enemy of their benefactors, the Dinii."

The nobles shook their fists. The royal governors gathered in a group and argued among themselves. Most of the ministers kept their thoughts to themselves.

Iegani noticed it was the ministers who studied him

with purpose.

The great gong sounded. The crowd grew quiet.

Queen Abisola stood beside Iegani. "I have seen this treaty. It is legitimate. We are allowed to live in Hasan Daeg in a symbiotic relationship with the Dinii as long as we cooperate within the guidelines of this treaty."

One noblewoman strode toward the dais. "Let's kill the Dini!" she cried.

A guard jumped in her way and knocked her down, placing the point of the lance at her throat.

Queen Abisola's heartbeat quickened but her expression did not change from one of stoic reserve. "I will let Prince Iegani address this issue."

Prince Iegani bowed to Queen Abisola. He jumped to where the noblewoman had been knocked down, pushing the guard out of the way. He picked the woman up and carried her back to the dais, holding her up by the throat. Spreading his magnificent wings, Iegani rose to the top of the ceiling and dropped the woman to the floor. "Leave her be," he ordered, fluttering down and resting his taloned feet upon the moaning woman.

Others stood in awe.

Iegani held out his hands and, with each finger, released a razor-sharp talon. "Take a good look at these," he boasted, displaying his hands to the assemblage. "Even with your current weaponry, there is neither shield nor armor that will protect you against these. Our females are ten times stronger than your most powerful female. We do not need fire. The cold and wet do not bother us. We rarely get sick. We can out run you, out jump you, out hunt you, out distance you, out endure you. Oh, did I mention that we can fly?" Iegani smiled for effect.

Stepping off the woman, he motioned for the guards to gather her. "She has only a couple of broken bones because I was just toying with her. What do you think I could do if I were angry?" Iegani placed a talon to his pursed lip. "I wager," he said, turning around sharply, "I could kill most of you in this room before you could kill me. No. I wager I could kill all of you before you could kill me." He sat down.

The room went cold with silence.

Abisola gave him a warning glance. He was going too far. She smelled the stink of fear in the room. "Let me remind you that we have lived with the Dinii for two thousand years without serious repercussions. In fact, our association, though a shock to many of you, has been extremely beneficial to our social and political development."

She looked appraisingly at Iegani. "Yes, the Dinii are tremendous in both strength and height, but until this day, they have never shown unwarranted aggression toward us. Most of you had never seen one and thought they were mythical."

Iegani returned Abisola's gaze. He knew when he was being reprimanded. He bowed his head slightly in acknowledgment.

One of the ministers approached the dais. "Great Mother, may I speak?"

Abisola nodded.

The minister stood on the bottom step of the dais and faced the crowd. "I am Jon, minister to Governor Petenptope in the northern state of Kinton. In our region, we have heard many stories of Dinii sightings for generations from our people." She glanced back at Prince Iegani. "Until now, I believed the stories were a product of an overactive imagination or too much ale. I also would like to state that Kinton receives more intruders than any other region. For the past five years, spies and deserters have encroached on our territory. As consistent with current policy, we have led them back out with plenty of food and water, but I want everyone here to understand that these newcomers are not like the wanderers and travelers of old. These new men are cruel and their nature is something unfamiliar to us."

Jon pointed back to Iegani. "I'm glad the Dinii are here. I'm glad they are fierce. I'm glad they are on our side. Let us keep the treaty. Our interests are compatible." Jon thanked the queen and stepped down.

Another minister stepped forward. "If we were to fight Zoar, how would this be accomplished?"

Iegani liked these ministers and was pleased with the intelligent questions rather than the high emotions running among the nobles. He answered, "Hasan Daeg has a military that is little more than an honor guard. You have not fought a war in six hundred years. However, your population density is high. You have over three million people. Your entire population will be turned into a fighting force.

"The Dinii have over ten thousand warriors. We have started a new breeding program. We hope to have twice that many in ten years.

"We will combine our forces and make a stand in Hasan Daeg at the border. We know the terrain. Zoar does not, and he is currently occupied tearing Anqara apart, which gives us time."

The queen, her stiff robes rustling, reiterated, "You see the importance of what we are trying to accomplish. The war is no more outside our country. It is here. It affects us now. No matter what doubts you harbor, this treaty is going to be honored. You will swear your allegiance to me now or you will die. The choice is yours." Abisola returned to her throne and leaned back. Sweat beaded on her upper lip.

Any of the nobles could have rushed the throne and killed her before the guards could intercede. She was a tempting target, except for Iegani beside her.

Iasos sensed danger also, but dared not change his position. Before coming into the audience room, he had inserted a dagger into his boot. He prayed that he would be quick enough to use it if needed.

The governors and ministers seemed resigned. They were known to be more progressive and favor change if it was for the good.

Iasos studied the faces of the nobles. There he registered anger, surprise, and shock. The nobles would resist, for they were the most conservative element of the population.

No one moved. No one spoke.

Finally, there was a cough and a rustle of stiff, rich fabric.

The audience moved aside for Riza, the most respected of all the queen's nobles as she hobbled forward leaning upon her staff. "I was a little girl when you had been queen for many years. We have had peace and prosperity all this time. If you say there is danger, then I believe you. You have never made strong demands before."

Riza struggled to kneel when several of the ministers helped her. "Therefore, I swear allegiance to you, Great

Mother, and will do my utmost to save my queen and country, even at the sacrifice of my life or my children's lives." She bowed her head.

Scribes entered the room and took their places before Queen Abisola.

The ministers and governors kneeled one by one, pledging allegiance to Abisola.

The nobles were the last to swear their oaths, many scowling as they knelt.

After the oaths of fealty were given, Queen Abisola raised the royal fan. "Let this be entered into law. From this day forth, Hasan Daeg males shall have all the rights, privileges, and duties as Hasan Daeg females until the Queen's pleasure is withdrawn."

The great gong sounded.

"From this day forth, all persons from the ages of fourteen to fifty shall be conscripted into the military until the Queen's pleasure is withdrawn."

The gong sounded.

"From this day forth, taxes shall be raised one-eighth until the Queen's pleasure is withdrawn."

The gong sounded.

"From this day forth, the treaty with the Dinii shall be recognized and honored by the current population until the Queen's pleasure is withdrawn."

The gong sounded.

"This is law until the pleasure of the Queen is withdrawn."

At Queen Abisola's command, the guards raised their lances and retreated from the room. Abisola felt victorious. She felt Iasos place his hand on her shoulder for just a brief second. It comforted her. She rose and retreated from the room. Court was dismissed.

Iegani left for the City of the Peaks immediately. There was no grand farewell. He flew out a window as the court gasped in awe and fear.

19

Worry followed Queen Abisola.

It finally caught up with her on her private balcony. She gazed upon the twinkling lights of O Konya and heard Iasos enter her room. She looked at him questioningly as he joined her.

"It is really a beautiful place, isn't it?" he whispered as he gazed upon the city. He placed his hands on the railing and breathed deeply. "I joined the military today."

"You what!" exclaimed Abisola.

"Yes, this afternoon. I walked down to the headquarters and joined up. Of course, it took a bit of doing. They didn't believe I was serious at first, but I finally convinced them. It will be announced tomorrow."

"You're mad," scolded Abisola angrily. "Your place is with me, not in some cold barracks."

ABIGAIL KEAM

"No, my love. You are wrong." Iasos turned toward her. "My place is being an example. How can we expect others to do what we won't sacrifice ourselves?"

"Isn't our daughter a sacrifice enough?"

"What have we really sacrificed there, Abisola? That she is safe for the time being. That she is being trained to fight her enemy in order to save her life. Could we have done that for her?" Iasos shook his head. "We offer her nothing at the moment. Surely not safety. No, the Dinii are a blessing." He looked toward the heavens. "Maura is better off where she is. You know that."

Abisola stood beside her husband and kissed him. "How would I fare without you?" she cooed, smiling.

"Very badly, I expect."

"So do I."

Iasos returned her smile. "What now?"

"We need to contact that old buzzard, Iegani."

"He's an owl-man."

Abisola rolled her eyes. "You know what I mean."

Iasos laughed. "Should queens roll their eyes like school girls?"

"Only if they feel like it."

"Just tell the wind what you want. Iegani will come soon enough."

"Really?"

"Haven't you noticed, dearest? Ever since our contact with the Dinii, we have been under constant surveillance. Just tell the little songbirds what you want. Any bird will do."

Abisola swirled around and studied the walls of the palace. Nooks and crannies were filled with birds of all kinds. She was surprised and noted that security would have to improve. Abisola called out, "I want to speak to Iegani!"

A swirl of sparrows, twittering nervously, flew into the night sky in all different directions.

"Some will report to Gitar, no doubt," complained Abisola.

"No doubt," replied Iasos, pulling Abisola toward her chamber. "But the night is young, and Iegani might not come tonight, which leaves us time for other pursuits."

"That's right. I can't send a soldier off without a kiss."

"I was thinking of something more."

"Aren't you being bold for a male?"

"Well, now that I have equal rights with females, I might as well take advantage of them," Iasos crowed, pulling Abisola down on the bed.

Abisola rolled on top of him. "Almost equal, but not quite," she quipped, nipping his nose.

"It will do for now," teased Iasos as he blew out the lamp.

20

Maura was an enigma to her people.

She would swoop down upon the back of a great hawk, followed by falcon guards, who would drop her off on the roof of the palace.

At first, this unsettled the people, especially when the great Bird People tarried in the city—walking upright, speaking to frightened citizens in their mother tongue, drinking ale in taverns, and singing bawdy songs with drunken Sivan merchants.

The Sivans seemed to know the Bird People well and did not find the female hawks strange with their painted feathers, tattooed faces, or hands with retractable talons. They deferred to the Dinii.

Children also wanted to be with the Bird People. They loved to creep up behind a hawk, pluck a feather, and then run off screaming with delight. The purloined feathers were placed in the hair or worn around the neck in the form of a necklace. The children rebuffed fathers loudly if they tried to cut out feathers from tangled hair or untie a Dinii feather necklace in order to wash a dirty face and neck.

Scores of hawks and falcons of all colors and sizes entered the city frequently, flying in a V formation and landing right on the palace grounds. They would stay for months and work with the high-ranking officers of Her Majesty's army. They inspected storehouses, weapons, and fortifications. Then, they would strap nervous Hasan Daegian officers to their bodies and fly out into the countryside to study each small village's preparation for the inevitable conflict. They always would exhort in their high-pitched voices, "Not good enough, not good enough," to the dismay and frustration of the ministers and governors.

Only when the combat-hardened mercenaries, recruited by the Sivans, trained the grumbling Hasan Daegians in the art of swordplay, ax throwing, and hand-to-hand fighting with a mace did the Dinii relax a little.

In the early days, the mercenaries taunted the observing Dinii to spar with them in front of their pupils.

A hawk would good-naturedly lumber over to some arrogant, over-muscled soldier of fortune and wait to be rushed. Hovering just out of reach from her opponent, the challenged hawk would jab at him with her taloned feet. Otherwise, she liked to catch his face and hold him at arm's length while he struggled to break free.

Yesemek issued a decree putting an end to the fighting when it was discovered the mercenaries nearly suffocated with each encounter.

The real reason the challenges stopped was that the mercenaries realized the hawk soldiers, especially the females, were too powerful and quick.

A new game of rivalry ensued soon after. Several mercenaries would attack a lone hawk in the streets, usually at night. The fight concluded quickly with one of the mercenaries being thrown into a wall or another landing on his head in a water tank. The attacked hawk or falcon would quietly gather a coin from the pocket of each of her attackers, salute, and saunter off to the nearest tavern to drink ale that the Dinii were becoming increasingly fond of.

The wounded mercenaries collected themselves and, with their heads aching, tried to figure out what they were doing wrong. As the years went by, the attacks became more elaborate and ingenious. Once in a while, they would successfully overtake a Dini and, as a symbol of their achievement, pluck out some tail feathers and proudly display them on their shields. It was very prestigious, but rare.

As Maura grew older, the presence of the hawks and falcons was more accepted in the city. She would join them in the streets to walk along the wide boulevards, look at fresh fruit in the bazaar, and sip colla water.

Behind her followed Queen Abisola's personal bodyguards, aware that their presence was superfluous. They could not hide their boredom. There was no fool born who would try to harm Princess Maura with a seven-foot birdwoman holding her hand.

Sometimes, she rode on the shoulders of the Dinii, giggling while taking care not to injure their wings as she leaned over to yank people's hair or pull their hats over their eyes. Of course, the hawks would get the blame as Maura innocently blinked her wide eyes and cried loudly if anyone persisted in scolding her.

Hasan Daegians took great pride in their appearance and were sorely vexed if hair or adornments were out of their proper place, but the sight of their future queen bawling in the street, even if she deserved reprimand, was too much for them.

Princess Maura and her hawks were soon given wide berth, much to her dismay. She did so like causing a commotion.

Every winter and spring, Maura came home to the safety and luxury of her parents' palace. And every year, she would have to be reintroduced to court etiquette.

While Dinii chicks were encouraged to be inventive and daring in their play, Hasan Daegian children were to be quiet and unassuming when adults were present, and even well behaved when they weren't.

"Don't wipe your nose on the tablecloth, don't pull ladies' dresses over their backsides, don't hide food in your pockets, don't spit at other nobles' children, don't burst into your mother's receiving room when she's conducting a private audience only to show her the morning's finds of bugs, don't laugh out loud if you think someone is funny looking, don't wear your father's undergarments on your head, don't, don't, don't!"

When her tutors and nannies admonished her, Princess Maura would look genuinely overcome with shame and hug them, saying with complete sincerity that she would never do it again. They relented by stroking her hair and giving her a treat. They couldn't help but spoil her.

At the City of the Peaks, life was different. Princess Maura was taught the knowledge of the outdoors. She grew astute in understanding the sights and smells of nature and their meaning. By the age of five, she could track any animal. By the age of eight, she could camouflage her body to match any surrounding. She was taught how to wrestle, throw daggers with deadly accuracy, and eat bloody meat without flinching. Even with the Dinii's exceptional sight, they sometimes had a hard time discerning her in a grain field or from a limb of a tree.

Maura grew accustomed to being outside in any kind of weather as were the Dinii. They spent most of their lives outdoors, so most of the buildings in the City of the Peaks were of a semi-permanent nature.

As a very young child, she wore very little until the Dinii found the sight of her naked, pale, indigo body without the covering of feathers almost obscene. Several of the craftsmen made a little leather shift and a plumed hat for her, taking feathers from their own bodies. They periodically replaced her clothes as she outgrew them.

When she came home to O Konya, her little brown shift and feathered hat were stored away. She was dressed in the finest robes, her hair washed with scented soap and braided with flowers, the most costly of oils rubbed into her skin, and her feet encased in the softest of shoes.

Maura was taught manners, geography, mathematics, history, herbal medicine, dancing, and military strategy. Above all, she was taught to rule.

Queen Abisola was away for much of the year, touring the country and encouraging her people during these stressful times, but she always made sure she was home for her daughter's visits.

Although Abisola was not a demonstrative parent, Maura sensed her mother's fierce pride in her. She realized her mother expected great things of her and was careful not to disappoint her. What these great things were, she did not yet know, but she guessed it had something to do with the uneasy pact between the Dinii and her people. Of course, being a child, she never thought about it long.

When Princess Maura wanted hugs and kisses, it was to her father, Iasos, she ran. He would always be there for her when she received scratches and bruises. He even defended her the time she caused a playmate to cry by practicing the Dinii death grip on him.

Iasos always stroked her dark bluish hair and gave her a big wet kiss. His eyes seemed moist most of the time, and there were evenings when he looked at her and could not speak. He was never harsh with her. Her father was a constant factor in her life with love, kindness, and understanding.

Maura also loved the Dinii and wondered at the confusion her people seemed to have when confronting them. She loved the rough way the Dinii smelled of leaves, trees, mountain air, and musk. She loved the softness of their feathers. When she wanted to sleep, she would just curl up against any one of them. Many Dinii mothers would find the sleeping princess nesting with their chicks. They would always let her remain. Everyone in the City of the Peaks, down to the lowliest servant, knew Princess Maura and protected her, fed her, and generally kept an eye on her, hoping to curb her mischievous ways.

The princess loved Empress Gitar, regarding the empress as her second mother. She loved Gitar's children whom she thought of as her siblings ... especially Chaun Maaun, Empress Gitar's only male chick.

From the very beginning of Princess Maura's placement in the royal nest, Chaun Maaun seemed fascinated with the featherless chick who was blue and cried out loud. He would always scoot next to her, placing his little undeveloped wing over her arm. Chaun Maaun liked sharing the royal nipple with Princess Maura until she was given her own Hasan Daegian wet nurse. He did not understand why the wet nurse would shoo him away when he tried to nurse from her too. Chaun Maaun wanted to drink from the big, soft breasts with the pink nipples after smelling the milk on Princess Maura. He would become irritable, flapping his wings and hissing whenever the nurse approached Maura, but he never turned from the princess. He tried to share his regurgitated food with her always until Empress Gitar explained that Hasan Daegians could not properly absorb the already digested meat. They were used to plant matter, not meat.

Princess Maura, in turn, doted on Chaun Maaun. She would cry if separated from him for too long. She loved to play with his feathers as she outgrew her allergies. The smell of them calmed her so much that finally Queen Abisola was forced to ask Empress Gitar to collect Chaun Maaun's downy feathers so a quilt could be made for the princess when she was staying in the royal palace.

As they grew older, they became close companions, growing uneasy when apart from each other for very long. The years went by comfortably for Princess Maura as she grew into a strong-willed, powerfully built young woman.

When Maura received word that Empress Gitar and Chaun Maaun would visit O Konya for the princess's eighteenth birthday, she was overcome with excitement and joy. Running into her mother's morning room, she stopped short, gathered herself, and then continued gracefully to her mother's breakfast table on the veranda.

Queen Abisola sat regally at a handsome table carved with flowers and mythical beasts. Her robes were a shimmering blue, edged with beaten silver that formed a simple geometric design. Her hair was braided with rare flowers, as Hasan Daegian custom dictated, and was piled lustrously on her head.

Maura suddenly realized that her mother was no longer beautiful by Hasan Daegian standards. She had gray in her hair and her face was starting to line, but the princess could not take her eyes off her mother.

Queen Abisola seemed to radiate a beauty beyond the merely physical. Sitting there quietly in the morning light, Queen Abisola shined with an otherworldly glow, and power emanated from the Queen's skin.

Princess Maura thought to herself, *This is how I shall always remember my mother—dressed in beautiful robes, sitting on the balcony, overlooking her kingdom. Forever vigilant. Forever resolute.* Maura felt panic. How could she rule after a great queen like her mother? She feared she would never measure up.

"Maura, why are you staring at me?" inquired Abisola, gingerly picking up her colla cup.

"I'm sorry, Mother. I think you look so beautiful this morning."

Queen Abisola smiled warmly at her daughter. "That's very nice for you to say. I don't feel very beautiful." She sighed.

"Maybe we'll find the Mother Bogazkoy this year."

"Perhaps we shall. That would be a great blessing for us both," Queen Abisola said. "Our Bogazkoy is dying and provides little support to me now or I to it, I'm afraid. One day we shall talk about the Bogazkoy and its meaning to the rulers of Hasan Daeg. You did not run in only to say good morning to your mother. What news have you?"

Maura grinned. She handed her mother a letter, which her mother scanned quickly.

"So, the Dinii are learning to write."

"On no, Mother. Queen Gitar has hired a scribe through the Sivans to write all her correspondence."

"Of course, Gitar would never lower herself to become literate."

Maura paled at her mother's harsh words. "Mother, you know how they feel about written symbols. They are not stupid."

"How well I know. They are a very intelligent race." Abisola beckoned her daughter into a chair. "I'm sorry if I sound rude. In a few months you will go back to them, and the palace will seem empty for your father and me." The Queen shook her head. "I know I must sound bitter, but how would Empress Gitar feel if Chaun Maaun spent half his life growing up away from her in a strange land?"

Maura plopped her elbows on the table. "That's what I've come to tell you. Chaun Maaun and Empress Gitar are coming for the celebrations. Isn't that wonderful!"

Queen Abisola winked conspiratorially at Sari, who had just brought them fresh colla tea and fruit.

Sari stood behind her mistress, not wanting to miss any gossip.

"I know, dear. I too have a letter from Empress Gitar." She held up a beautifully written scroll detailing the date and time of the Dinii's arrival. "They will arrive tomorrow."

"Not much time for preparation," snorted Sari.

Maura replied, "They don't need much."

"If the palace were a forest, that is. We'll have to equip all the bedrooms with tree limbs and hunt down fresh game, beating the meat until it's nice and bloody, just the disgusting way they like it."

"That's enough, Sari," admonished Abisola. "We will be able to accommodate any special needs of the Dinii. Don't you worry, my dear," she said to Maura. "We will make them feel right at home." Abisola folded her napkin. "After all, they have taken such good care of Maura all these years."

As she rose, Maura bowed in respect.

"No, no, finish your breakfast. I need to start my day. I will see you later at dinner."

"Is my father coming home?"

Abisola's face softened at the mention of her husband. "Yes, with all haste. He sent word last night. Now I must go. I will see you tonight."

Princess Maura bounced in a chair, stuffing a pastry in her mouth. Cream smeared on the corner of her lips.

Sari glared at her.

"I don't care if you disapprove," argued Maura with her mouth full. "I tire of doing everything correctly and according to tradition. Blast tradition!"

"That's fine, little one, for now, but never let your mother see you conducting yourself so. She's spent the last seventeen years battling problems this country never anticipated, and it would not do her heart good knowing she was leaving her people in the hands of a willful girl who stuffs food into her mouth and slurps like a common Sivan merchant. You lack discipline!"

"I lack nothing, you old busybody," spat Maura, crumbs falling out of her mouth.

Lady Sari walked away in disgust.

Maura swallowed and wiped off her mouth. With great care, she sipped her tea and then gathered the crumbs off the table, putting them in a nice little pile on her plate. Peeling one of the green fruits offered by a servant, she graciously gave the man leave to go. Sitting very straight in her chair, she would occasionally wave to a passerby who would wave back with gusto. Although she was very happy about her upcoming birthday, Sari's words rang in her ears. Maura's growing fear that she was not made of the stuff of queens kept encroaching upon her happy thoughts.

I will do better, she thought. *I will make Mother and Father very proud of me. I will not embarrass them in front of dignitaries who already think I am a half-wild Dini. I will be the perfect Hasan Daegian princess.*

She smiled. The next week was going to be glorious, and she was not going to miss a single moment of it. She was going to eat, dance, laugh, wear gorgeous clothes, and, most of all, be with Chaun Maaun.

Soon she would tell her parents they intended to be married. Perhaps that's why Chaun Maaun was coming—to tell them himself.

She giggled, thinking of the wondrous days to come—of flying in Chaun Maaun's arms in the cold night sky, the stars their only companions, and joint-ruling the Dinii and the Hasan Daegians with him by her side. Maura dreamed of a future where both races intermingled in peace and prosperity.

Healers, scholars, musicians, writers, and great artisans would gather in the streets of O Konya. Together, she and Chaun Maaun would make Hasan Daeg one of the most beautiful places in the world. Everyone would love her and her king, and she would be the greatest ruler of all time. She shivered with girlish anticipation.

Princess Maura simply did not understand why her mother took everything so seriously and made life so hard for herself. With the characteristic self-involvement of the young, Maura's mind drifted to thoughts of pleasure. She changed her clothes and went to the archery range to practice. She wanted to show Chaun Maaun how good she was with a bow and arrow.

Yes, that was why Chaun Maaun was coming. He was going to ask Abisola for her daughter's hand in marriage.

Maura giggled.

Life was ripe.

21

The princess practiced archery.

Abisola went to her work chamber, a massive room filled with paintings and tapestries. Fresh cut flowers were cheerfully arranged in hand-blown glass vases standing on the tops of polished tables and chests. As always, two scribes, three personal secretaries, and one servant who tended to the queen's personal needs stood at attention.

The queen nodded to Consul Rubank. As with all consuls before him, his tongue had been cut out voluntarily. In order for him to advise Queen Abisola, she had to ask direct questions to which he could nod or shake his head. It was said that no Consul in the history of Hasan Daeg had ever divulged the confidences of his ruler—hence the absence of the tongue.

Abisola sat down in her chair behind the gleaming

desk. "Are most of the preparations for my daughter's birthday ready?"

The consul nodded yes.

The queen looked pleased, asking the consul's assistants, "What is left?"

The consul motioned one of the young men forward.

"Well, Great Mother, everything is in readiness. However, we feel if Princess Maura is to ride in a parade through the city, security needs to be tightened. Of course, we recommend that she does not ride in the parade at all."

"The people need to see their future ruler, a young girl with vitality and strength. Not some aging relic as myself."

"There have been threats on her life. We do not think the parade a good idea."

"I know some of the nobles have formed a secret cabal sworn to bring this dynasty down and put their own queen on the throne."

"Why don't we just arrest them? It would make our job so much simpler."

Queen Abisola cocked her head to one side. "Because it would create sympathy among the rest of the nobles. We need their support. We need them to fight when the time comes. I can't afford to cause unrest among them right now. We must present a strong and unified front. They must think the throne is in strong hands."

"Great Mother, I don't mean to be disrespectful, but how long can you fool everyone that you are all right? Your health is failing. Your endurance is low. At this rate, you will not survive until Princess Maura's fortieth birthday," advised the assistant in low tones.

The consul gave the assistant a threatening look.

"I understand your concern. I am worried myself. We must find the Mother Bogazkoy. The ruler of Hasan Daeg must look in peak condition or the nobles will swoop down like the Dinii on an unsuspecting boaep." Queen Abisola paused. "That is my present concern. Empress Gitar will be arriving tomorrow and staying through the birthday celebration. We must make ready. I want everything perfect for her."

"Will the Dinii princesses be joining her?" inquired the assistant.

"No," replied the Queen. "Only Chaun Maaun."

The consul raised an eyebrow.

The queen studied his face. "Yes, I know," she replied to Rubank. "I don't like the looks of it either."

"I'm sorry, Your Majesty, I don't understand," confessed the assistant.

The queen looked away from Rubank. "It's nothing," she sighed. "Please make sure all beds are removed from their chambers. Have large tree limbs brought in and placed there instead. Make sure each room has an ample supply of straw and soft animal hair for their nesting. Lady Sari will help."

"I don't know if we can buy enough meat on such short notice," stated the assistant.

"Go through the Sivan guild here in the city. If I know the Sivans, they knew about this visit before I did. I'm sure they have in stock everything we need to make the Dinii comfortable. Just tell our cook their food is served warm but not cooked, and it must be bloody. Oh, and tell him the Dinii like the meat cut into ribbons."

The assistant nodded and motioned to the scribe to give him a copy of everything that had been said. With copy in hand, the assistant was given leave to finish his preparations for the birthday celebration.

Queen Abisola turned her attention to Rubank. "I want to examine yesterday's report again."

Rubank went to the opposite side of the room and unlocked a door, which led into a stone-lined archival chamber for important documents and reports. He immediately went to yesterday's report from the eastern border.

Queen Abisola took the report and slowly went over

it again with a heavy heart. It was not good.

Zoar was advancing in an erratic line, looting city after city, always heading in Hasan Daeg's general direction. After being quiet for almost ten years, Zoar was on the move again, conquering with the same terrible swiftness and finality that marked his earlier campaigns.

Once conquered, the enslaved territories were assimilated into the Bhuttanian Empire. If the population resisted, it was decimated.

Queen Abisola hoped Zoar would break off before reaching her border, but in her heart of hearts, she knew he would keep marching. She was glad Gitar was coming, for she could share this burden with the Dinii empress.

Abisola looked up from the report. "The day after my daughter's birthday, Hasan Daeg will go on war alert. The armories are to be opened in O Konya, and all citizens are to be armed. Zoar is much too close to our borders to ignore his threat."

Rubank nodded.

"For the time being, triple the guards on the eastern borders. I will ask the Dinii to extend their patrols when Empress Gitar arrives. We must know every move Zoar makes. I find this report too vague. I wish for more detail." She handed the report back to the consul.

Rubank saluted and left the room almost at a run to execute Abisola's orders.

Abisola sat back in her chair, wiping the perspiration off her forehead. She wondered when Iasos was going to arrive. She needed to hear his soft voice and feel his velvet skin beneath her. Everything was becoming too much for her to handle by herself. She did not feel well. Abisola steeled herself. *I must survive until Maura can ascend the throne.*

She nervously rubbed her hands together. Gathering up documents from the desk, she signed several papers while her thoughts always went back to Zoar. It was just a matter of months now. She was sure of it, and she was truly glad Empress Gitar was coming. Maybe they could fly Maura back to the City of the Peaks until the war was all over? Deep in her heart, Abisola knew that was not going to happen. No one was going to be spared.

Least of all her daughter.

22

Empress Gitar flew into O Konya.

Residents of the city stood in the streets and watched as the Bird People entered with a precision that took the Hasan Daegians' breath away.

Falcons with black geometric designs painted on their wings flew in a cross formation, diving suddenly in single file as though they would crash into the palace roof. At the last moment, they arched upwards, creating a fan-shaped effect in the sky. The designs on their wings looked like pairs of eyes staring down at the people.

The thrilled Hasan Daegians in the streets below and on rooftops clapped enthusiastically.

The falcons jetted down again, spinning as if out of control until, at the last second, they flipped up and landed on chimneys of various roofs. They remained immobile and looked as though they were statues.

Next, the hawks entered. There were thousands of them. They flew in a giant star formation with the red hawks creating the form of a five-point star while the gray hawks formed the outline of the star. With the wing of one hawk touching the wing of another, they flew in perfect formation, all wings moving in unison. As the red hawks had white chests and bellies, the star was white and surrounded by the dark outline of the gray hawks' wings.

With one rotation, the red hawks rolled over and flew upside down, exposing their red wings.

People cheered and hollered with glee as the white star suddenly turned into a red one and then turned back again to white.

The Dinii flew off into the darkening eastern sky. As soon as they were out of sight, drums sounded from every rooftop in an almost deafening cacophony. Trumpets joined and heralded the arrival of the Dinii empress.

A thousand moving lights lit up the sky as more hawk, owl, and falcon Dinii soared, each holding a torch. They flew in a spiral formation. In the center flew their Empress surrounded by huge silver and white flags dancing gaily in the dimming sky. As the spiral approached the palace, the Dinii spun outward, creating an explosive effect. Empress Gitar dropped out of the center of the lights and landed with her party onto the roof of the royal palace.

Queen Abisola and Princess Maura approached the Dinii party and bowed. "We welcome you to our home," said Abisola. She could barely hear herself speak over the roar of the crowd in the streets below.

Empress Gitar smiled and nodded. She beckoned Queen Abisola to her side, and they stood together near the edge of the roof, waving to the people watching from below.

Empress Gitar spread her mighty wings. The diamond dust she had sprinkled on her feathers twinkled in the fading light. It looked like small bolts of light flashing.

The crowd erupted with cheers.

Empress Gitar turned toward Queen Abisola, and they clasped hands, raising their arms in a sign of unity.

The roar of the applause was deafening.

Queen Abisola smiled brightly. She beckoned to Princess Maura and the young girl shyly joined them.

Cheers sounded in the air again.

After much waving, the queens and their entourages moved indoors where they could speak. Instead of entering the throne room, Empress Gitar was shown to a private audience chamber where chairs and tree limbs were strategically placed.

Gitar turned to Queen Abisola. "How very thoughtful. We can sit as you, but not for very long periods of time."

Queen Abisola waved toward a limb.

"First, Your Majesty," said Gitar, "I would like to formally present my son, Prince Chaun Maaun, to you."

An eagle with markings like his mother's stepped forward and bowed low to Queen Abisola and Princess Maura. "Great Mother," he addressed Abisola, "the last time we met, I was quite young. I see Her Majesty's beauty still complements her legendary wisdom."

Abisola nodded to Chaun Maaun with pleasure. She loved compliments when they sounded sincere. Out of the corner of her eye, she noticed a strange gleam in Princess Maura's eyes as she gazed upon the striking royal son.

Queen Abisola did not think this a good omen, but she gave no sign that she noticed her daughter's apparent infatuation.

Empress Gitar did the same.

"Princess Maura," said Chaun Maaun, tenderly turning toward her.

Maura returned his gaze longingly.

"And, of course, you know my uncle, Prince Iegani, Great Divigi," quickly said Empress Gitar, trying to push down her anger with her son for his public display of affection.

Iegani stepped forward and bowed.

Queen Abisola extended her hand. "Always a pleasure, Prince Iegani," she lied.

Iegani caught the sarcasm and chuckled. He always liked Queen Abisola's candor.

She said to him, "I have prepared your usual room." Queen Abisola clapped her hands and asked the servants to bring refreshments.

Maura looked up and answered Iegani, who was sending her telepathic messages. "Yes, Great Divigi, I have been practicing as you taught me, but I still cannot send over long distances." She lowered her eyes. Of all her teachers, Iegani was the one who instilled fear and uneasiness in her. She greatly respected her mentor but never could relax around him. Maura was always afraid she would make a mistake, and she frequently did. His disapproval was keenly felt.

Chaun Maaun reached over and patted her hand. He frowned at Iegani.

Princess Maura felt relieved and looked appreciatively at the visiting Prince.

Chaun Maaun was not afraid of Iegani as she was. He was not afraid of anything.

Iegani pursed his lips and slowly breathed out.

Empress Gitar gave a warning look at both Chaun Maaun and Iegani as if to say, "behave!" She knew they were sending messages to each other telepathically.

"I can hardly believe Princess Maura will be eighteen tomorrow," teased Empress Gitar. "It seems like only yesterday she was driving me to fits with her constant crying as a baby."

Maura blushed, glancing at her mother.

"May we expect the Royal Princesses from the House of Gitar?" asked Abisola, tactfully changing the subject.

"Someone needed to stay behind and keep order," quickly answered Gitar. "My people are not responsible like yours," she said, referring to their combined troops. "My hawks have become too fond of ale and are smuggling kegs into the City of the Peaks."

Queen Abisola took a sip of her drink, noting that Gitar had spoken too quickly. She did not believe her. No, there was a specific reason that only Chaun Maaun was present. Queen Abisola started to speak, but the door to the chamber burst open.

"Father!" squealed Maura as she rushed forward to embrace her dirty and sweating father.

"Not too close," he said, laughing and holding his daughter at bay. "I smell as bad as a decaying borax."

Maura wrinkled her nose after getting a strong whiff

of him.

Iasos bowed to Empress Gitar. "I've only just arrived and come to pay my respects to my wife and child. I did not know you were present, or I would have bathed before presenting myself. My apologies, Empress."

Empress Gitar stood up and towered over Iasos. "No apologies needed. Please excuse me. I need to rest. May your servants show me to my quarters?"

"Of course," replied Queen Abisola, rising. "It's been a long day for us all. Lady Sari will be your personal servant while you are present in O Konya. You have only to ask."

"You are so kind." Empress Gitar started to follow Lady Sari out of the room when she turned to Chaun Maaun. "Coming?"

Chaun Maaun bid his hosts good night and sheepishly followed his mother and great uncle to their quarters.

Once the door was closed, Abisola rushed to Iasos, branding him with a kiss and staining her splendid golden gown with dirt and grease. "I thought you would never get here," she confessed breathlessly.

Iasos returned her passionate kiss and, grabbing Maura, held them both tightly. "Nothing could keep me away from my daughter's birthday."

Maura looked at them both with delight.

Iasos smiled at his daughter and then returned Abisola's gaze.

Maura knew when it was time to leave. She politely excused herself and left her parents to their own devices. Her day would come tomorrow. She could wait for their complete attention. This night belonged to them.

23

Maura barely had time to change.

Looking sheepish, Chaun Maaun squeezed himself through the narrow window of her bedchamber.

She gaily ran over to him and they embraced. Maura loved the feeling of security and tenderness when he surrounded her with his broad wings. He was smaller than most Dinii, so Maura didn't feel overwhelmed by his size.

"Did anyone see you?" she asked.

"I don't think so," he whispered.

"You don't have to talk so low. I have sent everyone away for the night."

"Don't you think that will cause them to be suspicious?"

"No, I often sleep without servants or nurses. I'm not a baby anymore. They still try to treat me as such though," Maura pouted. "Besides, I'm a Hasan Daegian of legal age now. I may do as I please."

Chaun Maaun laughed. He picked her up and swirled her around. Her laughter joined his. Laughing and kissing, he took her over to the bed, placing her gently in the middle of it. "Do you think it will hold me?" he asked.

She nodded enthusiastically.

He cautiously joined her and snuggled closely.

"Did you talk to your mother?" Maura asked.

Chaun Maaun busily untied the blue ribbon to her nightgown. "I have tried for several weeks, but every time I tell her I need to see her, she has some excuse. I think she knows about us and doesn't want to talk to me. Tomorrow, I'll corner her and make her listen." He reached into her gown and pulled out a breast, slowly sucking on a nipple. "Mmmmmm, delicious."

Maura giggled and pulled away. "We need to talk, Chaun. We need to make plans."

"Right," he said, leaning on his elbow and grinning. "Talk all you want. Did you tell *your* mother that we want to get married?"

Princess Maura looked apprehensive. "No. I tried. I really did. I just couldn't get the words out." She started chewing on the end of a ribbon from her gown. "I thought I would wait until Father got home. He's more reasonable, and I thought he could talk to Mother."

Chaun Maaun gave her an appraising look.

Maura snapped, "Oh, don't look at me so. This is not going to be easy."

"Doesn't she like me?"

"Oh, Chaun!" she said, scooting next to his face. "It's not personal. My mother will probably say that I should marry one of my own people, because I'm going to be queen one day."

"You could tell her by marrying me, the treaty between our two nations would be strengthened. Royalty from other countries marry for the same reason all the time." He rolled on his back and pulled her on top of him.

She lightly kissed his chin. "I don't think my mother is the problem. What if Zoar comes?"

Chaun laughed. "He doesn't even know we exist."

"Mother says he's moving west."

"He will come to the mist and, seeing nothing but his doom if he tries to enter, turn back. He will think it is the end of the world. He won't bother us, but if he does, the Dinii will take care of him."

"I don't know. Mother says he's awfully determined."

"I don't want to talk about Zoar. I don't want to talk about our mothers. I want to kiss you again and again and again." He kissed her passionately.

Maura responded warmly.

"The night is ours. Let's not waste it," he whispered, giving her a rakish look.

Maura grinned and put out the lamp.

24

Maura pushed Chaun Maaun out the window.

Neither of them saw Iegani standing in the window of the apartment across from them, watching silently in the darkness.

Chaun Maaun crawled contentedly into his room and fell asleep while Maura began preparing for her big day. The servants found her already bathed and brushing her hair.

Upon entering the chamber, Sari smelled both the foreign odor of a Dini and the familiar smell of love-making. She looked at Maura, but decided not to say anything. It was Maura's big day, and Sari did not want to spoil it. Besides, there was nothing anyone could do. Maura was of legal age.

Already she had left the Queen, who was terribly

upset with a new report that Zoar was moving ever closer to their border. Iasos was dressing in the Queen's room, hoping his presence would calm his distraught wife.

Hurriedly, a message had already been sent to Empress Gitar that Abisola wished to have an audience with her immediately.

Sari wished to spare Maura this awful news and her parents' anguish. "Nothing is going to spoil this day for her little one," she muttered to herself.

"What was that?" asked Maura, looking at her strangely.

"Nothing, my wild bird baby."

"I thought you said something."

Sari shook her head and began supervising the dressing of the princess.

Maura donned a gown of white with gold buttons and trimming. Her headdress was a gold crown with a matching white veil, which was sheer and fell to the floor behind the dress. Her slippers were the color of gold and covered with Mother of Pearl. The design of an uultepe was on her right breast. She wore no jewelry. Her pale indigo skin gleamed under the various applications of oil.

Sari looked at her with satisfaction.

The girl standing proudly before her looked every

inch a princess.

Sari felt tears come into her eyes. "Two Hasan Daegian queens I will have served."

Maura laughed while looking into a mirror. "I'm not a queen yet."

"You soon will be," said Queen Abisola, standing in the doorway. She walked toward her daughter. "I'm so proud of you. Here, let me look."

Maura twirled around in her dress.

Sari fussed at her. "Your hair!" she nagged.

"She looks fine, Sari," admonished the queen.

"Mother, what is it! You look like you've been crying."

Abisola held her daughter's hands. "Nothing that can't wait until after the celebration. You have your eighteenth birthday only once. Isn't that right, Sari?"

Sari nodded enthusiastically.

Maura looked suspiciously at her mother. "Something's wrong. I can tell."

"Can you tell that your father is waiting impatiently at the breakfast table with a big present for you?"

"He is?" asked Maura excitedly. Picking up her skirts, she rushed to the dining room.

Sari blocked her path. "Oh no, you don't," scolded Sari. "You are going to act like a princess all day, even if it kills you."

The queen winced at Sari's words, but no one noticed.

Sari and Maura glared at each other in a standoff.

Abisola coaxed, "For once, let's do as Sari wants. It would make her so happy."

"All right, Mother, but when I'm queen, no one is going to boss me around."

Lady Sari looked heavenward as though beseeching the great goddess, Mekonia.

"Walk slowly with your head held high," instructed Abisola. "Show the people they can have confidence in you. Go on. I will follow shortly."

"I'm going. You will come soon, promise?"

"Absolutely. I'll be there in a few minutes."

Maura turned and, with exaggerated slowness, walked out of the room.

Sari turned to her cousin in exasperation. "When is she going to grow up?"

"Soon," replied Abisola. "Very soon."

25

Guests rose.

Queen Abisola and Empress Gitar entered the great dining hall and took their seats at a massive table. On Abisola's right sat Empress Gitar looking as forlorn as her hostess. Moments before, they had discussed Zoar, and both knew war was imminent. The very thing they had been dreading was now upon them.

Empress Gitar had trouble focusing on small talk with the Hasan Daegian nobles and governors who had gathered for the breakfast. Her voice was higher-pitched than usual, and she sometimes lapsed into Dinii clicks.

Abisola gave the empress a reassuring smile.

Gitar brightened.

At the end of the table sat Iasos with Maura on his right and Prince Chaun Maaun seated across from her.

Prince Iegani sat uncomfortably between two ancient noblewomen, who complimented him on his still-powerful physique, attempting to stroke his lap under the table. He wanted to slap their silly over-powdered faces, but pretended he did not notice them. He was troubled about the report, but strove not to show it.

Stealing a look here and there, he saw that both Abisola and Gitar were pale and drawn. In the trying times ahead, Iegani hoped the two rulers would bond together as true sisters and not as rival queens. He looked to his left. Chaun Maaun and Princess Maura were enjoying the day. Chaun Maaun looked sleepy. *No wonder*, Iegani thought.

Maura looked fresh and cheerfully picked at her food, impatient to begin her official birthday procession.

Sensing Iegani was thinking of her, Maura looked up and met his eyes. He quickly turned his head.

Odd, thought Maura as Iegani's actions left her with a feeling of uneasiness. She became angry, for she did not want her day spoiled. With childish impudence, she threw her chin out in defiance.

The breakfast continued at a slow pace with people chatting gaily and loading their plates with food. Musicians played lively tunes. Servants poured drinks, running back and forth with platters laden with food from all parts of Hasan Daeg.

For Chaun Maaun, the meal dragged on with endless toasts to Maura and songs in her honor. He wanted to go out into the city and be away from these old relics—both Hasan Daegian and Dinii. He wanted to have fun.

A commotion sounded outside one of the doors.

Chaun Maaun turned and strained to see what was happening.

A guard emerged from the hallway and went to Queen Abisola. She whispered into the queen's ear.

Queen Abisola stood. "I'm sorry to leave this wonderful gathering, but duty calls. Please continue in my absence. I shan't be long."

The guests stood as Queen Abisola left the room.

A few moments later, a guard came for Empress Gitar and Prince Iegani, escorting them out of the dining hall.

The guests murmured anxiously among themselves.

Iasos continued chatting, even though his daughter looked at him questioningly.

Outside the windows, Maura could hear the dancers, acrobats, fire-eaters, illusionists, exotic animals, and escort guards lining up for the parade. She knew she ought to be in the courtyard and getting ready to mount the float decorated just for this occasion. Craftsmen had spent weeks designing the elaborate structure with thousands of flowers and topiary statues. She began squirming in her chair, desiring to be off. Her father gave her a stern look. Chastened, Maura remained quietly with her hands folded in her lap.

The guests made no pretense of small talk now. Everyone sat hushed, and either stared out the windows or picked at the food on their plates. Only the melodious tune from a lone flute sounded in the immense room.

A soldier strode into the room, saluted, and handed Iasos a note. Iasos cut the seal open with his plate knife and silently read it. Putting the note in his pocket, he returned the salute and gave the soldier leave. He stood and, for a moment, had to steady himself against the table.

"Father?" questioned Maura, rising to help him.

Iasos waved her away. "Countrywomen, kinsmen, honored guests, I have the sad duty to tell you that our day of joy celebrating with your future queen, Princess Maura, has been postponed to an indefinite date."

Iasos paused, trying to calm his nerves. "You are to gather your belongings, children, and servants, and make ready to return to your homes."

Everyone gasped.

Iasos continued, "Before you leave, Queen Abisola has commanded that you attend a royal audience inside the throne room within the hour. Those who do not attend will be imprisoned. I'm sorry for this—this inconvenience. You are dismissed until the bell strikes the next hour. Then we shall meet again."

Chairs were thrown back as guests rushed to their quarters to gather their husbands and belongings. Servants scurried beside their mistresses, receiving their instructions, and ran off to complete their tasks. Everyone noticed that the number of guards had doubled in the hallways, and Dinii hawks and falcons were standing at attention near any royal apartment.

The dining hall was empty except for Chaun Maaun, Princess Maura, and Iasos.

Sari entered the room from the servants' entrance. "Sire," she gushed with tears in her eyes, "Her Majesty wishes you and Princess Maura to change into military dress and join her in the throne room shortly before the new hour. Prince Chaun Maaun, you are to wait with Empress Gitar in her apartment. This is your mother's wish."

"What has happened?" Chaun Maaun croaked.

Sari shook her head. "All will be made known to you. That is all I can say." She turned to the stricken princess and took the young girl's hands in her worn ones. "I'm so sorry. It just could not be helped."

Maura stared at Sari's gnarled hands—hands which had bathed her, fed her, hugged her, kept her from danger, and helped her take her first step. She looked into Sari's moist eyes. "I know it must be something awful to cancel my celebration. I have something better than a parade or presents. I have my parents and you. What more is there?"

Iasos hugged his daughter and pushed her toward the door. "You'd better hurry if you want to change out of that garb."

Guards entered and escorted Chaun Maaun from the room.

Maura hurried out into the great hallway as well.

Alone in the room, Iasos fell into a chair and stared at the empty room. In a fit of rage he jumped up, sweeping serving dishes off the table and throwing crystal against the wall. He threw centuries-old china out the window, pulled apart massive flower arrangements, and hurled fruit at the large portraits of previous Hasan Daegian rulers and their consorts. When he came to the portrait of Abisola, he fell to his knees sobbing.

Servants, hearing the tumult, ran into the dining room.

Embarrassed, Iasos hurried out through a side door.

Aghast at the disarray the consort had left in the room, they began the awful process of cleaning and restoring order.

26

Y eti and Tarsus fell in step with Maura.

Tarsus made way for Maura through the ribbons of people streaming past in the great hallway.

"Panic is not a pretty thing," murmured Yeti, pushing people out of the way.

Maura felt a rush of air behind her. It felt unnatural, and she swirled around to see the blur of a silver blade coming toward her chest. A cry sounded, "No war!" Instinctively she parried with her forearm and felt something slice her skin. Hearing screams, she felt Yeti push her out of the way. Lying on the floor, she could see upward between the powerful legs of Yeti who was now standing protectively in front of her.

Tarsus had in his hands a youth struggling in vain against the powerful Dini. Tarsus held the boy's head in a lock and released his killing talon.

Maura mouthed "NO" in horror as Tarsus slit the boy's throat, throwing him against a marble wall, cracking his skull open.

The would-be assassin twitched several times and then fell still.

Tarsus picked up the boy's dagger and instructed the newly arrived guards to remove the body for examination.

The senior guard officer assessed the condition of the princess and ordered four of her soldiers to stay with the Dinii, while the rest dragged the body away. Many of the soldiers spat on the boy's body before touching him.

Yeti bent down and pulled up Maura who moaned as the hawk brushed her cut arm. She clicked to Maura in the Dinii language.

The princess nodded and walked behind Yeti, hiding her wound, with Tarsus following to Maura's private chambers.

Once inside Maura's suite, Yeti tore off the birthday dress, searching for other injuries while Tarsus bathed the cut in water. Maura acquiesced silently. Her beautiful dress was ripped and ruined with blood. The crown and veil were removed quickly as were the rest of her clothes.

"It's not so bad," announced Tarsus. "Just a few

stitches and you'll be good as new." He tore apart some bed sheets and wrapped them around her arm. "This should stem the bleeding until your healer can attend."

Yeti shook Maura gently. "Maura, put this behind you. You need to join your mother in a few minutes."

Maura sat bewildered, trying to make sense of what had happened. "I know that boy. He is Baroness Mikkotto's son, Yubuto. I used to play with him. He is, I mean was, my cousin. Lady Sari is his grandmother." She looked pleadingly at Yeti. "Why did he try to kill me? I've never done anything to him. I liked him."

"There is no time for this. You must think on your feet. Remember all we have taught you. Here is your uniform. Get into it. Tarsus will help you."

"You shouldn't even be in here," snapped Maura.

Tarsus grinned. "I used to see you running naked from house to house in the City of the Peaks causing mischief. I doubt you have anything I haven't seen before."

"Oh, for goodness sake," scolded Yeti. "Maura, get in your uniform. Wash that makeup off your face. There isn't time for false modesty."

Tarsus went through many closets trying to find suitable underclothes. He did not understand how Hasan Daegians could stand cloth next to their skin. He ignored Maura's blushes as he and Yeti helped put on her pants and boots.

Yeti buttoned her top. "Maura, you will have to design a uniform that you can get into yourself. You need to be as independent as possible. Haven't we always taught this?"

"Yes, but my mother thinks it's unbecoming for a Hasan Daegian princess to dress herself." Maura stopped, realizing she was sounding like a fool.

Tarsus checked the dressing on the wound. It was holding. No blood showed through.

"We must go now," announced Yeti.

"I think we should go through the servants' hallways," cautioned Tarsus.

Maura got to her feet and followed Tarsus and Yeti out through her chambers the back way. She was relieved to find guards stationed at every door. This was a momentary comfort, for she realized that if the conservative nobles wanted her dead, they would find a way. Twisting and turning through a maze of corridors, Yeti and Tarsus finally arrived at the main hallway.

Seeing the nobles were beginning to arrive, Yeti placed Maura between herself and Tarsus. Spreading their wings as shields, they marched her into the throne room. Toppo and Benzar met them and escorted them to the conference room at the back of the chamber.

Inside, Gitar stood alongside Abisola, looking at a

massive map of the continent.

Yesemek was pointing out spots on the map, explaining strategy to military staff that stood politely behind.

Maura scanned the room quickly.

Iegani sat in a corner with his eyes closed.

I know you can hear me, thought Maura. *Open your eyes, Great Divigi, and speak to me.*

Iegani opened the first set of his eyelids. The second set was still over his eyes, but almost transparent, so Maura could see his orbs vibrating.

Maura knew he was in a deep trance. She didn't care. *Why did young Yubuto try to kill me?*

He thought by killing you, your parents would be so distraught they would not fight Zoar.

That is the surface explanation. What is the deeper meaning?

We have taught you well, my daughter. Certain elements of the nobility do not believe we can win a war against Zoar. They wish to protect their interests by collaborating.

Why kill me? Why not try to kill my mother?

They perceive you to be the greater threat. You have been trained as a warrior. You know how to fight. Your mother does not.

Why was I trained as a warrior?

Because we were told to do so.

By whom?

Iegani did not respond to the question.

Who told you to make me a warrior?

Iegani closed his first set of eyelids, and Maura knew she had lost him for now. She would try again later.

Chaun Maaun entered the room and stood next to Maura. He nudged her. "Are you all right?" he asked. "Did the bastard hurt you?"

"You already know?"

"Everyone knows. When I think of what that lunatic might have done! I'm so glad Yeti and Tarsus were there to protect you."

"Yes, isn't it a fortunate coincidence they were standing right outside of the dining hall," she replied sarcastically.

"If they hadn't been there, you could have been killed."

"I can take care of myself," Maura shot back.

"If you were as good a warrior as you think, he never would have gotten near you. You would have sensed him."

"I'll be more careful from now on."

"You had better be or you might be dead next time," shot back Chaun Maaun, angrily. He left and joined his mother at the map.

Ashamed, Maura followed discreetly and placed her finger in the palm of his hand. He squeezed back gently.

Yesemek turned to Abisola and Gitar. "Are there any questions?"

"Yes," said Iegani, still sitting in the corner with his eyes closed. "Why don't we open the Forbidden Zone? Why have we not looked for the Bogazkoy there?"

Yesemek pondered this. She knew enough of her husband to know that his words always carried wisdom. She was open to discussing the idea.

Queen Abisola spoke, "We have always held the land to be a danger to our people. We have never ventured into the Forbidden Zone."

"Do you know why it is forbidden?" asked Iegani, opening both sets of eyelids.

"I do not know why. Perhaps someone from the House of Magi could tell us."

"They will not know. I know, but I will not tell you now—only this. There is no inherent danger to the people of Hasan Daeg or to the race of the Dinii in the Forbidden Zone. Beyond the Forbidden Zone is the sea."

"I have never seen the sea," responded Queen Abisola.

"March to the sea," advised Iegani.

There was silence in the room.

Yesemek turned to Queen Abisola. "Great Mother, we can discuss this matter later for we have other urgent matters at hand. You must speak to your people. They are waiting."

Queen Abisola adjusted her official robes and proceeded into the audience hall. She paused as she was announced and then made way to her throne. Consort Iasos and Princess Maura stood beside her.

Empress Gitar followed and sat in a chair made of rare wood one step higher than Abisola. Prince Chaun Maaun stood to the left of his mother.

Queen Abisola opened her fan, rose, and faced the agitated crowd. "It is my sad duty to inform you that last night Zoar, Aga of Bhuttan, camped just outside our border."

The court murmured.

"This morning he began sending soldiers through our wall of mist. The soldiers were met on the other side by our warriors. The Bhuttanian soldiers died quickly and without pain. Their armor and weapons have been confiscated, and their bodies removed for burning. The total of Bhuttanian casualties has been over seven hundred so far. We have suffered none."

The court gasped and moaned for the poor Bhuttanian soldiers.

Abisola lifted her fan for all to see. "I, Queen Abisola de Magela, Great Mother, ninth ruler of Hasan Daeg, Daughter of Queen Hagar, find the acts of Zoar,

Aga of Bhuttan, to be of bold naked aggression against the people of Hasan Daeg. Therefore, it is my duty to proclaim war against Zoar, Aga of Bhuttan, and all other peoples who make war against citizens of Hasan Daeg."

The great gong sounded and it was made law.

Abisola took a step down on the dais. "I, Queen Abisola de Magela, do hereby formally petition Empress Gitar, Overlord of Kaseri, Queen of the City of the Peaks, to acknowledge the treaty between our two peoples and proclaim war against Zoar, Aga of Bhuttan." She turned and looked at Gitar.

Empress Gitar rose, keeping her eyes on those assembled. She motioned for her attendants. Several hawks brought two pairs of snowy white wings made with the feathers of royal eagles. "I have saved these royal feathers for many years to make these symbolic pairs of wings. I present them to you, Queen Abisola and Princess Maura, heir apparent, as symbols of kinship and enduring bonds between my race and yours. You are both now full-fledged members of the Dinii."

Both Abisola and Maura bowed to Empress Gitar and held out their arms so the wings could be slipped on over their garments. Abisola tried not to stagger under their weight. Both the queen and princess were instructed to pull a leather strap that allowed the wings

209

to spread to their full glory.

The court erupted with delight.

Gitar, smiling broadly at the cheering crowd, cried, "I, Empress Gitar, Overlord of Kaseri, do acknowledge the ancient treaty between the Hasan Daegians and the Dinii. I also proclaim war. Thy enemies are my enemies."

The great gong sounded.

Gitar returned to her throne on the dais.

Abisola stepped forward. "I, Queen Abisola de Magela, do hereby sentence the body of Yubuto Sumsumitoyo, to be burned, and his ashes cast adrift with the wind. His mother, Baroness Mikkotto Sumsumitoyo is to be executed upon sight for the attempted assassination of Princess Maura de Magela. All properties belonging to the Sumsumitoyo family will be confiscated for the Crown. Baroness Mikkotto's children will be hung if found guilty of conspiracy."

Maura found her heart growing heavier with each pronouncement. She saw her future slipping away. She was beginning to doubt if she would ever marry Chaun Maaun. She stole a glance at him. From the expression on his face, she knew he was thinking the same. She would be expected to behave like a ruler of Hasan Daeg, sacrificing whatever was needed. No longer would she be able to fly with Chaun Maaun to some distant peak and spend the day lounging in a nest of down, watching the clouds roll past. Her destiny had finally caught up with her. Maura did not think she was going to like it.

27

Accept your destiny! Accept your destiny!

Iegani stood in the doorway.

Maura knew the message was for her and felt his eyes bore into her back. She refused to turn her head to look at him. Instead, she watched her mother proclaim edict after edict.

The great gong sounded each time with finality.

When Abisola was finished, she snapped her fan shut and returned exhausted to her throne.

Queen Abisola's First General, Kimtemee, addressed the worried governors and nobles. "It is Her Majesty's wish that you return to your homes and begin enacting the primary plan. Word will be sent to you regarding further orders. I wish you good luck! You are dismissed."

The crowd fled the room and hurried home to make

ready for war. A few of the older noblewomen lingered and approached Queen Abisola.

She answered their questions and listened to their concerns.

One apologized for the actions of Baroness Mikkotto, but warned of unrest among the nobles. The others nodded their heads in agreement.

"Thank you for your warnings and kind support. They are greatly appreciated," answered Queen Abisola.

The ancient noblewomen said their good-byes and slowly left the throne room aided by their daughters or male servants.

When the chamber was empty, Rubank approached Queen Abisola, taking the heavy ceremonial fan and crown to storage.

Gitar turned to Abisola. "How do you think they reacted?"

Queen Abisola looked at Iasos. "I couldn't see everyone."

"I think the governors and ministers will back us totally. After all, the Crown employs them," said Iasos. "However, the nobles are another matter. The older families will support us totally. It would be treason not to do so, but the younger noble families are less concerned with honor than with money. Still, we have been preparing them for years. They ought to accept this war."

"What of the attack on Princess Maura?" asked Empress Gitar.

"We know that Baroness Mikkotto is behind the attack and used her son as a pawn. There are other conspirators. We are sure of it, but we only have suspects currently," replied Queen Abisola, watching the reaction of her daughter.

Princess Maura seemed to be studying the pattern in the marble floor.

"Could the boy have acted on his own?" Empress Gitar questioned.

"In our culture, it is rare for a boy his age to initiate an act of this magnitude unless he is insane. No, this was the act of a woman, a ruthless one at that! May her bowels be scattered to the buzzards while she still lives!" seethed Iasos.

Queen Abisola smiled at her husband's passion. "The baroness has fled. We shall apprehend her soon enough."

Maura ventured an opinion to Empress Gitar. "Mikkotto's lands are near the border where Zoar is approaching. She has much to lose if Zoar enters that sector. I think she will probably try to regroup with her personal guards and perhaps make a deal with Zoar. Mother, I think it is imperative we find her."

All those attending looked appraisingly at Maura. A new respect entered their eyes.

Iegani stepped forward. "So our little fledgling is finally spreading her wings. Good. Good. This is what I've been waiting for—clean logic. Not some prattle about a ridiculous party or a new frock that your mother had made for you." He turned to Empress Gitar. "See, all our efforts are reaping just rewards."

Empress Gitar's face fell into a sad expression. She turned to Abisola. "Our little girl is no more," she whispered. "Iegani, perhaps you do not understand something has happened here, which does not pertain to war, but is just as important to a mother. Something precious has been lost and, for all your wisdom, you do not even see it."

She leaned on Chaun Maaun. "I wish to go to my room to rest. I will talk with you and your generals later this afternoon before I fly back to the City of the Peaks," Gitar said to Abisola.

"I understand," answered Abisola.

"I know you do," replied Gitar.

Iegani bowed as his empress left the room with her confused son.

"Mother, what do you mean?" Chaun Maaun asked quietly so the others would not hear.

"Oh, my precious dear, our little Maura, who used

to run naked through our streets, is no more. Princess Maura de Magela, future ruler of Hasan Daeg, Great Mother to her people, now resides in this palace of cold stone. I have lost a daughter and gained a rival." Empress Gitar could barely keep from weeping in the great marble hall as she walked back to her chambers.

Maura sorrowfully watched the Dinii depart. Throwing back her shoulders, she returned to the conference room with her mother and father.

The three of them began the business of war.

28

Zoar watched the sun set.

The wind gently blew from the west and played with the coverlet draped over his lap. He felt so cold these days.

Knowing his healer would scold him for being out in the brisk air rather than in his tent near a warm fire, Zoar stroked his beard and ordered his litter moved closer to the mist. If his healer annoyed him, he would just get another and then another, until he found one that would let him do as he pleased.

At the moment he was *pleased* to study the wall of mist which taunted him. For ten days he had sent men into the mist, and they had never returned. Over two thousand men had met their fates beyond the wall. *But what fate?* thought Zoar. *What is behind the wall? There is something there. I can feel it.*

He told his men to stop and lower his litter. They did not dare get too close. The mist made Zoar sleepy. He wondered if his soldiers had fallen asleep in the mist and died in a peaceful dream. Or were they met by some terrible fate? Perhaps paradise was behind the wall, and they did not wish to return. Frustrated, Zoar beat the arm of his litter chair with his fist. *If I weren't crippled, I'd go myself!*

Ten years earlier, a horse had thrown Zoar during the last days of war with Anqara and fell upon him. The carnage in Anqara had been so severe that it had taken Zoar's men several days to find him. By that time, Zoar's severely shattered leg could not be set correctly. Zoar swore he would be in the saddle in no time, but could not keep his promise.

As the years passed, Zoar's body betrayed him more and more until he was nothing but an arthritic old man who complained daily of aches and pains. A day did not pass when Zoar did not go over the events of that fateful incident. He had saddled the warhorse himself, checking the tack as always, and had kept the horse with him ready to mount. There was no way anyone could have gotten to the animal. Yet, there was a tiny cut on the girth, which caused the leather to finally pull apart and with it—Zoar. Suspicion remained with Zoar, ate at him, and totally consumed him. What if? What if?

Zoar pondered on his life as he watched ducks fly over the mist. He noticed they did not seem to be bothered by it. Back and forth went Zoar's thoughts from the mist to battles fought long ago, women ravished, and the feeling of invincibility he had once possessed. He wondered what would have happened had he had not been possessed by bloodlust. Would he have built instead of destroyed?

But he *was* building for the future, damn it! He was building a great empire with one central government instead of petty city-states or weak countries floundering in ineptitude and indecision. One culture, one language, one nation! That was his dream. And it took the flowing of much blood to make it happen! Now an old man, Zoar questioned not his dream, but his methods. "Too much blood," he muttered.

"What, Father?"

"Dorak, I didn't hear you approach." Zoar looked at his son.

Dorak had grown into a beautiful man, looking much like his mother. His skin was a honey caramel, encased in a tall frame. His hair was raven black, and it highlighted his dark, intelligent eyes and aquiline nose. His mouth was full and pouty.

How different from me, thought Zoar, who was short and squat.

"I've ordered the men to stop entering the mist. I don't see the need for wasting valuable resources."

Zoar noticed the hint of disapproval in his son's voice. "What would you have done differently, Dorak?"

"I would have sent scouting parties, but when they did not return, I would have come up with a creative solution."

"A creative solution? I do not know what that means. I do know whatever is beyond that mist can dispose of two thousand men without so much as a sound. I also know I can faintly smell smoke coming from the west. And where there is smoke, there is fire. That means there is man!"

"The fire could be caused by lightning."

"There hasn't been a thunderstorm in two weeks," countered Zoar. "No, Dorak, look at the mist." He pointed. "Follow the lines. They are not natural. It must be man-made. Always the same height, always without a break regardless of the topography. It's rather magnificent," he said with admiration.

"Father, do you remember those stories KiKu used to tell about singing plants and streams of different colors in a land to the west?"

"Yes, I remember his babble. I almost cut his head off for those lies." Zoar coughed phlegm into a vial.

"I've sent to Bhuttan for copies of any report suggesting these things, and none are to be found. But I remember quite distinctly being in the room with you when KiKu reported these wonders."

"It was during the last campaign before I was blessed with this broken body." Zoar thought back to the days when he was strong. Now his hair was shot through with gray, and his body was withered.

"But I did find reports about men dressed as birds who could fly. In fact, there is a report back in my tent which states you saw such a creature yourself at Anqara."

Zoar looked away. He did not want his son to see fear and confusion in his eyes. "Dorak, it was not a man dressed as a bird, but a man who was a bird."

"I don't understand. How can that be?"

"Nor do I, but it was not a costume. He was real. An immense creature who had the body of man, moved like a man, talked like a man, but had feathers covering him except for his feet, hands, and face. He had great wings on his back, and he flew out a window. I remember running to the window to see if he had fallen. I heard laughing and looked up, and he flew past me with the tip of a wing brushing my face. He said we would meet again. There was nothing mechanical or artificial about him. He was as real as you or I. Even now, the telling of it leaves me shaken."

Dorak was surprised at his father's intensity. "I'm sorry, Great Aga. I did not mean to upset you," he said with sincerity.

Zoar clasped his son's arm. "I will listen to any plan you may have. What are you if not a capable advisor? It is the reason for this one last campaign. You must proceed as you wish. The men must learn to trust you, and they will. It just takes time."

"Time is what we don't have. Our world is starving. The land is depleted. We must find fertile land to grow food until our fields recover."

"What do you propose?"

"I want to hear more about Anqara."

"Anqara?"

"Yes, it was after the campaign of Anqara that these reports dry up. No more leads after that. I think there might be a connection. Weren't you planning to keep moving west?"

"That's right," replied Zoar animatedly. "But my accident happened, and I was ill for a long time."

"How interesting."

"Yes, isn't it," replied Zoar grinning. "I think we should speak to KiKu, don't you?"

"There is a problem with that."

"Oh?"

"He is nowhere to be found. He has disappeared

with the wind."

Zoar took this news in silence.

Dorak stood waiting.

"Son, that night in Anqara when I found the bird-man in the room of the High Priestess of the House of Magi, he was attempting to destroy her writings. I had the fire put out, and the papers stored."

"Are there any other priestesses alive who can interpret the writings?"

"All the priestesses from the House of Magi disappeared that night. No trace of them at all."

"And you think this birdman had something to do with their disappearance?"

"I can feel it in my bones. I've often wondered what strong magic he possessed to steal those women past my men."

"Maybe he just flew them away," joked Dorak.

"Maybe he did," replied Zoar. "I have often wondered about the possibility." Zoar shifted in his chair and rubbed his hands together, blowing on them. "What do you propose to do about the mist, Dorak? We cannot sit here forever."

"I will send for the writings of this woman, and see if we can glean anything from them."

Zoar snorted in disgust.

Dorak maintained his position. "I'm not going to

continue sending men into this fog."

"Perhaps, that is the reason why you should. Test the boundaries. Tie ropes around the men before you send them in. Do something. Our women back home are starving."

Dorak shot back, "You've starved women before, and it never seemed to bother you."

"If you are referring to your mother, I did everything I could. What did you want me to do . . . force her mouth open and pour soup down?"

"Yes, I did!" said Dorak fiercely.

"Ah, we've been over this a hundred times. She wanted to die and so she did. There was nothing I could have done."

Dorak started to speak, but thought the better of it. There was no use arguing about a terrible event that could not be changed. He motioned to the litter bearers to get up. "It's time to go inside now, Father. You must rest."

His father put up no resistance as the bearers led him down the hill to the campsite.

Dorak followed at a brisk pace. He would do well not to anger his father. He needed the old man's cooperation to gain power among the generals.

The campsite was spread over several hills with Zoar's tent in the middle. They followed the main trail to his tent.

Soldiers, who were polishing their weapons, sparring for fun, or playing dice, quickly stood and saluted as Zoar passed in his litter chair borne by four sweating and grunting men.

Zoar paid them no mind, for he was in pain again and wished to be in bed. The desire to conquer worlds left him as the pain grew stronger. As they approached, both Dorak and Zoar heard a loud commotion and screams coming from the aga's tent.

Dorak came to the side of the litter, ordering the men to stop.

The tent flap was pushed aside by two guards tenuously holding on to a woman who was fighting with all her strength. She bit the hand of one guard and as he let go, she swung around and punched the other guard in the face. Quickly grabbing the fallen guard's sword, she sliced both men.

The soldiers held their hands to their wounds, crying out.

The woman looked about and was about to flee when she saw the aga's litter. Realizing who was before her, she flung herself at the litter only to be repulsed by Dorak who threw himself in front of her. Dropping the sword, she fell to her knees.

Dorak strolled over, pulled her head up by her hair,

and prepared to cut her throat.

"Great Aga!" she cried out. "Don't kill me! I come from beyond the mist!"

Zoar roared, "DORAK! STOP!"

Dorak's knife nicked the woman's throat before he released her. A thin line of blood trickled down her neck. The woman fell unconscious on the ground.

"Bind her wounds and bring her to me," Zoar commanded.

Dorak obeyed and called for a physician who had to push his way through a crowd of curious men gawking at the strange woman. Kneeling by her side, Dorak looked for concealed weapons.

The healer had the woman taken to a nearby tent where he could tend to her as well as the two injured guards.

While being examined, the guards told Dorak they had been following their routine, checking the aga's tent when they discovered the woman lurking inside.

"Explain to me how one woman can get past forty thousand men!" shouted Dorak. "Get that woman ready! I want to question her."

The physician bandaged the woman's neck and caused her to awaken with a horrible smelling solution he kept in a borax stomach.

She pushed the foul-smelling bag away, and sat up

shaking her head as if to straighten her thoughts. Seeing Dorak out of the corner of her eye, she immediately became still and waited in silence.

He studied her coldly, and she turned to return the stare. He was surprised by her boldness.

The woman was in excellent shape for being middle-aged. She was very tall and muscular. Her clothing looked of rich quality, though now dirty and torn in places. She had all her teeth. Her hands were strong, but lacked the look of a manual laborer.

This is no peasant woman, thought Dorak. "Come, my father will see you," said Dorak. He motioned to her to follow. "Do you understand me?"

The woman nodded and swung off the table. Passing the soldiers she had wounded, she smiled patronizingly at them.

Obviously uncomfortable, they looked away.

Four guards fell into step, marching behind Dorak and the woman. They passed the aga's horses being brought in for the night, a small group of musicians, numerous advisors, attending guards, and servants bringing shaybar and cheese.

Zoar's concubines lounged on couches. They became alarmed when the strange woman was brought in.

Zoar was drinking shaybar—a bowl of boiled borax milk mixed with blood his healer had brought while having his feet bathed in scented water by a concubine.

Dorak knew his father was using this time to study the prisoner.

Finally, Zoar waved the healer away. He belched loudly and gave the bowl to a waiting servant.

The captured woman was forced to her knees by a guard.

Dorak approached his father and whispered in his ear all that he had learned.

"Who are you?" asked Zoar after listening to Dorak. "Can you speak my language?"

"I can speak Sivan, Great Lord," answered Mikkotto in the Sivan language.

A scribe, who could translate, hurried to the aga's side.

"Where do you come from?"

"Hasan Daeg, the land beyond the mist. My name is Baroness Mikkotto from the House of Sumsumitoyo."

"Why are you here?"

"I have come to serve the Great Aga."

"Liar!" shouted Zoar, his face turning red.

For the first time, the woman felt fear. "No, it is true," she stuttered. "I have come to serve you against the royal house of Hasan Daeg."

"Why would you betray your king?" asked Dorak.

"I've come because I want blood revenge. The ruler,

Queen Abisola de Magela, killed my only son. I want her to die as well as her offspring, Princess Maura," Baroness Mikkotto professed maliciously.

"Why did the queen kill your son?"

"Because she wanted him as a consort and he refused her. Out of a jealous rage, she had my son murdered," lied Mikkotto.

Zoar and Dorak exchanged glances.

"Let's try another answer. If your son refused the advances of his queen, then he deserved to die. You would not betray your country over that. What is the real reason?" asked Dorak. "Be quick or I really will slit your throat this time."

Mikkotto's hands flew up to her neck. "I tried to have Princess Maura, assassinated, but my child was killed instead."

Zoar threw back his head. "Ah, truth finally enters the room. Pray, truth, be seated."

A chair was brought for Mikkotto and she gratefully sat.

"Why did you want the princess to die?" asked Dorak, fascinated by the woman sitting before him.

"I do not want war. I want to make a treaty." She stopped and caught her breath before continuing. "My lands are on the border and will be decimated. I stand to lose everything."

"And yet it seems you have," claimed Zoar.

"Perhaps not," Mikkotto implied.

"I will not deal with a woman. Where is your husband?"

Mikkotto bristled. "Our husbands do not deal with public life. That is reserved for the females. You will make your deal with me or better yet, let me speak to the woman in charge here."

Zoar's concubines gasped, staring at Mikkotto in awe. They had never heard of such concepts before.

Dorak's mouth fell open, but Zoar let out a lusty guffaw. "I like you, Baroness," he laughed. "You will provide me with much entertainment and information about this Hasan Daeg."

Mikkotto eyed Zoar suspiciously. "Only if we can come to some agreement."

"Even without an agreement. There are things worse than death, Baroness Mikkotto. And before your death, you would tell me everything I wish to know. But why such rancor? We can become friends. Come lie beside me on these comfortable pillows," he offered, pointing to his side.

"We will dine and listen to beautiful music sounding like a woman weeping when she is being made love to. After you have rested, we will talk like old comrades." Zoar paused for a moment. "What choice do you have, my lady?"

The baroness listened calmly to the translator knowing she was trapped. She smiled convincingly at Zoar. "Great Aga, surely you do not want me to lie next to you in these filthy rags? I am a woman of high rank—noble blood. I should dress accordingly."

Dorak motioned to the oldest of Zoar's concubines who rose and went over to him. "Arrange for Baroness Mikkotto to have suitable clothes for one of her station, and a private tent with a bath waiting for her."

The concubine nodded and left with several servants.

"May I compliment you on your choice of bedmates," remarked Mikkotto looking at all of Zoar's concubines.

Zoar laughed. "That's all they are, Baroness. Mates to keep me warm, and nothing more. But a man could make love to a woman like you even with only his mind. Come. Lie next to me. Talk to me," he cooed entreatingly. "Let us learn one from the other."

Mikkotto rose and sat down beside Zoar.

Servants placed pillows behind her so she could sit up without straining. Another pillow was gently eased under her neck. Women pulled off her boots and bathed her feet with warm water and oils. Mikkotto, used to being served, relished the attention. Her outer garment was pulled off and her hands were placed in bowls of scented water. The musicians played sweet music, almost lulling Mikkotto to sleep. She opened her eyes to find both Zoar and Dorak staring at her curiously. It startled her.

"I apologize for being so rude," uttered Dorak, "but we have never seen a woman so powerful as you. You are tall and almost as muscular as a man."

"All the women from my country are my size or larger. I find it strange that your women are so delicate."

"Why do you have no hair on your body?" asked Zoar.

"It is the custom of my country that both women and men shave all hair except for their heads."

"Even down there?"

Mikkotto caught Zoar's meaning. "Especially down there." She felt exasperated. She had expected to be talking about matters of war with the king, not the hygiene of her countrywomen.

Zoar and Dorak were conducting themselves like two adolescent schoolboys after their first kiss. It disgusted her, but she would answer anything they asked. As Zoar had put it, what choice did she have?

"What do the men look like?" asked Zoar.

Zoar's advisors gathered closer. They too were fascinated by the large woman, who moved like an experienced warrior. Even the servants put down their platters so they could overhear what was being said.

"Our men are beautiful and very graceful. They wear their hair long and usually braid it with flowers. They are smaller and taught in the ways of poetry, art, stewardship of the home, and lovemaking. That was until our queen decided to make them like women," lamented Mikkotto.

"And you think this is bad?" asked Zoar.

"I think it is unnatural."

"So you are a traditionalist in your country. A noblewoman who wants to preserve the old ways."

Mikkotto said nothing after listening to the translator.

"My dear, this conflict tearing at your heart caused you to sacrifice your son and risk your life entering the enemy camp, making you dangerous indeed for you are a fanatic! Fanatics will not listen to reason, and they are hard to control. I'll tell you something else too. I wager you have daughters, but you would not sacrifice them to assassinate the princess because you knew in all probability the assassin would be killed." Zoar took a drink from his goblet.

"Wanting to preserve my way of life doesn't make me a criminal or a traitor, but a patriot!"

Dorak stifled a laugh.

Zoar too was amused. "What is it that you desire, my pretty traitor?"

"I want to rule Hasan Daeg. I would be a much better queen than that hag who now rules," Mikkotto declared bitterly.

Zoar turned to Dorak. "You see, my son, that all things come down to greed, power, or lust. With a fanatic, it is usually all three."

The translator refused to repeat Zoar's words to Mikkotto.

Still, she knew she had been berated by Zoar through his tone of voice. Insulted, Mikkotto pulled her hand away from Zoar's touch.

"Baroness, why should I make you ruler over Hasan Daeg and not put one of my own governors in or even my son?"

Mikkotto licked her lips before speaking.

Dorak thought she had the look of a poisonous snake before it struck.

His hand steadied on the hilt of his dagger.

Mikkotto spoke slowly. "I want my country to be as it was before Abisola started meddling in our culture. I want to preserve our heritage. What she is doing goes against nature and against our religion. In return for allowing me to restore the natural balance, I will serve you loyally. I know your world is in desperate need of food and medical supplies. My country can supply these things in abundance. We can feed your world!"

"What happened to my men?" asked Dorak.

Mikkotto chose her words carefully. "The mist is a powerful narcotic spray emitted by the caromate plant when its leaves are disturbed. With caromate plant beds, we have put other plants that draw small animals, birds, and insects not bothered by the mist. There is constant activity in the plants due to the movement of the small animals, so there is constant mist."

"Go on," encouraged Zoar.

"Anyone who enters the mist becomes drowsy and disoriented. We are immune to the plant so we can simply enter and do whatever we want. Your soldiers were taken out and given a heavy sedative. They died peacefully in their sleep. I can assure you they were not molested or disrespected in any way. Their bodies were taken away and buried according to our custom." Mikkotto seemed pleased with the telling of the story.

Zoar's face grew red with fury. "You have denied my men an honorable death!"

"I don't understand."

"In our world, a good death is one in which a warrior meets his end fighting a worthy opponent. It ensures peace for the soul of the deceased. Allowing the men to die defenseless means they will walk the land without rest."

Mikkotto was alarmed. "I am sorry. We did not

know. We thought we were being merciful." Mikkotto slid to her knees. "Great Aga, my country has not had a war in over six hundred years. We have forgotten the ways of the warrior. Do not place blame on my people, who thought they were doing right. Blame the bitch who brought this all about. Make me queen so I may serve you. You will not regret it."

"I already regret it. Get out of here. Go bathe. You stink. Then come back later. You will tell me more of your country." Zoar looked at her lecherously. "Maybe there are other things you can show me."

Mikkotto barely suppressed a shudder. "Sire, I am too old for you. I have spent a life of being pleased rather than one pleasing. I would not know what to do."

"As you are taking your bath, you may reflect. I'm sure you can think of something to benefit the both of us."

Mikkotto bowed her head and left the tent, eager to be away from Zoar.

Dorak turned to Zoar after she had left. "Surely, you are not serious about taking that odious woman into your bed. She would sooner kill you than look at you."

"I am too old and sick for such ventures, but she doesn't know that. I like to torment her. It gives me a new interest in life. I'll make her beg and say sweet things, knowing all the time she is retching inside," said

Zoar, smiling sweetly.

"But why waste the time? Let's just torture her and get the information we need."

"Dorak, you have no instinct for sport. Besides, I don't want her tortured by anyone but me. She interests me. She excites me."

"She's the enemy. She ought to be treated like a prisoner of war."

"She's a woman. What real harm can she do?"

"Try asking the wounded guards."

"Luck. They were careless."

Dorak could not believe his father's stubbornness. "Father, she fought like a trained soldier. It was not luck bringing her to your tent. It was skill. She is very dangerous. Too dangerous for a bed toy. Please let me interrogate her."

Not wishing to continue this line of conversation, Zoar changed the subject. "Do you believe her? I mean, it sounds fantastic—a country run by women who have built a barrier from simple plants. Can it be true?"

"It sounds very much like KiKu's stories."

"KiKu," mused Zoar. "Yes, let's make every effort to find him. We have many things to ask him." Zoar flicked a moth off his sleeve. "You concentrate on KiKu and the spy network, and I will concentrate on the woman. Between the two of us, we should be able to overrun this Hasan Daegian queen within a full turning of the big moon."

Dorak did not believe in the methods of his father, though they usually had merit. If his father wanted to play with this woman's mind, who was he to say it would not be effective? He bowed and left the tent. He had much to do that night. He paused for a moment outside, looking at the mist looming in the distance. He made a silent vow that whatever was discovered beyond the wall, he would not let his father carve it up as he had other conquered lands. Too much waste and destruction for Dorak's taste.

He remembered the fall of Anqara. The city was still not inhabited. It was considered a place haunted by the dead. Thousands of people had been killed during the siege until the streets turned red with their blood. Many others had vanished. No, he would not let that happen to Hasan Daeg. Whatever was there he would try to preserve. And if it took working with the distasteful baroness to achieve it, he would do it.

Some soldiers began singing around a fire.

The singing caused Dorak to break his concentration. He regarded the soldiers for a moment, almost wishing he could join in their revelry. Pushing this thought from his mind, he headed for his tent with his way lit by several servants bearing torches.

29

Mikkotto bathed a long time.

A blue-green kimono and cork sandals were brought to her. "These are the clothes of a courtesan," barked Mikkotto in the Sivan language. "Bring me leggings and a tunic."

Zoar's concubine bowed low. "I am sorry, Baroness, but this is the court attire for a noblewoman. My lord would be most offended if I dressed you like a man. It would not be fitting."

"This foul country with its stupid practices," ranted Mikkotto, snatching the robe away from the concubine. "Get out. I can get dressed myself."

The concubine bowed low again. "I'm sorry. If you do not look presentable, I will lose my head. I cannot allow this to happen, so I must stay. You may kick me if it will make you feel better, but you will look presentable. After all, a kick is better than death. Do you not agree?"

Mikkotto looked at the concubine. "I have a daughter about your age," she said softly.

"That is good. Perhaps you will take pity on me and be kind," pleaded the concubine, putting ivory combs in Mikkotto's hair.

"In my country, women are treated with respect. We would kill a man who talked the way Zoar did tonight."

"Perhaps one day I will be allowed to visit your country. I would like once before I die to pick a man of my own choosing. Is that possible in your country?"

Mikkotto nodded.

The concubine smiled with great pleasure. "Baroness, you have given me something to dream about. I thank you for this great honor of serving a most independent female. Perhaps you will remember your most humble servant and call for me in the future?"

"We shall see."

The concubine lowered her voice. "Zoar has no intention of mating with you. He cannot. The most he can do is fondle. You can stand that, surely. It is Dorak you must watch."

Mikkotto did not respond to the concubine's words, but fussed with her hair. "What is your name, girl?" asked Mikkotto.

"KiKusan. I am the daughter of KiKu, the hetmaan for my master."

Mikkotto realized she had made a valuable friend. She smiled warmly at KiKusan.

KiKusan tied Mikkotto's sandals. "It is time for us to go," she announced.

The older woman followed the young concubine to Zoar's tent.

Mikkotto took a deep breath before entering. She was again assaulted by pungent odors. The smell of horse dung, incense, cooked meat, and body sweat permeated the air. She hoped she would not get a headache.

On the aga's couch lay Zoar with several of his women. The girls had already fallen asleep, but he was still awake and motioned to her.

Picking her way carefully through the various flung-out limbs of sleeping bedmates, Mikkotto made her way beside Zoar on her side, facing him.

Zoar appraised Mikkotto. "You look very handsome," he said in the Sivan language.

"Thank you," replied Mikkotto, knowing now that he had understood every word she had uttered. Zoar had never needed an interpreter. Still, she was grateful for his compliment. She knew she was not pretty, but striking in appearance. She pulled at the kimono folds.

Zoar raised up on one elbow, "No, don't do that. I want to look at you." He pulled the kimono apart. "Did you suckle your children?"

Surprised by the question, Mikkotto answered quickly, "Yes, I did. Only with the girls. My son had a wet nurse."

"There is something very pleasing about a woman who has suckled. These girls are all very beautiful. Their bellies are without blemish, their breasts high and firm, their lips eager to be kissed, but they bore me."

Mikkotto laughed, not believing him.

"No, it is true. I am bored with their beauty and youth. You told me you are used to being served. Then let me, Great Aga of the Eastern World, serve you. Let me stroke you. You need not respond if you do not wish to. Just tell stories about your homeland. What would you do if I made you queen? Talk about anything until you fall asleep."

Mikkotto did not move away, but her mind was full of astonishing thoughts. She did not feel repulsed as she thought she would. Instead, she felt lulled by the soft music playing, Zoar's murmuring voice, and the gentle snoring of the girls lying with them on the huge couch. She found Zoar's large rough hands soothing.

"It has been a long time since I have had pleasures such as this," she sighed.

"Tell me about your husband."

"Which one? I have had several."

"You tell me your story, and I will tell you about my wives. You remind me of my first wife."

"Did you have feelings for her?" asked Mikkotto, closing her eyes.

"I certainly love the memory of her. Now I have told you a truth about myself. You must tell me a truth."

"I married my first husband for dynastic reasons. He was an only child whose land doubled my holdings. I had my first child by him."

"And then you had him killed, right?"

Shocked, Mikkotto sat up, pushing Zoar away.

"Don't be so defensive. It only makes sense. You did not love him and, being an only child, he was probably a big baby. You could not bear the thought of spending the rest of your life with him, so he met with an unfortunate accident."

"No one knows," hissed Mikkotto.

"I do now. Your reaction tells me my guess is true. Lie back down, and I will tell you a secret about me. Come, come. Don't be shy. We are getting along so well." Zoar looked thoughtful and weighed his words before he spoke. "My first wife. I loved her desperately, but she did not love me. She was in love with another."

243

"You saw them together?"

Zoar shook his head. "She would never have betrayed me. She was very honorable. But I couldn't stand the notion that she thought of another when she was with me. It drove me nearly insane. One day we were out hunting and a borax attacked. I hesitated killing the animal, and that mistake cost her life. It was during her funeral, I realized I had wanted her to die, and that's why I had hesitated. Strangely, her death set me free."

Zoar paused and looked at Mikkotto. "I wish to love again, Mikkotto. Let me love you, and I will make you queen of Hasan Daeg."

"I have no wish to recapture your past with you and die as did your queen."

"I am an old man long past all such vanities. I know you would never love me as you are past such grand passions yourself. I wish only to love on a small scale. I want to touch this time with clarity, not the drunkenness of lust. I want to talk about old glories. I want a woman who wants to be pleasured instead of sniffing around me like a hound in heat. Give me a little passion, a little companionship, and I will make you queen of Hasan Daeg."

"It is such a tempting offer. I must say you are not as repulsive as I thought you would be."

Zoar winked. "Tell me the truth. Isn't this more

pleasant than rotting away in some prison?"

Mikkotto smiled. "I accept your offer, Great Aga. May we both not live to regret this foolishness."

"Call me Zoar, please. Now move closer, my pet. Let me feel your belly. That is all the energy I will have left for tonight. If you need more, you must satisfy yourself."

Mikkotto moved closer and untied her kimono. "Maybe we can satisfy each other?"

Zoar grinned with anticipation. "We can try, pet. We can certainly try."

30

Dorak took a deep breath.

"Tell me again. Who are the Dinii?"

"We have been over this countless times. I am tired. I want to go to sleep," complained Mikkotto.

"Not until I understand."

Mikkotto sighed. "The Dinii are the Overlords of Hasan Daeg. They are the real owners of the land. We cultivate the land which attracts the wildlife upon which they feed."

"And they are birds?"

"Yes. No. Yes!" cried Mikkotto, exasperated. "They are birds, but they are people as well."

"Are they intelligent?"

"Extremely. They are a very old race and great warriors. Your shields and swords will be no match for them."

"Dorak, I don't see what good it is to go over the same information time and time again," interjected Zoar. He, too, was tired and wanted to go to bed.

The Prince held up his hand. "I must see if her information is consistent. Please try to be patient."

"Can't you see that she is exhausted?"

"Which is why I want to continue questioning her, Father, to see if there are any cracks in her story."

Mikkotto gave Dorak a vicious glare. "I've told you all I know. If you fight the Hasan Daegians, you must also fight the Dinii."

"If it is the Dinii's land, where did the Hasan Daegians come from?"

"I don't know. I just know it was the Dinii's land before we came."

"Where did you come from?"

"I don't know," spat Mikkotto.

"As you told us, Hasan Daegians have various ethnic appearances. Don't you think it strange that Hasan Daegians have different skin colors and hair textures from each other?"

Zoar said, "I don't see the point."

"Father, don't you see? In every country we have been in, all the people have looked similar except for the slaves, which were brought in from other places. This has always been consistent."

"We are not slaves," protested Mikkotto, very insulted.

"How do you know? You can't even tell me the origin of your own people. You could be manipulated by the Dinii and not even know it."

Zoar countered, "Suppose they are the descendants of slaves, how does this information help to invade Hasan Daeg? Tell me. I would truly like to know."

"We could use this information to help break the treaty between the Dinii and the Hasan Daegians," answered Dorak hoarsely, his throat feeling dry.

"Bah, this is silly." Zoar turned to Mikkotto. "Pet, how would you invade Hasan Daeg?"

Mikkotto tried to suppress a yawn, but could not. "There is only one river which enters Hasan Daeg from the east. Across this river, they run huge, stationary barges filled with dirt in which they have planted caromate plants. It is here the mist is the weakest. Have your men destroy the barges, and you will have a pathway into Hasan Daeg." She lay down by Zoar's feet and curled up. "Leave me alone now. I must sleep."

Dorak started to kick Mikkotto but Zoar caught his leg, shooting him a warning glance. Dorak bowed and went to the table to replenish his wine goblet. He did not like his father's fascination with this woman. For weeks, the army had remained stationary while Zoar amused himself with his new plaything. Their relationship interfered with Dorak's plans.

Outside a thunderstorm raged furiously. A thunderclap woke Mikkotto, and she groggily struggled to rise.

Zoar helped her.

Dorak thumbed through scrolls on the table and continued his interrogation. "Do you recognize this drawing?" He held up a picture.

"It is the Bogazkoy tree."

"What is that?"

"It is the rarest species of plant life in Hasan Daeg. There is only one specimen rumored to exist, and it is owned by the Crown."

"Why does Queen Abisola want this plant?"

Mikkotto coughed, "May I have some water?"

"Answer the question first," said Dorak.

"It is thought the Bogazkoy tree is used to prolong the lives of the rulers. It gives them and their offspring the blue color. The blue skin is a sign of royalty."

"True blue bloods, eh, Dorak," croaked Zoar. He thought it amusing.

"How does it do this?" asked Dorak, ignoring his father.

"I don't know. It is just a rumor of how the de Magelas got their blue skin. Probably superstition. You said I could have some water."

Dorak handed her a goblet of wine.

She drank greedily.

Zoar observed them both quietly. His intuition told him that Dorak was planning something unpleasant for Mikkotto. He would have to keep an eye on his son to prevent him from doing something that would cause misery between the two of them.

"You have seen this Bogazkoy tree?"

"No one has ever seen it."

"Then how do you know this picture is of the Bogazkoy?"

"That same picture is in our religious texts which we use to worship our goddess, Mekonia."

"Where is this tree planted?"

"Probably the palace, but I don't really know."

"You don't know. You don't know," mimicked Dorak. "You are worthless!"

"Stop it! Stop screaming those endless questions at me. It is driving me crazy, I tell you," shouted Mikkotto. She feared she was breaking under the strain of constant interrogation for the past four days and nights.

Zoar had done little to interfere.

She looked pleadingly at him.

"This is enough for tonight," said Zoar, motioning for his men to raise his litter.

Dorak started to protest.

"Enough, I said," countered Zoar forcefully. "What good is she to us if you drive her to exhaustion with your constant pestering?"

"But Father!"

"She has told you how to enter Hasan Daeg. Isn't that a start? Why don't you start planning a strategy to get us inside? Why are you asking questions about their culture, habits, their royalty? We will know all of that soon enough when we enter. Your questioning is wasting precious time. Fall will be here soon, then winter. I want to be back in Bhuttan by the first snow."

"Father, I only ask on your behalf."

"How is that?"

"If this Bogazkoy tree prolongs life, perhaps it can restore part of your vigor. Maybe your health entirely. Remember, these Hasan Daegian queens are renowned as healers!"

"Dangling a carrot on a stick, son? I know all about this Bogazkoy tree. I've known about it for years from the papers of the High Priestess from the House of Magi." Zoar pulled the coverlet closer to his chest. "The High Priestess was named Mehmet. She kept a personal diary, which was partially burned in the fire set by the Dini I witnessed in her room. She was found on a rooftop with her neck broken."

Dorak scattered through his scrolls, looking for a

translation of the diary. "I have no such copy of this diary," he complained, puzzled.

"You were given none by my orders," replied Zoar, looking pleased. "I have the only copy and it is locked away. It took years to translate it. She had written it in no known language, but in her own coding system. This woman would have made a great spy," Zoar said admiringly. "Her code was finally broken two years ago."

"That's when you started planning this campaign."

"Correct. From the scraps of the diary, I realized the significance of the Bogazkoy tree. There was hope again that I would be able to walk." Zoar's eyes glowed with anticipation. "How the tree works, I don't know yet. But whatever happens, no one from the house de Magela will be killed or injured until I have discovered their secret."

Zoar pointed to Mikkotto leaning against the litter chair asleep. "And she is going to help me."

"She knows nothing."

"You do not give Mikkotto credit. She is a brave and resourceful woman. She is also connected to the royal house by kinship. This poor creature may know the answer to the Bogazkoy mystery, but does not realize that she does. That's why my method is more fruitful. If she is not intimidated, she will divulge more."

"Is that why you treat her kindly?"

Zoar stroked his beard. He regarded Dorak coldly, his voice ringing with deadly earnest. "I treat Mikkotto well because she is the key to Hasan Daeg and because I care for her."

"What!" exclaimed Dorak. "Surely you're joking?"

"No, Dorak. After the campaign, I intend to marry Mikkotto and make her my empress." Zoar mused, "With a little luck, she still might be able to conceive."

Dorak grabbed the table to steady himself, betraying his inner thoughts. "I don't understand. You have only known this woman for a few short weeks."

"At my age, that is long enough."

"But you cannot perform." Dorak felt as if he had been kicked in the stomach by a warhorse. His mind was quickly calculating the damage if Mikkotto were made empress and conceived. Could Zoar, in his ardent passion for Mikkotto, proclaim a new heir presumptive? No, Dorak could never allow this possibility. He and his mother had suffered too much.

"I am feeling better all the time. As I said, Mikkotto is a remarkable woman. Now I wish to retire." Zoar motioned for his bearers to lift Mikkotto into the litter chair. He stroked her hair absently while bidding Dorak good night and left for his own tent.

Sickened, Dorak fell into a chair. He brooded for

hours and did not hear the trumpet herald the new morning.

His servants found him slumped over a table, his hands clutching scrolls. Gently they removed him to his couch and undressed him. Pulling the tent flap closed, they let him sleep until dusk. When Dorak awoke, his future course had been plotted. He knew he could not turn back.

31

It took weeks for the preparations.

The river was surveyed as much as possible while great rafts were constructed. Huge catapults were dragged into place on both sides of the river before the mist wall. Archers practiced shooting with their longbows the distance Dorak said would be required to set the barges on fire. Men, hand-picked by Dorak, spent hours swimming back and forth across the river. It was very difficult as some of the men lost their way and drifted into the mist. They became sleepy and drowned.

Foot soldiers practiced hand-to-hand combat while the cavalry ran their warhorses through daily exercises. The tanners made extra bridles and gloves. Armor and weapons were polished until they were blinding in the late summer sun and checked over and over again.

The Camaroon population was rounded up and interrogated. When Dorak was satisfied they knew nothing about what was beyond the mist, he used them as slave labor to gather firewood for his army, tend the animals, and satisfy his men at night. The captured Camaroons, crying out in agony, were heard by Hasan Daegian soldiers standing watch on the other side of the mist.

On the last night before the invasion was to begin, forty thousand men along with ten thousand servants, slaves, and camp followers celebrated Bhuttan's most sacred holiday, the mating of Bhuttu with Bhutta to create a new world order.

Tables, laden with food and drink, were stretched from one end of the camp to the other. Huge fires were built, and the soldiers danced feverishly around them.

Those in Zoar's tent were also celebrating. Paper mache replicas of phalluses were placed all around the tent. Zoar's concubines dressed gaily in bold colors and danced lasciviously in Bhuttu's honor. Some had fake phalluses attached to their costumes and pretended to mate with other girls.

Mikkotto watched the girls with quiet disdain and was glad when the food was brought in. It gave her an excuse to be distracted from the entertainment. She looked at Zoar and saw that his eyes glittered with excitement. She thought him an old lecherous fool.

Dorak strode into the tent, his face tense. He went up to Zoar. "Father, I thought there would be no spirits tonight."

"The men need something more than just water to wash down their food."

Dorak curbed his tone. "I realize tonight is a special celebration, but we are going into battle tomorrow. The men will need clear heads and steady hands."

"Tomorrow will pose no problem for us," laughed Zoar. "Mikkotto has told us everything we need to know about the Hasan Daegian army." He smiled sweetly at her. "We could go in with only twenty thousand men and mop up before dusk."

"I wish I could be so confident," said Dorak, lowering his voice. He smiled at the advisors and honored guests of his father's, not wishing to cause a scene.

"Relax, sit down beside me and enjoy the festivities." Zoar motioned for a servant to get some wine for Dorak. "You worry too much."

Dorak sat down, trying not to scowl. His brain was racing. He noticed Mikkotto was looking around Zoar at him. *Even she thinks this is ridiculous*, thought Dorak.

Zoar was stuffing himself with food and drink. He wiped his greasy hands on his robe. As soon as he was finished with one dish, Mikkotto offered him another and then another dish. She teased him, coaxed him, and baited him. Zoar laughed uproariously. He slapped his knees with mirth at performing clowns who juggled small boaeps. Suddenly he grabbed his middle and let out a loud belch. "I think I need to make water," Zoar announced.

Servants rushed over to help Zoar to his litter.

"I will go with him," offered Dorak, rising to follow his father being carried out.

The servants placed Zoar's litter by a tree and lifted his robe to allow him to relieve himself.

Dorak told the servants to leave. "I will call you when he is ready to go back in," ordered the prince.

The servants, always impressed with Dorak's concern for his father, gladly left Zoar in his hands. They wished to watch the clowns.

Zoar babbled incoherently, his mind befuddled by too much drink. He leaned precariously from his chair as he began urinating.

Dorak looked about. There was no one to be seen.

With the strength of a powerful warrior, Dorak quickly grabbed his father's face, placing his hands over Zoar's nose and mouth.

Zoar struggled hard, grabbing at his son's hands and twisting, almost causing Dorak to lose his grip. But Dorak held on for what seemed to be an eternity.

Zoar's squirming slowed until it ceased all together. Finally, he slumped against Dorak's chest.

Dorak checked for a pulse. Finding none, he gathered Zoar gently in his arms and carried him into the tent. In a loud voice, he cried out, "My father's ill. Someone help!"

Tears of sorrow fell from Dorak's face.

32

Princess Maura could not sleep.

She stood staring into mist listening to the revelry from the other side.

Before dawn, her soldiers would slip through and attack Zoar's army. They would try to inflict as much damage as possible before they retreated beyond the wall again. It had been decided that the Hasan Daegians, even though well-trained, were no match for Zoar's crack troops and would have to resort to guerrilla tactics.

She looked behind her.

All through the forest, trees were filled with the darkened outlines of the Dinii who had perched for the night. Beneath the shelter of the trees and the watchful eyes of the Dinii camped thousands of Hasan Daegians, Anqarians, and mercenaries from other countries. They all looked asleep in their bedrolls, but Maura knew her soldiers were awake, listening to the sound of singing coming through the mist wall.

Chaun Maaun came up behind and placed his arm around her.

She rested her head on his chest, grateful for his small kindness. As always, Maura deeply inhaled his scent for she loved the woodsy smell of him.

He kissed the top of her head. "I guess I shouldn't be kissing the new commander-in-chief," he teased.

Maura said nothing. Since her birthday, they had spoken little, both realizing they had no future together. Saddened by the thought that they might die soon, Maura clasped her arms around Chaun Maaun and sobbed into his chest.

He held her tightly, rocking her back and forth with soothing sounds. "You mustn't cry," Chaun Maaun said softly. "You must stay strong for everyone's sake."

"I don't feel very strong," she hiccupped, tears streaming down her face.

"You want to know a secret? I'm frightened too."

"You, Chaun Maaun!"

"Even me."

"But you've fought before. You've even killed. I don't know that I can."

"When you see a double-edged ax coming toward

your face, you'll kill without even thinking about it. Trust me on that. The instinct to survive will not let you down. Just let it guide you."

The princess wiped hot salty tears from her face. "Chaun, I have terrible fears that I will be a coward, hiding until the battle is over. How will I be able to live with myself if I dishonor my family?"

"Maura, you are not alone. I remember the first time I fought with a poacher. I was so scared. I had the same thoughts, but you cannot run away even as I could not. There is something inside us that won't allow it. Trust your instinct. Pull from your center all that Iegani has taught you."

"I wish my mother had never made me commander-in-chief. I begged her not to. Yesemek should have been in charge. She's a true warrior."

"Yesemek is not Hasan Daegian. She would never be able to inspire the people as you do. They will follow you, but will always have a seed of mistrust of Yesemek because she is a Dini. Your mother is correct about this and far-seeing in her choice."

"You are right. I am being a fool. It's a little late to have second thoughts."

Chaun Maaun laughed heartily. "That's an under-statement!"

She joined with him laughing.

Yesemek flew down beside them. "Shh, do you want to alert the enemy?" she hissed angrily.

Princess Maura blushed furiously. "I am sorry, General Yesemek. It was most unwise of us, but as I am commander-in-chief, I will remind you not to publicly reprimand me again. Good night," she said brusquely. Marching to her tent, the princess left the general astounded and Chaun Maaun grinning.

Yesemek gaped after her and turned to Chaun Maaun.

He shrugged his massive shoulders and said, "I guess she's taking her new title very seriously."

The Dini general flew back up to her perch making clicking noises.

Suddenly the singing from the other side stopped.

Anxious cries could be heard.

Chaun Maaun listened carefully.

Maura ran back and joined him.

The entire Hasan Daegian camp got up from their bedrolls and waited.

"Get Yeti," commanded Princess Maura to a Dinii sergeant.

Within a few minutes, Yeti and Benzar appeared at Maura's side. "They are not celebrating anymore. See what's happening and report to me here," she commanded.

Yeti and Benzar flew off with barely a sound.

A stool and a blanket were brought for Maura.

Chaun Maaun and Yesemek stood beside the shivering princess, both of them realizing she wasn't shaking from the cold. They knew their presence brought her some measure of comfort.

Yesemek silently prayed that Maura's years of training with the Dinii would instill her with courage. She wished Iegani was present so that he could reassure the princess as he always did. He had flown off to some secret place for a retreat. He needed to communicate with his inner self, he had said. *What balderdash!* Yesemek had thought when he came to say goodbye. He was needed now, and no one knew where to find him.

Maura, Chaun Maaun, Yesemek, along with all the other warriors waited in silence.

Twenty minutes later, Yeti and Benzar flew into the camp. They were hot and panting, but they looked jubilant.

"What has happened?" asked Maura, standing abruptly.

Yeti cried, "Zoar is dead!"

"What!" echoed Chaun Maaun, stunned.

"Yes, he died this very night during the feast of their gods. The entire camp is in mourning. They think this a very bad omen."

"This means the attack will be called off!" exclaimed a jubilant Chaun Maaun. He shook his fists into the air and did a little dance, skipping and hopping around Maura and Yesemek.

"Is Dorak, the son of Zoar, still alive?" questioned Yesemek.

"Yes, he was with his father when he passed away," said Benzar.

"How did Zoar die?" asked Maura.

"They don't know for sure, but it is thought from natural causes. Dorak claims Zoar was relieving himself and grabbed at his chest as though in pain. Zoar was dead by the time a healer could be called. There were no marks on the body."

Yesemek gave a deadly look at Chaun Maaun. "You say Dorak was with Zoar when he died?"

"Yes, General," answered Yeti.

Yesemek turned to Princess Maura. "It may be Dorak will take his troops home out of respect for his father. However, I would like to point out if Dorak does leave, he will lose face with his men and might never regain their trust again. If I were he, I would still attack, if only to remove the memory of the former ruler."

Maura inclined her head. She turned to Yeti. "You say the men are upset. Are they drunk?"

"Some are, Your Highness," replied Yeti. "It is certain that they are disoriented and low in spirit."

Maura pondered on this information. Everyone was looking to her for guidance. She felt her heart beating faster and not sure what to do. "I wish to be alone," she barked.

Everyone bowed and left except for Chaun Maaun. He looked at her expectantly.

"You too," she said more softly.

Looking hurt, he lumbered down the hill and joined Yesemek.

Pulling the blanket around herself, she slumped down. For a moment, she had the very strong urge to suck her thumb. She wanted to go home. Disgusted with herself, she put the thought out of her mind. Surely, Dorak would not attack with his father dead.

Closing her eyes, the princess struggled to meditate as Iegani had taught her so many years ago. Deeper and deeper she reached into herself until there was a blinding light flashing from behind her eyes. It caused Maura great pain causing her to double over. Through the light, she saw Iegani in a strange watery place reaching his hand out toward her.

"Trust your inner self," he said.

Maura held her head as she felt a grinding pain near her ears. She was sure she cried out. In the blinking of an eye, the pain released her and she slumped back into her chair. Sweat matted her hair, and her skin was covered with goosebumps. A strange tingling crept up her spine and then left her body through her eyes. She felt it dissipate.

Maura was unable to move. She tried lifting her arms, but could not. Finally, after some exertion, she could move her fingers. They felt as if they had been burned. The princess lowered her head toward her chest. Her hands and legs began to twitch. She tried to sit up, but couldn't. Straining, she tried to call, but this time no sound came forth. Suddenly she heard Chaun Maaun.

"Yesemek, help me! The princess is having a fit!" cried Chaun Maaun, rushing to Maura's side.

Yesemek blocked his way. "Let her be! She is on the Path of Seeking."

Chaun Maaun angrily pushed Yesemek aside, but too late. Princess Maura fell out of her chair.

The Dinii Prince fell to his knees to hold Maura, but felt a blow to the back of his neck. Bewildered, he swung around.

Yesemek warned, "Don't touch her. You don't want to be where she is."

Strong vibrations surrounded the trio. The very air seemed disturbed and unsteady. An angry buzzing noise sounded around the princess, then slowly faded.

Yesemek watched the young woman and knew her to be suffering.

Chaun Maaun sat back on his haunches, waiting until the spasms grew faint.

With her face still contorted, Maura slowly opened her eyes. Upon seeing Chaun Maaun, she struggled to talk.

Sensing the danger was past, he pulled her into a chair and called for a healer. He pulled hair out of her eyes and brushed leaves from her robe.

"I did not understand at first why Iegani left," confided Yesemek to Maura. "I thought it very odd. When I saw you go into a trance, I realized Iegani went to one of his special places of power. He was waiting for you, wasn't he?"

"She is not ill?" asked Chaun Maaun.

Princess Maura shook her head. "I was in a strange place. I wasn't really there, but then again, I was. It seemed like a spirit walk, but it was in water. Water surrounded me, and yet I could breathe and walk without hindrance. There was a bright yellow light, and I followed it. Before I could find the source of the light, Iegani stood before me encased in a huge orb. It shimmered in the light as water cascaded over its façade. He beckoned, telling me not to be afraid. I was going to be shown my destiny, but I would not be alone. His words calmed me until a strange-looking woman came up from behind and pushed him out of the way. Her hair floated in the water current, and she wore no clothes. I could see inside her body. I saw her heart pumping with blood running through her veins." The princess shivered, looking beseechingly at Chaun Maaun.

"Continue," encouraged Yesemek.

"The woman talked to me telepathically. She said she knew me and was going to show me a dark and terrible future if I did not fight. She said she knew I was thinking about returning to O Konya. From the corner of my eye, I saw Iegani struggle to move between us. The woman blew her breath at Iegani causing him to float away. Then she held out her hands. In the middle of each palm was an open eye, which moved independently from the other. She told me to look at the eyes.

"I said to her, 'No, I don't want to', but I could not look away. She took no pity on me. I was carried into the future, and it was a future without me. I knew I had been dead for a long time. The planet was scarred beyond recognition. Where once green valleys had nestled, there were now deserts. The land was cracked and scorched. Water was scarce and worth more than gold. Most of the animals were gone. People moved in bands, scavenging what they could. They were poor and ragged, without hearth or home to call their own. Everything that I had loved was gone. Hasan Daeg did not exist, nor did the Dinii. It was a world without hope because even the tools to rebuild no longer existed. It was a miserable existence for those who survived. I was glad that I was dead!

"The woman pointed a finger at me. 'You are responsible for this because you were weak. You did not take up the sword when needed, letting the enemy overrun your land. You could have stopped this. You are responsible!' Then I awoke." Maura mumbled again softly, "You are responsible." She stood unsteadily.

Chaun Maaun threw out a hand, but she dismissed it. She smiled gently at him. "I understand now what I must do. Please help me."

"Always!" cried Chaun Maaun alarmed.

"My dearest friend, you will not always understand my ways, but I beg of you to be patient with me. I am led down a path that I do not fully understand except I must follow it. The thought of turning my back fills me with such foreboding, I can do nothing else but go where I am called."

"I swear to you before all this company, both Dinii and Hasan Daegian, I give my personal fealty to you regardless of the relations between our two races." He bowed before Maura and kissed her hand.

Overcome with emotion, Princess Maura's hand flew up to stroke the feathers on his head before she summoned her soldiers.

"Get me Queen Rosalind's sword," she commanded of a servant.

The ancient sword of the first queen of Hasan Daeg with its jewel-encrusted hilt was handed to the princess. She raised the sword high over her head. In a loud voice she proclaimed, "I, Princess Maura de Magela, Heir Presumptive to the Royal House of Hasan Daeg, Little Mother of the Weak, Healer of the Infirm, do swear before this good company that I will fight and defend all that is mine and thine!"

"Aye! Aye!" shouted the crowd. "We love you, Princess. We will follow you unto death!"

Maura stood before the cheering crowd, her sword rising into the air, her legs apart and arms akimbo. Her eyes seemed ablaze. Her countenance was one of rapture. One by one, the soldiers began to bow down before her and proclaim their allegiance.

Maura turned to Yesemek and Kimtimee. "We attack just before dawn."

Yesemek snapped to attention and saluted. "Yes, everything will proceed as planned."

"Our goals are to knock out the catapults and rafts. After that is accomplished, kill as many as you can before retreating," said Maura.

Surprised, Yesemek ventured, "I thought we would only concentrate on military weapons systems."

"I have changed my mind," Princess Maura said, looking at her coldly. "Knocking out a few catapults is not going to change Dorak's mind about invading, but bloodshed might."

General Kimtimee offered, "Or it might make him angry."

"Do as you're told," snapped Maura.

Kimtimee and Yesemek bowed their heads and left to execute Maura's new orders.

Yesemek passed the word along to the Dinii. No one in the Dinii camp realized her concern about attacking the army itself. Were the Hasan Daegians ready for such bloody confrontation?

Chaun Maaun looked questioningly at Maura.

"You gave me your oath," she remarked bluntly.

"So I did and so I shall act," he replied. "I hope you don't lead us down the path of perdition."

"I don't know what that is," Maura retorted.

Chaun Maaun looked at the mist. "I imagine Dorak doesn't either." He turned and strode away, leaving her in the gloom of a dwindling torch.

33

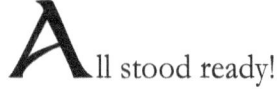

All stood ready!

Princess Maura rode her pony, Beca, to the head of the soldiers anxiously awaiting her signal. Solemnly dressed in black leather, she sat stoically on the back of her prancing horse. Taking a deep breath, she extracted an arrow from her quiver and put the shaft in a cauldron of fire. With one swift movement, she withdrew the flaming arrow and notched it in the taut bowstring of her longbow. Deliberately, she raised the longbow to the heavens and, with a sudden cry of emotion, released the bowstring.

This was the signal to attack.

Watching as the flaming arrow arched upward over the waiting troops, the Dinii sprang into action. From the limbs of hundreds of trees, groups of Dinii flew in formation to scaffolds where Hasan Daegians awaited with small clay pots filled with burning oil. Each pot was in a leather sling with a long circular strap. The pots were hoisted up by the Hasan Daegians on tall poles. The Dinii would straighten out their formations into two lines, fly in low, snatch the flaming pot by the strap, and then regroup into their previous formations. With horrific battle cries, they flew by the hundreds over the wall of mist into the camp of the Bhuttanians. Once over their targets they simply released their slings with their burning fuel. So acute was their eyesight in the dark, they rarely missed snatching the slings or dropping them on their targets.

The Bhuttanians, demoralized and confused by the death of their king, stumbled out of their tents without benefit of armor or weapons. They stood perplexed, watching the catapults and rafts explode into flames as demon-like creatures flew across the dark sky. These creatures terrified them with hideous screams, their red eyes highlighted by the flames and sparks shooting into the air. Thinking their god, Bhuttan, was sending an army of banshees to avenge the death of Zoar, many of the soldiers ran screaming into the night only to die later as the Dinii hunted them down, one by one.

As soon as the first catapult was afire and gave enough light, several thousand male Hasan Daegian archers emerged from the mist. Taking aim with their small bows, they released a deadly rain of arrows, which found its mark in more than one man's chest. As soon as they released, they kneeled and began rearming their bows.

From behind stepped forward the female archers with heavier and stronger longbows. They lit their arrows and aimed for any target that would burn. Once they released, they kneeled and rearmed. The male archers then stood and began the process over again.

Step-by-step, arrow-by-arrow, they began to advance upon the encampment of Zoar until at last they were given the signal to retreat.

Out of the mist stepped Maura. Her dark hair framed her camouflaged face. The only mark of her station on her black uniform was embroidered uultepes encircling a Bogazkoy tree on her chest. Armed with a mace, sword, dagger, and shield she led her soldiers into battle with a mighty swing of her morning star mace.

The women, excited by the smell of blood in the air, cried out and descended upon the camp in a frenzied state. They were fighting for their land, their homes, and their children. They realized they would never have another opportunity like this again to destroy the enemy, so each blow must count.

Maura struck the first blow. A soldier, his eyes wide with fear, blocked her way. He swung at her with a sword. She parried with her mace.

The soldier, confused, hesitated.

Princess Maura immediately struck the side of his head.

He looked strangely at her, falling with the mace embedded in his skull.

She put her foot on his neck while trying to pull the mace out of the soldier's skull. Seeing another man approached from the left side, she whirled around, pulling out her sword. Falling to her knees, she placed her shield before her and thrust upwards with her sword. The stunned soldier dropped his ax and grabbed his belly.

A Hasan Daegian soldier came from behind and finished him off. She then helped Maura up. The princess murmured thanks and continued on.

Slashing, cutting, hacking, and thrusting, the Hasan Daegian foot soldiers made their way steadily deep into the enemy's camp. Behind them followed dismounted members of the cavalry, scavenging for useful weapons, carrying back their wounded, and killing any enemy soldier who was found still alive. Unable to bring their ponies through the mist, they were still eager for a fight until they saw the carnage left by Maura and her warriors. More than one was heard to say, "This isn't right."

Another soldier snapped back, "What do you think they would do to us, if given half a chance?"

By this time, the archers had moved around to the right of the encampment and, stepping out of the mist, they began their reign of terror over again.

Looking up, Maura gauged she only had about a hundred feet to go before her people would start making contact with the arrows. Coughing because of the thick smoke moving throughout the camp, she called to her next-in-command to signal a retreat.

The lieutenant shot an arrow with a red streaming tail into the air.

Dinii, watching from nearby trees, called to Kimtimee to retreat. She commanded the Hasan Daegians to blow the signal on their trumpets.

The trumpets sounded, and the Hasan Daegian women began moving back.

Bhuttanian soldiers from the rear of the camp had had time to dress and gather their weapons. Delayed by the stampede of borax and horses, they still made their way to the center of the camp where the Hasan Daegians were fighting.

Hearing a great cry from behind her, Maura swirled around, dodging a sword. She fell and quickly rolled to her left to bring up her shield. A heavy blow met it. She rolled to the right and threw up her shield. A blow rained down again and was so great that it split the shield. Sweat dripped into her eyes, making it hard to see. She parried her sword upward only to have it knocked from her hands. Rolling to her left, her opponent's sword struck the ground about her face. She rolled to the right and the same thing happened. Realizing her opponent was now playing with her, Maura charged forward only to be knocked down.

Breathing heavily and wiping sweat from her face, Maura glanced quickly about her. She was alone. Her soldiers and personal guards were fighting several hundred feet beyond her. Realizing she was captured, the princess pulled open her shirt and bared her throat to her victor. She would not be taken prisoner.

"Upon the brow of the goddess, it's the princess!" she heard a familiar voice cry out. "Look, see the blue skin!"

Maura looked hard at the small group of the enemy now encircling her. "Mikkotto!" Maura gasped. "You, here! Traitor!" Princess Maura spat at her.

"Tsk, tsk, is that any way for a royal princess to act?" baited Mikkotto, her eyes narrowing. "May I introduce your host to you? Prince Dorak, this is Princess Maura de Magela of the Royal House of Hasan Daeg. Princess Maura, the man with the sword at your chest is Prince Dorak. I am so sorry. I mean to say, Aga Dorak."

Maura shot a look at Dorak.

He slowly sheathed his sword, never taking his eyes off her. They were dark and seemed to penetrate her with their questioning stare.

Maura found she could not look away. And what was more, she did not want to.

He extended his hand to her.

She shook her head and stood on her own, feeling a little woozy.

"Please call off your warriors, Princess," requested Dorak politely, "I have taken you prisoner. It is considered very bad form to continue fighting after one's leader has, shall we say, fallen."

"You can't be serious," sputtered Mikkotto. "Kill her now and all resistance will fall in Hasan Daeg. Keep her and they will fight to the death to get her back."

"I don't believe you are on my staff of advisors, Baroness," Dorak warned coldly.

"Your father would have listened to me!"

"My father is dead, and you were nothing but my father's passing fancy."

Mikkotto's face grew red with fury. "Your father swore an oath to give me Hasan Daeg and she stands in the way!" The baroness, with lightening speed, withdrew a dagger from her sleeve and pushed past Dorak.

A black and white blur flew past her in front of

Maura. Chaun Maaun stood facing the baroness.

Mikkotto gasped and stepped back. Even Dorak seemed unable to move, so frightening was the sight of Chaun Maaun towering over them.

"Here's something to remember me by, Baroness," Chaun Maaun said contemptuously. He reached out a taloned hand and scratched her left cheek. "Every time you look in the mirror."

Mikkotto screamed and, dropping the dagger, put her hands up to her face. Her hands were bloody.

Chaun Maaun smiled and, then stretching out his mighty wings, he took to the sky with Maura hanging on to his back.

Dorak watched them fly away until they were out of sight.

34

It was mid-morning.

Both sides were taking stock.

Dorak's camp was ravaged. Only a few hundred tents, out of thousands, stood. The armory tent, mess tent, and the medical tent were burned to the ground. Horses and borax that the Dinii had not slaughtered were scattered throughout the hills. A third of Dorak's men were missing or dead.

Patrols came back with horrid stories of finding their comrades, who had fled during the night, hanging upside down from tree limbs with their throats slit.

Each report made Dorak more livid until he thought his brain would explode. He sat exhausted on his father's couch, his head hung low. From the corner of the tent, he heard a low chuckle. "Go away from me," Dorak growled. "Torment some other poor fool!"

"A fool is what you are, Dorak," sneered Mikkotto. "You let an eighteen-year-old girl get the best of you. I wonder what your men are thinking of you right now. Are they saying Dorak is a great warrior like his father?" She laughed heartily. "Or are they saying that you are nothing?"

"Be careful how you tread, traitor," cautioned Dorak.

"Oh, you won't do anything to me. At least, not for a while. I'm too valuable. I know the terrain of Hasan Daeg. I know its people. I know the traits of the leaders. I know where the City of the Peaks is. No, you won't touch one hair on my pretty head."

"In my current mood, I would torture you for pleasure."

Mikkotto gave a tight-lipped smile before sitting on Zoar's couch, stretching out alongside Dorak.

Dorak thought she looked like a cat lounging in the summer sun.

"Dorak," she cooed, "have you any magic?"

"What?"

"Obviously, it has occurred to you that you might not be able to enter Hasan Daeg with brute strength, not as long as the Dinii are fighting with the Hasans. You need another tactical advantage."

"Such as?"

Mikkotto thought Dorak an idiot like his father, and tried to hide the irritation in her voice. "Maura won today because of the advantage of surprise. If your soldiers had not been so overcome by the loss of your father, they would have responded more quickly. That, together with their first sight of the Dinii and women as soldiers, unnerved them even more."

"The Dinii are a frightening lot."

"Your men are mentally prepared for them now. Haven't I heard you say time and time again that your soldiers are the best troops in the world? Don't you believe that still?"

Dorak looked at her, trying to see through his fog of despair. He felt lost and the guilt of his father's murder ate at him. Surely, Bhuttu was punishing him for his crime by this horrible defeat.

"Listen to me, Dorak," said Mikkotto, her voice taking on new authority. "You need to find a way to enter Hasan Daeg. Once inside, your soldiers can overcome any resistance."

She slid over to his side seductively and whispered in his ear. "Hasan Daeg is a jewel worth conquering. She is rich in minerals and precious gems. Her land is fertile, her timber virgin. Our cities are spacious and clean with wide boulevards and gardens with fountains. They are not like the crowded, starving, dirty towns of your world. Our population is tall and strong, free of disease. Treat Hasan Daeg well and she will lick your hand. Your father never conquered any country as rich in natural resources. You can really build your empire with Hasan Daeg's help, not some dogged villages with dirt roads patched together here and there, but a real empire. An empire to last a thousand years or more!" Mikkotto sat back and studied Dorak's face.

A vein in his temple pulsated strongly. He turned toward her. "Everything you say is true."

Mikkotto smiled smugly.

"And I despise you for saying it," he continued.

The baroness was startled.

"I despise the fact that you are a traitor. I hate you for being my father's woman and thus being a threat to me. I loathe you for daring to give me counsel."

Mikkotto began to move away from Dorak, but he grabbed her arm, causing her to wince in pain.

"But as you say, I need you. That, for the moment, is the only thing keeping you alive." He shoved her off the couch. "I will enter Hasan Daeg, and I will become her conqueror and king. You will be by my side the entire time. But I warn you, if you ever try to kill one of the de Magelas again, I will kill you by cutting one inch of your skin off at a time until there is nothing covering your body but muscle. How long do you think it would take, Mikkotto, slicing off skin one inch at a time until you look like a skinned boaep? Nod if you understand."

Mikkotto, terrified, nodded.

"That's a good girl. Now go run and play. Your lord and master needs time to think." Dorak leaned back on the couch and closed his eyes.

Mikkotto rose silently, tiptoeing out of the great tent. Her skin felt clammy as she breathed heavily. It was one thing to deal with a vain, pompous, old man. It was quite another to deal with a maniac. She would have to think long and hard about this boy.

35

Order was brought to the camp.

Throughout the day, Dorak's men managed to right their camp, even though they were constantly harassed during the morning by arrows shot through the mist wall. Dorak ordered the camp to move out of range and sent companies of men out foraging. What they could not buy or borrow, they stole. Some of the borax were found, and immediately killed and skinned to set on the roasting spits. At night the men readied themselves for another attack, and they were not disappointed.

The Dinii circled the camp and came up from behind, dropping a hail of rocks on the camp. As swiftly as they appeared, the Dinii flew off again, howling like night demons.

The camp was constantly harassed by arrows. More than one man died in full armor with an arrow through his neck.

Dorak sat in grim silence in his tent. He did not respond when his advisors begged him to retreat until reinforcements and supplies could be sent. He calmly drank his wine and watched his father's body being prepared for burial.

The next morning, Dorak, in full military dress, accompanied his father's body onto the battlefield in front of the mist. A handful of men erected a funeral pyre and carefully placed the body on it. Dorak ordered the men to join the other Bhuttanians, also in full armor, standing on a ridge watching.

Alone, he stood on the platform facing Hasan Daegians who stood at the edge of the mist watching. Dorak paid them no heed. The Dinii flew over the mist and roosted in trees away from Bhuttanian soldiers, but close enough to witness the funeral.

With great exaggeration of movement, Dorak snatched a large amulet from his father's corpse and set fire to the pyre. As the flames shot into the air, he took off his plumed helmet. Standing very rigid, he began to recite incantations as he began moving clockwise around the pyre. His voice became louder and more urgent. Round and round he walked gesturing to the heavens.

Princess Maura, flanked by Yeti and Benzar, stood

in a cluster of noblewomen.

Chaun Maaun strode over, scattering women in his path. "What's he doing?" asked Chaun Maaun.

"I don't know. I wish Iegani were here," responded Maura with a worried look on her face.

Suddenly, a great dark cloud appeared in the clear sky. It rumbled loudly, and an occasional bolt of lightening struck the ground near Dorak.

"I don't like the look of this, Your Highness," pleaded Yeti. "Perhaps we should get behind the wall."

"No. I must see what is happening," Maura answered stubbornly.

Dorak reached up into the sky with both hands with the amulet encircling his fingers. Calling forth in a strange tongue, he threw the amulet into his father's pyre. A great cloud of smoke burst from the pyre, and from its midst emerged a man clad in a black robe and hood who stood on the burning body of Zoar. His face was hidden.

The Bhuttanians cheered loudly and beat their shields with weapons.

The man in black stretched out his dark leathery arms and rubbed his hands together.

"Oooohhh! This isn't good!" exclaimed Yeti.

Maura stood riveted by the sight of the man in the black hood. "General Kimtimee, do we have reports of the Bhuttanians using magic in battle?" asked Maura, fearing the worst.

"Not for decades. We have reports Zoar banished all wizards from his court for meddling in politics."

Yesemek fired back, "It seems he kept a spare."

Frightened, Yeti advised, "Princess, I don't think we should be standing here. This is black magic at work."

Maura agreed and ordered all her people back except for herself and her advisors.

Flames from the funeral pyre were now leaping about the man's face, but he didn't seem to burn.

The princess watched as a ball of purple and yellow light shone from the man's hands. Lightning continued striking about the black-robed man and Dorak, who commanded the figure to throw the ball of unearthly light at the mist.

"Here it comes," cried Yeti as she picked up Maura and flew way beyond the wall. The blast almost knocked Yeti out of the sky. She saw many of her feathers scattered on the wind. Looking back, she saw Chaun Maaun and Benzar carrying the rest of the small group to safety. She descended with the princess, but another blast hit and knocked everyone to the ground. The sky was filled with the acrid smoke of Zoar's burning body and waves of purplish, yellow light.

Maura crawled behind a crop of rocks yelling orders

over the rumbling of the thunder and the explosions.

Yesemek managed to crawl to Maura's position. "Whoever he is, he's blasting a hole in the mist!" the general screamed over the continuing explosions.

BOOM! Another explosion hit.

Clods of debris landed on Maura and her company. She climbed up to look over the boulder.

There was a forty-foot-wide hole in the wall! The barges were sinking as bits of the caromate plants were strewn everywhere. There were holes on the riverbank where the ball of light had struck. Giant yagomba trees burned as their leaves withered.

Someone grabbed Maura's foot and pulled her down. She turned around and faced an angry Chaun Maaun. "What in the gods' names do you think you are doing?" he shouted over the din.

"The Dinii don't believe in the gods," answered Maura.

Chaun Maaun ignored her remark. "They are going to come through."

"I know." She turned to a dirty and frightened high-ranking officer. "Tell my generals to meet me by the north shore of the Sacred Lake. We will all rendezvous there. I will take this fight away from the population and into the great woods. Evacuate the people in the southeast corridor. They are to go to O Konya. Burn everything in Dorak's path. Leave nothing for the Bhuttanians to scavenge."

The officer saluted and turned to withdraw.

Maura grabbed her sleeve. "All soldiers! Go now. Hurry!"

"Yes, Your Highness," said the officer, now alive with purpose. She was gone in a flash.

BOOM! Another explosion hit.

Princess Maura ducked down and covered her face. She coughed from the smoke whirling in the air.

"Why are we retreating?" asked Chaun Maaun. "We should make a stand."

"It is too exposed here. Dorak still outnumbers us two to one."

BOOM! BOOM! The ball of light, the color of an angry bruise, came dangerously close to the crop of rocks. Everyone lay facedown on the ground. Clumps of dirt sprayed the Hasan Daegians and the Dinii, who wanted to fight, not hide behind stone.

Maura continued, "We need the cover of the forest. Dorak would decimate us on the plains."

Yesemek nodded in agreement.

Yeti turned her back to Maura. "Climb aboard, Princess. I'll have you at the lake in no time."

"I'll go with Chaun Maaun. You are to make sure everyone gets away safely."

Yeti opened her mouth to speak.

Maura interrupted. "Don't argue. There isn't time. Move out now!"

The princess held on to Chaun Maaun, gripping with her legs and wrapping her arms around his neck.

He spread his great wings and they took off. Yesemek followed closely behind. As they flew higher, Maura could see the first wave of her soldiers moving out, carrying supplies and the wounded as best they could. She smiled as she saw many Dinii, who had suffered no casualties in the fighting, take the injured and fly off to O Konya where medical treatment awaited. The Dinii, after dropping off the wounded, would report back to the north shore of Yappor Lake where their prince, Chaun Maaun, would await them.

36

Chaun Maaun reached the Sacred Lake.

He settled Maura on a moss-covered rock by a majestic waterfall. Tired and dirty, he dove into the crystal clear water to refresh himself. Hearing a splash, he found Maura swimming beside him, washing the day's dirt and sweat from her skin. Had this been another time, he would have indulged himself with her, but now he could only worry. He jumped out of the crystal clear water and lay out on a flat rock, spreading his wings to dry.

A few minutes later Maura joined him.

She sighed. "You think I'm wrong."

Chaun Maaun rose up on one elbow. "You let them enter the country. You are now fighting a war in your own territory."

"How could we fight Dorak's wizard? We have never seen power as this. We have only heard of such magic. His bolts would have destroyed us. At least this way, we still have an army to fight another day." She touched his cheek. "The Dinii can simply fly away. But my people can't outrun this wizard's power."

Chaun Maaun acknowledged the logic of Maura's thinking. "What do you propose to do now?"

"I have sent messengers to the High Priestess of the House of Magi. Until I get more information about this sorcerer, I don't know what I can do except delay Dorak as much as possible. I dare not confront him openly at this time."

Chaun Maaun leaned over and kissed Maura tenderly.

She returned his kiss ardently.

He stroked her hair and kissed her neck.

Maura climbed on top of him and they made love, slowly, wondering if this was going to be the last time. Again and again, they mated until hearing the beating of wings in the sky; they parted from each other and quickly dressed.

Yesemek descended accompanied by the rest of the generals, both Hasan Daegian and Dinii. In the rear of the group, four Dinii were bearing a specially constructed litter carrying an imposing woman dressed in a blue velvet cape. On her cape were gold buttons gathered together in the shape of constellations throughout the material. She had, on either side of her litter chair, leather bags stuffed to capacity. One of the Dinii helped her off the litter. She thanked the Dinii with calm regal authority and threw back her hood as the Dinii gathered her bags.

Princess Maura and Chaun Maaun approached the newly arrived guest.

The woman bowed. "Greetings, Your Highness and Good Prince. I bear messages from both your mothers." She handed them letters bearing the royal seal of Hasan Daeg.

Chaun Maaun looked hopelessly at his.

"I hope you understand the high level of anxiety they feel."

Princess Maura inclined her head. "Greetings, No-abini, High Priestess of the House of Magi. I appreciate you bringing us our mothers' salutations."

"I bring you more, Your Highness. Your mother is quite distressed that the enemy has entered Hasan Daeg, and our army has retreated before them."

Maura felt like a schoolgirl being scolded by her teacher. "There was no other plan of action possible," she declared.

"I quite agree," replied the High Priestess, "but, unfortunately, your mother does not."

Princess Maura stopped herself before nervously biting her lip. "What news do you bring of this wizard?"

"You are correct when you say wizard." The High Priestess opened one of her bags and went through it. "I have searched all of our records about Bhuttanian magic. The one who dressed all in black is called the Black Cacodemon. He is the most revered and feared of all of Bhuttu's priests, but seldom seen. He is known as the harbinger of destruction and is said to drink the blood of sacrificed victims during Bhuttu's high holy days."

"I have so many questions. Please be seated," said Maura.

The High Priestess looked around, and seeing no chairs, cheerfully sat upon a rock. "The Black Cacodemon was once a powerful person because of his dark magic. Zoar's father used him often to obtain control over stronger lords and gain territory.

"But Zoar was different. He felt the Black Cacodemon wielded too much power and wanted to loosen his grip. He did this by the most passive means without directly confronting the Black Cacodemon. He simply did not use him. Zoar really did not need help when it came to warfare. He could rely on his own amazing intellect and intuition to guide him. Over the years, the Black Cacodemon was seldom seen at court and his position fell into disuse."

"And now Dorak has brought him back," said Chaun Maaun.

"Yes. Dorak is young and has suffered a great military blow besides the untimely death of his father. He probably felt he needed the Black Cacodemon to solidify his position. And it worked. I am sure Dorak and his men are swarming through the hole blasted by his evil priest even as we speak."

"How can I fight such an opponent?" asked Maura.

"Somehow, the Black Cacodemon must be taken out of the equation," replied the High Priestess quietly. "You must make yourself impervious to the magic of this evil man."

"How shall I do this?" asked the princess, overwhelmed. It was one thing to fight a human enemy. It was quite another to battle a magician steeped in the arts of black magic.

"You must mate with the Mother Bogazkoy!" interrupted Iegani.

"Iegani!" shouted Chaun Maaun. "Where have you been?"

"Looking for the Mother Bogazkoy, impertinent boy!"

Maura felt relieved that Iegani was once again by her side. "You have found the Mother Bogazkoy?" she asked excitedly.

"It's no wonder we never found it," said Iegani. "It is in the Forbidden Zone in a cave underneath the sea. You must go to it and bind yourself with it. The Mother Bogazkoy is so potent that once you have mated with her, very little will be able to touch you. Not illness, not arrows, maybe not even death."

"How can she mate with a plant?" sneered Chaun Maaun.

"It's a figure of speech—a metaphor," replied Iegani disgustedly. Sometimes he wondered about Chaun Maaun's inability to grasp the obvious.

"You have seen the Mother Bogazkoy?" asked the princess.

"I have talked to her!"

"You have what?"

"She is waiting for you, Your Highness, and wishes your company very much. She needs to procreate. And without certain fluids from your body, she will be unable."

"She told you this?" asked the High Priestess.

Iegani nodded his head.

"I will leave at once. How long will it take me to get to the Forbidden Zone?" the princess asked, now anxious to be moving.

"If Chaun Maaun and I take you, almost a week to

get there and back."

"Can I travel by the Seeing State?"

Iegani raised his eyebrow. "The Seeing State will not work. You must meet the Mother Bogazkoy in person."

"Your Highness, may I join your party?" asked the High Priestess. "I will not be a burden, and I may be able to help you along the journey. If I impede you, you may send me back at my own risk."

Maura looked at Iegani.

He nodded.

Noabini smiled, flashing large white teeth.

"Yeti and Benzar will accompany us," stated Maura.

"Good," stated Iegani. "Toppo and Tarsus are waiting for us just before the Forbidden Zone."

Without warning, a Dini courier swooped down out of the sky and crashed into the ground.

Chaun Maaun ran over to him and helped him sit up. The courier was badly wounded.

"Greetings, Prince Chaun Maaun and Princess Maura. I bring grave tidings." The courier stopped and took a deep breath.

"Take your time," Maura said, feeling alarmed. A sense of dread overtook her.

"O Konya is under attack, Your Highness. Your mother is trapped in the palace. Empress Gitar and many Dinii stayed behind in the city to fight. Other

Dinii are picking up any Hasan Daegian they can find on the roads and flying them to the City of Peaks."

Princess Maura staggered a bit.

Everyone else cried out in shock, looking at each other in confused wonder.

Even Iegani looked bedeviled. "How can that be? It should have taken Dorak months to march to O Konya–not hours. And to overtake the city? A city like O Konya. It's impossible! You must be mistaken. It's just impossible."

"Magic, my lord. It's some form of magic. The Bhuttanians are moving so fast they look like streaks of colored light," gasped the injured Dini. "Who can fight against such an enemy? Even the Dinii are helpless before the Bhuttanians moving so fast."

Princess Maura fell to the ground and put her head in her hands. "How could I have been so stupid?" she moaned.

"You underestimated the power of your enemy," lamented Iegani, "as did we all. The Dinii have no knowledge of black magic. We possess no magic to fight this. We must wait until Dorak and his men come out of the spell and try to strike then."

"This spell must take an enormous amount of power. Dorak and his army will need to rest as well as the Black Cacodemon. We must be ready to fight," said

Chaun Maaun.

"But what if you are wrong?" questioned Maura tearfully. "I've already made a huge blunder." She stood on her feet and yelled at the heavens. "I swear by all that is holy, neither I nor my kin will rest until the Bhuttanians are thrown out of Hasan Daeg. If I have to lie, cheat, murder, and commit the worst of atrocities, I will set my country free or the heavens may curse me for all time."

Wind swirled around the group as the sky darkened.

"Oh, do not make such a vow to the heavens!" beseeched the High Priestess. "It will doom us all."

"Not only shall I vow it, but so shall ye all. Vow it now, or I will curse each and every one of you right now."

"Maura, think of what you are asking of us. The Dinii do not make such oaths," implored Chaun Maaun.

"Vow it!" screamed Maura. "Vow it!"

Iegani lowered himself to his knees. "I swear." He looked around at the others.

One by one, they kneeled before Maura and repeated her words.

Lightning struck near them as rain pelted from the sky. The ground shook.

The High Priestess wept. Maura had uttered a terrible oath and the heavens had accepted it. She wondered what monster Princess Maura would turn into for uttering such a terrible curse.

Hearing a gasp, she turned and saw what others were seeing.

Before their eyes, Maura's being was luminous, flickering like an oil lamp before the wick burns out.

Maura turned toward her comrades. "It is done. The heavens had accepted our vow. I'm going to O Konya. The Queen and the Empress must be saved. Do not try to stop me. The attempt must be made. Never fear. We will meet again soon, my friends."

Having said that, she climbed onto the back of Chaun Maaun. With wings outstretched, he flew into the foreboding sky, leaving the rest to go their separate ways to fight for freedom.

37

Chaun Maaun and Maura smelled smoke.

With his keen sight, Chaun Maaun saw buildings burning in the distance.

Maura could also discern an unholy light near the horizon. She sank her head between Chaun Maaun's shoulders.

Chaun Maaun beat his wings upon the night air faster and faster until he finally landed on the roof of the palace.

Maura rolled off the exhausted prince and stood riveted. Down below, the city's wondrous architecture was being put to the torch. The streets were blocked with the bodies of the dead.

Amidst the dying and wounded stood the Dinii fighting Dorak's men hand-to-hand, slashing as many throats as they could and throwing the bodies into heaps.

From other rooftops, Hasan Daegian archers rained arrows down upon the enemy.

But still Dorak's men came—waves and waves of them.

With a fury, Princess Maura unsheathed her sword and started down the staircase. She heard Chaun Maaun calling, but did not stop. Running as fast as she could, she reached the bottom of the stone staircase only to find fighting ensuing at the other end of a massive hallway. There she spied her mother, father, and several Dinii desperately fighting a group of Dorak's men.

Maura released a great cry of terror combined with anger, rushing toward the clashing throng.

Abisola, recognizing her daughter's voice, turned away from her opponent.

Seeing his opportunity, a soldier stabbed the queen through the shoulder, causing her to stumble and fall to the floor.

Iasos immediately threw himself on top of his injured wife, trying to protect her from any further blows.

Maura struck the Bhuttanian soldier nearest her, almost severing his head.

Smelling a Dinii next to her, she looked out of the corner of her eye and spied Gitar and Yeti fighting alongside her.

Gitar picked up a screaming soldier and, with one jerk, broke his neck. She then threw the twitching body at the on-rushing Bhuttanians.

Yeti began pulling Iasos and his wounded queen away from the fray.

Maura fought like a wild animal, snarling at her enemies and baring her teeth. Her skin glistened with blue sweat as red blood splattered on her. She did not think; just reacted, letting her instinct for survival take over.

It was just as Chaun Maaun said it would be.

"BHUTTANIANS, ALL WEAPONS ON THE FLOOR!" shouted a booming voice from behind the melee.

The Bhuttanians looked at each other in confusion and reluctantly dropped their weapons. The soldiers parted as Dorak emerged.

Dorak marched to the front of his men while sheathing his sword. Pulling off his dusty helmet, he revealed an exhausted face covered with the grime of battle. The dragon emblem on his chest was caked in blood, most of it still wet.

"Princess Maura, we meet again," Dorak chortled. He looked around the great hallway. "I see your party has dispatched more of my men. I'm afraid I will have to put a stop to that."

Maura said nothing, but watched his every move. He stepped closer to Queen Abisola, now being held upright in the arms of Iasos.

Maura and Yeti immediately blocked his way.

Dorak held up his hands in supplication. "I only want to speak to your mother," he implored. Looking past the princess, he said, "Queen Abisola, it is over. The city has been taken and is under my control."

Queen Abisola groaned.

Dorak continued in a soothing voice. "Your Majesty, I will give you the best terms for surrender. You and your family will not be harmed. Look, as you can see, my men have put down their arms." Dorak took a step closer. "It is not my desire to destroy this wondrous city. Your family may still sit on the throne as long as you pay homage to me as liege lord. My people need food. We need it desperately. Give me what I want and I will make Hasan Daeg a power to behold within the Bhuttanian Empire." Dorak took another step closer.

Maura brought up her sword.

Dorak walked up to the blade pointing at his throat. He stood so close that the point of the blade almost touched his skin. "Princess, I beseech you. Nothing can be gained from this last stand."

"I can kill you right now."

"Then you would sign your own death warrant. My

men would kill you and your parents before you made it to the roof," Dorak replied softly as though calming a frightened horse. "You would be of no use to your people then, I assure you."

"But neither would you."

Dorak chuckled softly. "You are a most unusual young woman. What a queen you will become. I do hope I will be present to witness your final blooming, but it is up to you."

When Maura did not respond, Dorak turned his attention to the failing Hasan Daegian queen. "Queen Abisola, think about your daughter. Surely you do not want to see her die? Surrender. It is all you can do."

The queen struggled. She coughed and blood seeped from her mouth.

Iasos quickly wiped the blood away with his sleeve.

Holding tightly to her husband's arms, she wept silently. "You may take me into custody. But all of the Dinii, including Empress Gitar and my child, are to leave now." She looked up at Iasos. "My husband will share my fate with me."

"Mother, no!" insisted Maura.

"This is my final command. Start withdrawing. Now!" croaked Abisola.

"I am afraid I can not allow this," interjected Dorak.

Queen Abisola measured her words carefully. "Dorak, I am over three hundred years old. Only recently have I begun to age. Even your magicians have no spells to do this. Do you not want to know my secret? Do you not want to live for a long time? How long did your father live? He wasn't even fifty, and he was used up." Abisola took a deep breath, which made a wheezing noise. "Just think of what you could accomplish in three hundred years or maybe more. Let my daughter go with the Dinii, and once they are safely away, I will show you how it is done." She let her words sink in.

"She is lying. The Bogazkoy will never accept a male bonding," cried a female from the shadows.

"Mikkotto!" exclaimed Iasos. "You traitorous mongrel!"

Dorak swung around and, upon seeing Mikkotto, his eyes narrowed. "How did you get up here?"

Mikkotto laughed. "Well, the front entrance was wide open. There was no one to stop me. It seems everyone is dead." She moved closer.

"Stop where you are," commanded Maura, her skin prickling from the tension.

Mikkotto cooed, "Is that any way to talk to your cousin?"

Dorak shot Mikkotto a surprised look.

She grinned. "That is right, my dear Dorak. I used to play in these very hallways as a child. My mother was

Abisola's first cousin and Lady Sari's daughter. I told you I was a kinswoman of the royal family. I just didn't tell you how close." She moved forward.

Dorak blocked her way. "I swear to you, Mikkotto, if you do not leave right now, I am going to kill you here with my own hands."

"I think you have forgotten we have a deal. I am to be queen of Hasan Daeg in exchange for certain services rendered."

"You, queen?" snorted Iasos in disgust.

"I have made no deal with you to be queen," denied Dorak. "I merely said I would let you live if you showed me the location of O Konya. I am sorry to say I regret my decision. I now have new plans for you."

Dorak, his expression one of hatred and anger, moved toward Mikkotto with deadly intent.

Realizing Dorak's intention, Mikkotto shoved Dorak into Princess Maura. "NOW!" she screamed.

Several soldiers pulled daggers from their sleeves and threw them at the royal couple.

One struck Abisola in the heart, killing her instantly.

The other hit Iasos in the stomach. He crumpled to the floor, his hands around the dagger, trying to pull it out.

Maura screamed, scrambling on the bloody floor. She threw herself across her parents.

At that moment, Chaun Maaun, having recovered from the arduous journey, rushed down the steps. He pushed his mother and Yeti behind him. Seeing Maura curled over the body of her mother and her dying father, he let out a muffled cry.

Dorak stood between the Hasan Daegians and his soldiers with his arms outstretched.

Other Bhuttanian warriors rushed forward to hold the men, who had thrown the daggers, prostrate on the floor.

Mikkotto was nowhere to be seen.

"No one move!" commanded Dorak, his voice like ice. Upon seeing Chaun Maaun's fury, he was moved to say, "I had nothing to do with this. Take your people and go. It is over."

Gitar leaned her head against Chaun Maaun's back while weeping.

Yeti stared in bewilderment at the fallen royal couple on the floor.

Chaun Maaun started toward Maura who was lying over her mother.

Dorak drew his sword. "It is over," he said again emphatically. "Take the empress and leave, Prince Chaun Maaun or I will kill Princess Maura. I swear it."

At Chaun Maaun's surprise that Dorak knew his name, Dorak said, "Yes, I know who you are. I know everything there is to know about this country."

"I will never rest until I kill you, Dorak. This I swear to you!" spat Chaun Maaun.

Dorak inclined his head in acknowledgment. "I will not harm her if you leave now. Go in peace."

Chaun Maaun picked up his distressed mother and swiftly left with Yeti covering his retreat.

Yeti looked back at the royal Hasan Daegian family she had sworn to protect, lying in a crumpled heap on the bloody floor. It had happened so quickly. "I will be back, little bird. Do not give up hope," she whispered.

She gave one last look at Dorak, who bowed to her as one honorable warrior recognizing another. Yeti turned and joined her group on the rooftop. "Can you fly, Empress?" she asked Gitar.

With great tears streaming down her face, Gitar clasped the hands of both Chaun Maaun and Yeti. "We must not blame ourselves. We did everything within our power to do. Dorak's evil magic was too powerful for us. There is no shame." She squeezed their hands. "Come now. We must live to fight another day."

Stretching out her mighty wings, Empress Gitar of the Dinii rose ghostlike into the night.

Chaun Maaun and Yeti followed, flanking her.

Empress Gitar flew about the city summoning the Dinii warriors to her.

One by one, they heard her call over the din of fighting and reluctantly joined her in the sky. When no more Dinii answered her lonesome cry, they flew toward the City of the Peaks.

A young Bhuttanian soldier, grieving over the loss of his best friend, lifted his longbow. With a quick release, he shot an arrow into the hellish night before he was cut down by General Alexanee, Dorak's first-in-command.

Dorak's conquest for Hasan Daeg was over.

But Maura had just started her quest for revenge, and she would not stop until she regained control of Hasan Daeg and Dorak was dead . . . or she was!

READ ON FOR A SPECIAL PREVIEW!
WALL OF PERIL
The Princess Maura Tales
Book 2

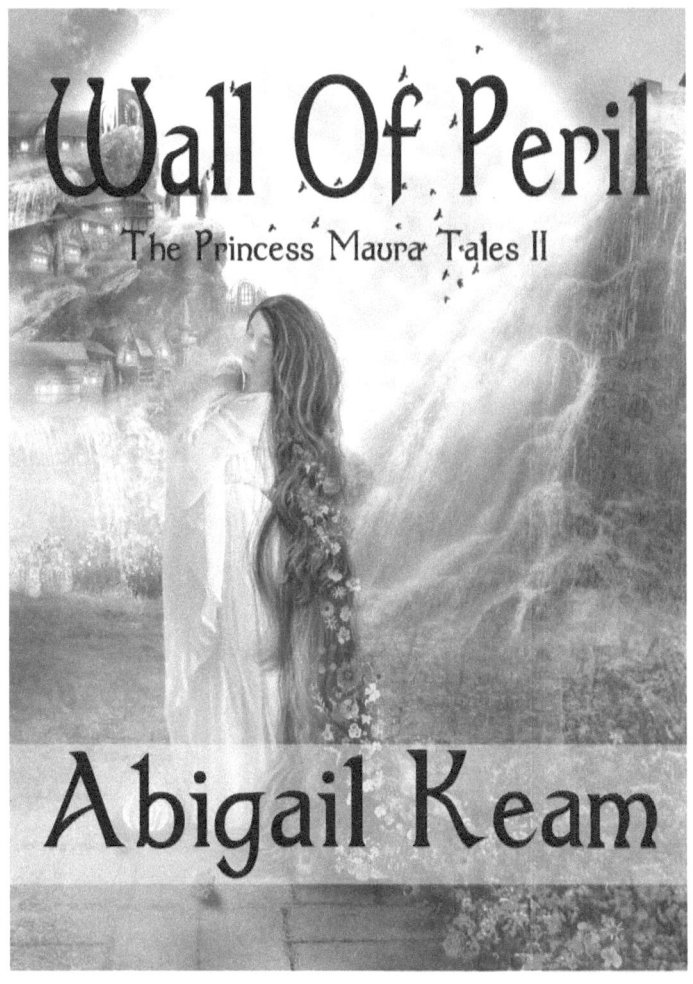

Prologue

Baroness Mikkotto pushed open the doors.

Through the majestic brass doors of the royal palace, its gleaming white walls and floors now stained with blood, she entered cautiously. Bodies of Hasan Daegians and the Dinii were strewn throughout the hall and staircase. Mikkotto ordered her personal guards to move the corpses out of her way, fearful that a soldier might play dead and stab her as she stepped over. Soldiers who moaned when moved were quickly dispatched by an axe to see their nature goddess, Mekonia.

The horrible chunking noise of the metal striking bone did not seem to bother Mikkotto, who calmly studied the carnage. Between the death throes of her countrywomen, Mikkotto listened for commotion in the palace. She knew Abisola and Iasos were somewhere nearby. Did they go downstairs into the bowels of the royal stronghold? Or were they on the rooftop waiting for extraction by the surviving Dinii?

It didn't matter. Mikkotto had placed guards at every exit point. She was searching for the royal family, and she must reach them before Dorak did.

Dorak! She had to hand it to him. He had made an inspired play by recalling the Black Cacodemon and using magic to invade Hasan Daeg. By using the wizard's powers, Dorak was able to conquer Hasan Daeg within hours rather than months or years. The Hasan Daegian army never stood a chance against the lightning speed of the Bhuttanian army in the grips of the wizard's spell.

As soon as Dorak had control of the capital O Kon-ya, the spell disbursed, and now everyone was moving normally. Mikkotto twisted her lips in annoyance. Too bad. She had wished the spell had lasted until she could discover the whereabouts of her royal cousin.

Mikkotto jerked her head up. She faintly heard Dorak ordering, "BHUTTANIANS! ALL WEAPONS ON THE FLOOR!"

She cursed knowing Dorak had entered the palace before her and had found Abisola and her consort. Fortunately for her, she had placed men among various squads, giving them instructions to kill the queen and her husband if they came upon them.

Grinning, she relished the thought that they would obey her and not Dorak, paying them with gold and the promise of more coins and land to come if they carried out her orders. Greed was a great motivator to get the unpleasantries of life done by those who valued money above all else.

Still, Mikkotto couldn't take a chance. She scampered up the grand white marble staircase, jumping over slain bodies until she reached the second floor. Hearing screaming, she ran up another flight with her women warriors behind her.

Motioning for her women to wait, Mikkotto peered into a doorway and saw Dorak and a few Bhuttanians threatening Abisola and Iasos, who huddled on the floor before a small staircase going to the rooftop. Between them stood Maura, brandishing a sword. Behind her stood two Dinii with their talons exposed and looking very threatening.

The Dinii gave Mikkotto pause. She did not care to have her face slashed again nor die from a quick cut across her throat with their razor sharp nails. If truth be known, Mikkotto was terrified of them, but that fear had to be put aside. Victory was given to the bold, not the fearful.

Mikkotto studied the Dinii, thinking the taller one

was Empress Gitar. She had seen her briefly at Maura's birthday celebration before her son bumbled Maura's assassination. Although the attempt on Maura's life had failed, Mikkotto had not flinched when told of her son's death at the hand of a Dini. She had little faith in her only son's ability and was only too glad she had not assigned one of her daughters to the task. Daughters were precious, but sons were expendable.

She motioned to her guards to be quiet while she listened to the conversation between Dorak and Abisola. If Maura and her parents were killed, Dorak would make her queen of Hasan Daeg. If he decided to spare them, she would have to make a daring move, and quickly too.

Moving closer, Mikkotto heard Dorak speak, "Princess Maura, we meet again." Dorak looked around the great hallway. "I see that you and your party have dispatched a few more of my men. I'm afraid I will have to put a stop to that."

Kill her. KILL HER! thought Mikkotto, hugging the darkness of the doorway.

Concentrating on Dorak, Maura did not see Mikkotto slinking closer and closer.

Dorak stepped nearer to Queen Abisola, now being held upright in the arms of Iasos.

Maura and Yeti immediately blocked his way.

Dorak held up his hands in supplication. "Princess, I only want to speak to your mother," he said calmly. Looking past Maura, he uttered, "Queen Abisola, it is over. The city has been taken and is in my control."

Queen Abisola groaned.

Dorak continued in a soothing voice. "Your Majesty, I will give you the best terms for surrender. You and your family will not be harmed. Look, as you can see, my men have put down their arms. It is not my desire to destroy this wondrous city. Your family may still sit on the throne as long as you pay homage to me as liege lord. My people need food. We need it desperately. Give me what I want, and I will make Hasan Daeg a power to behold within the Bhuttanian Empire." Dorak took another step toward Queen Abisola.

NO! NO! What is Dorak doing? I was promised Hasan Daeg by his father, Zoar. Dorak can't do this to me, Mikkotto screamed in her head. She had to make her move soon.

Maura brought up her sword.

Dorak walked up to the blade pointed at his throat. He stood so that the point of the weapon almost pierced his skin. "Princess, I beseech you. Nothing can be gained from this last stand. It is over."

"I can kill you right now."

"Then you would sign your own death warrant. My men would kill you and your parents before you made it to the roof," Dorak replied softly. "You would be of no use to your people then, I assure you."

"But neither would you."

Dorak chuckled softly. "You are a most unusual young woman. I do hope I will be present to witness your final blooming, but that is up to you."

When Maura did not respond to his words, Dorak turned his attention to the failing Hasan Daegian queen. "Queen Abisola, think about your daughter. Surely you do not want to see her die. Surrender. It is all you can do."

The queen struggled. She coughed, and blood seeped from her mouth.

Iasos quickly wiped it with his sleeve.

Holding tightly to her husband's arms, she whispered, "You may take me. But all of the Dinii, including Empress Gitar and my child, are to leave now." She looked up at Iasos. "My husband will share my fate with me."

"Mother, no!" insisted Maura.

"This is my final command. Start withdrawing. Now!" croaked Abisola.

"I am afraid I can not allow this," interjected Dorak.

Queen Abisola measured her words carefully. "Aga Dorak, I am over three hundred years old. Only recently have I begun to age. Even your magicians have no spells to do this. Do you not want to know my secret? Do you not want to live for a long time? How long did your father live? He wasn't even fifty and was used up." Abisola took a deep breath, which made a wheezing noise. "Just think of what you could accomplish in three hundred years or maybe more. Let my daughter go with the Dinii, and once they are safely away, I will show you how it is done." She let her words sink in.

Mikkotto knew it was now or never. "She's lying. The Bogazkoy will never accept a male bonding!" she cried from the shadows.

"Mikkotto!" exclaimed Iasos. "You traitorous mongrel!"

Dorak swung around, and upon seeing Mikkotto, his eyes narrowed. "How did you get up here?"

Mikkotto laughed. "The front door was wide open. There was no one to stop me. It seems everyone below is dead." She moved closer.

"Stop where you are," commanded Maura, her skin prickling from the tension.

"Is that any way to talk to your cousin?" cooed Mikkotto.

Dorak shot Mikkotto a surprised look.

Mikkotto grinned. "That is right, my dear Dorak. I used to play in these very hallways as a child. My mother was Abisola's first cousin and Lady Sari's daughter. For you see, Lady Sari is really Marchioness Sari and third in line to the throne. She gave up her title to serve the House of de Magela, stupid woman that she is." She moved forward.

Dorak blocked her way. "I swear to you, Mikkotto, if you do not leave right now, I am going to kill you here with my own hands."

"I think you have forgotten that we have a deal. I am to rule Hasan Daeg in exchange for certain services rendered."

"You, queen?" snorted Iasos in disgust.

"I have made no deal with you to rule," denied Dorak. "I merely said I would let you live if you showed me the location of O Konya. I am sorry to say I regret that decision. I now have new plans for you." Dorak, wearing an expression of hate, moved toward Mikkotto with deadly intent.

Realizing Dorak's intention, Mikkotto shoved Dorak into Maura. "NOW!" she shrieked.

Several soldiers pulled daggers from their sleeves and threw them at the royal couple.

One struck Abisola in the heart, killing her instantly.

The other hit Iasos in the stomach. He crumpled to the floor, his hands around the dagger, trying to pull it out.

Maura screamed, scrambling over the bloody floor.

She threw herself across her parents.

At that moment, Chaun Maaun, having recovered from the arduous journey, rushed down the steps. He pushed his mother and Yeti behind him. Seeing Maura curled over the body of her mother and her dying father, he let out a muffled cry.

Dorak stood between the Hasan Daegians and his soldiers with his arms outstretched.

Other Bhuttanian warriors rushed forward to restrain the men who had thrown the daggers.

Realizing that her bid for power had been thwarted, Mikkotto scurried away with her personal guards running interference before her. They collided into a squad of Bhuttanians loyal to Dorak. Thinking quickly, Mikkotto pointed and barked, "Hurry, your master is in danger. The Dinii empress is upstairs and threatening Dorak. Save him!"

She and her women pressed against the wall, letting the heavily-armed men rush past her to the third floor as they all heard Dorak shouting commands and trying to gain control of the grave situation.

Not wanting to linger where Dorak could seize her, Mikkotto pulled free a lance sticking out from the gut of a Hasan Daegian warrior and knocked a Bhuttanian soldier down from his warhorse with it.

Jumping upon the giant creature, Mikkotto gave

orders, "Get yourselves horses and catch up with me at my estate. We will regroup and hide with the Camaroons. There will be another way to the throne of Hasan Daeg, and I swear to you, my good women, I will find it."

Mikkotto kicked the anxious horse and rode off.

When Dorak rushed out of the palace with his men, not a trace of Mikkotto could be found even with a massive hunt looking for her.

It was as though Kaseri had swallowed her up.

Mikkotto was gone!

1

D orak carried Maura to her chamber.

He laid her carefully on her bed and summoned a healer. As he waited, Dorak smoothed Maura's furrowed brow and held her hand. Gently, he kissed the tips of her fingers.

A guard soon appeared with Meagan of Skujpor. Her traditional white robe was soaked red with blood. Seeing the patient was the princess, Meagan rushed to the bedside and pushed Dorak out of the way. She examined Maura with great care. Finally, she sighed with relief.

"What is wrong with her?" asked Dorak, offended by the healer's brusque treatment.

"She's in shock," replied Meagan, pushing red hair out of her face. She pointed to the princess' skin. "This blood is not hers."

"How do you know?"

"Because it is red. Her blood is blue." She paused for a moment. "It must be her father's."

"When will she recover?"

The healer looked at Dorak with distaste. "When her mind can absorb the shock of this terrible day. Until then, she will stay as she is." Meagan stood directly in front of Dorak, confronting him. "I will come back to check on the princess, but now I must go back to the wounded. They need me more."

Dorak did not stop her as she moved toward the door. "I will send an escort with you and have my personal physician accompany you."

"That is not necessary. I have seen your healers in action and do not approve of their methods." Meagan turned as if an afterthought. "If you wish for us to treat your men, send them over. They will have a greater chance of survival with our medicine."

"You would help your enemy?" asked Dorak, confused.

"It is you whom I wish to kill," replied Meagan simply. There was a moment of unnatural silence between Dorak and the woman he knew could help Maura. "I will help any injured animal, including your men," said Meagan, breaking the angry quiet. Then she was gone.

Dorak, relieved that Maura had no serious physical injuries, went out into the hallway and found his second-in-command.

The commander, yelling orders at his men, immediately came to attention and pressed his fist to his chest.

"Are there any survivors from the court or noble houses?" asked Dorak.

"Yes, Great Aga. They are being guarded in the royal stables."

Dorak raised an eyebrow.

The commander looked sheepishly at him. "Great Aga, this palace does not have a dungeon. I had nowhere else to put them."

"Get some of the noblewomen and have them stay with the princess—I mean, the queen—in her chambers. Then take the bodies of Queen Abisola and Consort Iasos to the throne room. Have women attend them." Dorak fell silent.

The commander waited a long time before Dorak spoke again.

"Also, there is to be no looting. Tell the men that no more citizens are to be harmed upon pain of death. Is that understood?"

"Yes, Great Aga. Your word is law." The commander waited to be excused.

"Send the Black Cacodemon to me. You will no

doubt find him lurking around the dying."

The commander's eyes widened. "Yes, Great Aga," he replied, his voice weak.

Dorak strode away, leaving the commander to search for someone else to carry his message to the Black Cacodemon. He would rather face ten hostile Dinii than speak one word to that foul wizard who stood among the dying inhaling their souls as they departed their bodies.

Finally, he spied a young lieutenant and called him over. With a faint smile, the commander gave the young man his instructions and watched the color drain from the boy's face. With a strong push to his back, the commander sent the lieutenant off and proceeded to the stables.

Dorak returned to Maura's bedchamber. From the balcony of her room, he watched his men putting out fires in the city and restoring order. The dead were being collected and laid into long lines. Tomorrow, he would let the Hasan Daegians mourn their departed loved ones and put them to rest according to their customs. He would honor his own fallen with purifying fires in accordance with the Bhuttanian way. Then he would start building his great empire. He looked at Maura. "The dead did not sacrifice in vain," he said. "Together, you and I will build a new order."

He leaned on the balcony railing, surveying the city. "The greatest the world has ever seen."

Maura did not hear Dorak. Dreaming, she heard only her own screams as a dagger pierced her mother's heart. Again and again, the scene replayed itself until her mother, dead on the floor, opened her lifeless eyes and said, "Leave this place of death and rejoin the living. I will always be with you."

A shimmering woman appeared. She floated toward Maura and held her hands against Maura's temples. "Sleep. Sleep. Find comfort in the darkness. Morning will come soon enough." The horrible images slowly faded from Maura's mind as she drifted into a deep slumber.

2

Maura opened her eyes.

The first thing she saw was the royal physician in clean white robes, bending over her bed with a puzzled look in her eyes.

"You look tired, Meagan," spoke Maura, noting the dark circles under Meagan's eyes.

Ignoring the remark, Meagan asked, "How do you feel, Your Majesty?"

Maura winced at the word *Majesty* and was overwhelmed with a flood of painful memories. "My mother?" she asked weakly.

The healer wiped a tear from her cheek and shook her white-capped head with wisps of red hair peeking out.

"Father too?"

"He died shortly after the queen passed away. I must

add that he died without much pain. He wrote a letter for you, but I do not know what happened to it." The healer sat on the bed and patted Maura's shoulder. "I want you to know that they were treated with respect and honor as befitting your mother's glorious reign."

Maura sat up, alarmed. "How long have I been unconscious?"

"Nine days!" boomed a masculine voice from the balcony.

Maura looked past Meagan, squinting her eyes and holding her hand up against the strong rays of the sun bouncing off the white balcony.

Silhouetted against the white-hot light, a dark figure emerged from the filmy curtains separating the room from the balcony. Dorak strode lazily over to the bed.

The healer bowed and left the room.

Dorak towered over Maura. He had a worried look on his face. He was unshaven, and his hair had not seen a comb for some time. Dressed in a black shirt with black breeches tucked into worn black boots, Maura thought he looked like a convict or, even worse, a privateer. His dark brooding look frightened her.

"I was very worried about you, Queen Maura," said Dorak, pouring her a glass of water. "I was beginning to wonder if you were ever going to open your eyes again."

Maura drank greedily. Her mouth felt hot and dirty.

The cool water soothed her raw throat. "I wish I had never awakened," she spat.

Dorak gave her an appraising look. "You look awful."

"So do you," Maura replied, returning the stare.

"Never at a loss for words, are you?"

"Why are you here with me? Isn't there someone who needs butchering somewhere?"

"Your . . . *our* country is in safe hands. Its citizens are safe. Law and order have been restored. The fires have been put out."

"You mean after you murdered the lawful queen and invaded a peaceful nation to which you have no legitimate claim?"

Dorak grew angry. "I had nothing to do with the death of your parents. I swear to you before Bhuttu!"

Feeling her eyes tearing, Maura struggled to retain her composure. "You will never know how much I hate you! I will not rest until you and your cohorts are thrown out of Hasan Daeg!"

A wicked smile grew on Dorak's handsome face. "That will pose something of a problem since I intend to marry you."

Maura gasped and drew back.

Dorak's smile grew broader as he saw her panic. "I am going to leave you now." He put out his hands as if to stop her from pleading. "No, my indigo queen, don't try to stop me. Matters of state. I am sure you understand."

Sneering, Maura turned her face away. "I'll die first before I marry you. You know I can make it happen."

Dorak pinched her cheek and laughed. He strode out of the room as if in good humor. Once out of her sight, Dorak's expression grew serious. He motioned to the healer Meagan, who waited in the hallway with several noblewomen. Meagan's white robes fluttered in the cool breeze of the marble hallway as she went over to him. She bowed and waited for Dorak to speak.

He seemed confused and rubbed his temples as if in pain.

"Do you have a headache, my lord?" she asked.

Dorak ignored her question. "The queen seems depressed. She threatened suicide."

"That is understandable considering the circumstances."

"I have heard stories that Hasan Daegian rulers can will themselves to die."

"Anyone can will themselves to death if unhappy enough."

"I want the queen watched. Make sure she eats. Stop her if she tries to do anything foolish."

The healer raised an eyebrow. "Sire, you can rest

assured that I will do everything in my power to ensure the queen's health returns. However, I will never help you enslave her."

"You people constantly surprise me. I would have anyone from my country killed who talked to me the way you just did. Since you are not Bhuttanian I give you allowance, but that will not last forever."

"Of course, my lord, but you came seeking us and not the other way around." Meagan bowed and briskly walked away, calling to her assistants who were struggling to carry her medical bags. She knocked on the queen's door before entering.

Behind her followed several noblewomen who had consecrated their lives to become healers. Gone were the necklaces made of precious stones. Gone were the flowers woven into the hair. Gone were the costly robes of rare cloth. Now they wore the stern black robes of the initiate, allowing only their family crest embroidered on their chest for adornment.

Hearing no reply, Meagan opened the door and peered into the room.

The queen lay on the bed in a fetal position with her eyes tightly shut. Maura did not stir.

Meagan checked Maura's eyes. Startled by what she saw, she called discreetly for Lady Sari so word would not pass to Dorak that something was wrong.

Lady Sari came as swiftly as her old bones would carry her. She hovered over Maura, wringing her hands.

"What is the meaning of this?" asked Meagan, pulling open Maura's eyes. The eyes had become a solid blue, blocking out any sign of a pupil or iris. The effect was chilling to one who had never seen it before.

Sari gasped at the sight.

"I have read ancient treatises that discuss the care and nurturing of the Royal House of Hasan Daeg. There is no mention that the queens' eyes ever turned a solid blue for any reason," stated Meagan.

"That is because we are not allowed to touch the body until it is over. By then, the eyes return to normal."

"Body? You talk as though this girl is dead."

Sari's face assumed a look of intense sorrow. "For all intents, she is. She has taken herself into the *death dream*. There is nothing more you can do."

"Hasan Daegian queens will only do that if they are over three hundred years old and have produced a suitable heir. She is neither old nor has she had a child."

Sari looked softly as Meagan. "You did not read enough. Hasan Daegian queens can will themselves to die if they are in terrible pain." She straightened Maura's coverlet. "And this child is in terrible pain. She does not have the will to go on."

Meagan blustered.

"You do not understand. They reach a certain nadir and this just happens. It is nothing they can control. Dorak must have said something to cause this."

"In most ancient writings, there is mentioned a tree as a giver of life to the Royal House alone. It is written that there is some sort of blending between the ruler and the tree." The healer took Sari's hand in her own calloused ones. "You have been with this family all of your life. Do you know of such a tree? I have done all I can. I fear that if I do not bring her out of this self-induced state, she will die this time."

Saying nothing, Sari went deep into thought.

Meagan was quiet. She was a healer, but she had been exposed to politics long enough to understand the significance of Sari's silence. "Do you know of a tree that can save this queen? Help me for I can do no more!"

The old woman shook her head slowly and clasped her hands in despair. She had the air of defeat about her. "There is such a plant, but it can not help her. It is also dying."

"How does it work? I must try something." Meagan felt Maura's pulse. "If her heart gets any slower, we are going to lose her!"

"I will take you to it, but we must bring the queen."

"How can we remove her from this room without suspicion?"

Sari gave a weak smile. "Not all of our teeth are gone. We can bite a little yet. Follow me."

Confused, Meagan ordered her assistants to carry the limp queen.

Sari went to a wall and pressed a certain stone.

Silently, part of the wall opened into a small, narrow hallway.

3

Sari entered.

She poked her head back out of the passageway and motioned for the healer to follow her.

Meagan grabbed an oil lamp, lit it, and taking a deep breath entered.

The black robed women followed, carrying the moaning queen. One of the noblewomen placed her hand over the queen's mouth. The door closed, leaving the group feeling isolated and confined.

"Watch where you are going," cautioned Sari. "We will soon begin descending. The steps are sometimes slippery."

The group silently followed the old woman down the stone steps, their footfalls echoing loudly against the massive hand-hewn walls. Down and down they went, descending far below the city. They could hear the noisy hubbub of the market place and the traffic of the main boulevard of O Konya.

With Sari leading the way, Meagan held the lamp high above her head so the light spread unevenly but brightly on the walkway. She was surprised that the ancient passageway was clean of debris. Her breathing was not impeded by mold or dust. She wondered who kept the underground passages clean.

Finally, they came to the bottom of the stairs. The initiates placed Maura gently on the stone floor and rested, panting deeply. Some wiped the sweat off their foreheads and the back of their necks with the hems of their robes.

Sari motioned them forward.

Without complaining, they picked up their royal cargo and resumed following the older woman deeper into the passageway. There were many corridors, but Sari consistently traveled down the farthest left.

Meagan took careful note of this, as well as the presence of a gentle breeze in the corridor, a fact she tucked away.

Sari took another left and came upon double wooden doors with carvings of ancient, mystical, and religious symbols. Although they were not locked, Sari did not have the strength to open the massive doors by herself.

Meagan and several of the initiates pulled at the iron

handles, which formed the image of pouncing uultepes.

Groaning, the doors opened an inch at a time.

One of the smaller women wiggled through a crack between the doors and then pushed from the opposite side as the doors opened out into the corridor. Frightened, she dared not look about her as she heard strange sounds. She was glad when the heavy doors finally opened wide, and lamplight spilled beyond it.

Sari and the Anqarian healer stepped beyond the doors into a voluminous chamber.

The older woman watched Meagan's face as she discovered the secret of the de Magela family. "Behold, the Tree of Life!" whispered Sari.

Meagan's eyes took everything in.

The cavernous chamber contained a small lake. Steam hissed from the water's surface, and Meagan could make out a small island of green rock at its center. In the middle of the island stood a blue plant with wide, flat tendrils extending beyond the rock and into the steaming water.

"There is a boat over there," Sari pointed. "You and I alone must take the queen. The boat will not hold all of us."

"That's the Bogazkoy?" asked Meagan, looking at the limp, unimpressive plant.

Sari barked a cruel laugh. "That's the Tree of Life or

rather what is left of it. It may be too weak to do the queen any good now. It has not been used for almost ten years."

"That is when Queen Abisola started to age," commented Meagan.

Sari nodded. "Queen Abisola wanted what was left of its power for her daughter." Sari instructed the initiates to follow her and place the queen into a small rowboat.

Meagan looked skeptically at the rickety boat, but tucked the hem of her robes in her belt determinedly. "Why is the boat in such poor condition?"

"As I told you. Queen Abisola did not want to use what was left of the Bogazkoy's power, so we rarely came down here. The hot water must have rotted the wood."

Meagan climbed precariously into the boat as it rocked back and forth. She tried to steady herself by grabbing the oars.

Sari climbed in after her and immediately sat down. She checked Maura's breathing. It seemed labored.

Taking the wooden oars from Meagan, Sari began rowing toward the green island.

Meagan placed her hand in the steaming water, pulling it back quickly. "It's very hot!" she exclaimed.

Sari nodded. "The lake is fed by a hot mineral

spring. The Bogazkoy needs the minerals to survive. Taste it."

Meagan gingerly placed her fingertip in the water and then to her tongue. "It tastes salty, but we are hundreds of miles from the sea."

Sari looked at her with a knowing smile. "Yes."

Meagan thought she saw something move under the water and peered down closer to get a better look.

"If I were you, I would not put my nose too close to the water," said Sari.

"Is there something down there?" asked Meagan, pointing to the black, bubbling water.

"I have never seen anything before, but things do not feel right to me. Maybe it is because my nerves are so fraught. Princess Maura has never been here before– I mean the queen." Sari looked uneasily around the chamber.

Meagan shuddered and put her hands in her lap. "Do you think we are safe in this thing?"

Sari dipped the oars silently into the lake. "I don't know. I have never done this before."

"What?"

"I always stood back where your women are. I have never been across the water. I cannot swim."

Meagan blinked several times. She felt her left eyebrow twitch.

Sari grew silent and would say no more, concentrating on rowing toward the island. Finally, the boat reached the rock island, scraping against it.

Meagan pulled the boat closer to the island dock and climbed out.

Sari handed her a battered rope with which to tie up the boat.

Meagan stood on the wooden dock, noticing that many of its planks looked rotten. She whispered a prayer that the boards would hold. Leaning over, she helped Sari pull Maura from the boat.

Sari, not used to such a heavy load, almost dropped the girl into the bubbling water.

Meagan heard her women cry out.

"Oh dear," was all Sari could muster, horrified at her lapse.

Suddenly, something large went under the boat and raised it out of the water several inches.

Sari fell back into the bottom of the boat.

With the heavy fog blowing in her face, it was hard for Meagan to see what circled the rowboat, but she knew it was large. Frightened, she reached down and pulled with all her might, dragging Maura from the boat. She felt the wooden planks start to give under her. With a mighty lunge, Meagan jumped onto a small outcropping of rocks with Maura on her shoulders.

ABIGAIL KEAM

Maura slid off and landed with a hard thud.

Meagan then rolled toward the dock and extended a hand to Sari. As Sari reached for the healer's plump but sturdy hand, the boat rocked again, and she lost her balance.

Meagan could see a green motley creature turn and make its way for the boat again. "Sari, hurry!" she cried.

The older woman looked over her shoulder and saw the monster swimming under the water toward her. Her eyes wide with fright, Sari scrambled to the edge of the rowboat and jumped up just as the boat was smashed into pieces. A great wave of hot spray hit them.

Tearing at Sari's hair and clothes, Meagan pulled her up.

They both clung to the dripping rocks, catching their breath.

Sari's hands and face were bleeding where they had scraped against the jagged stones.

Meagan held a huge hunk of Sari's white hair in her hand. "Here, I think this is yours," she said, trying to put the hair back on Sari's head.

Both women broke into laughter.

Meagan's attention was diverted when she spied the Bogazkoy extending its blue tendrils slowly over Maura's body. She suppressed a shudder. "It's alive," she mumbled.

"It knows the queen is here," said Sari, her breathing relaxing.

"What do we do?"

"Let us pull her closer to the center of the plant. Queen Abisola used to stand in the center, and it would wrap itself around her."

Grasping the queen under the arms, Meagan dragged Maura toward the center of the plant. If she stepped on tendrils, they would writhe upward as if in agony.

Sari followed, helping as best she could.

"Here! Here is the center of the tree," said Sari. They gently placed Maura down at the foot of the main trunk.

Meagan folded the queen's hands.

"Step back," cautioned Sari.

Meagan jumped over the moving tendrils and stood by Sari, reaching for her hand. They waited together, clasping their hands tightly.

Slowly, all of the Bogazkoy's tendrils retracted from the water and moved over the rock, searching for the queen. Upon finding her, they wrapped themselves around the unconscious girl until Maura could not be seen.

Alarmed, Meagan started forward.

Sari caught her arm and held her back. "This is what

the Bogazkoy does."

"She won't be able to breathe," argued Meagan.

"Yes, she will. Let the Bogazkoy do its magic if it has any power left." Sari shrugged. "And if it can not, what difference will it make for the queen to die anyway?"

Finding no fault in Sari's logic, Meagan sat on her haunches studying the Tree Of Life.

The tendrils had wrapped themselves around Maura so tightly as to become a second skin. An acrid smell filled the air. Maura began to twitch inside her cocoon.

Meagan glanced nervously at Sari.

Sari smiled. "It is injecting its serum into our lady. It has some life in it yet."

"What kind of serum?"

"I do not know, but when the queen arises, she will have little puncture wounds all over her body and her orifices will be sore."

"All of them?" asked Meagan incredulously.

"Yes," replied Sari, looking off into the rolling water. "That is why it is sometimes referred to as a 'mating.'"

"Oh," was all Meagan could comment.

The cocoon continued to jerk and twitch, seeming impervious to anything surrounding it.

Meagan soon gained the courage to touch the tendrils. They did not respond to her. Inside the cocoon, she could hear gurgling noises.

"Do not worry," comforted Sari. "This is normal."

"Did Queen Abisola ever complain about pain during this procedure?"

Sari grinned. "The only thing she ever said to me was that it was like being loved by six different men at the same time."

"Well, that could hurt," replied Meagan, feeling the conversation was taking on a disrespectful tone.

"Or it could feel like ecstasy," snorted Sari. "It just depends on one's frame of reference."

It was Meagan's turn to snort. She continued watching, taking mental notes. Then Meagan looked forlornly at the broken pieces of the dock and the rowboat floating in the water. She would think about getting across the water later. Right now, she had a queen to save.

The initiates waited patiently on the other side, occasionally waving and calling. Some prayed to Mekonia, their nature goddess.

A loud wail came from the cocoon. The cry wavered and then fell silent.

Sari rushed to the blue-wrapped mass. "Help me!" she cried. "This is not normal!"

Meagan helped Sari tear the tendrils from Maura.

They had become brittle and broke off, crumbling into dust. After removing many layers of plant wrap, they could see their queen. Her clothes were shredded.

Hastily, the healer pulled plant material from Maura's nose and ears. Realizing that the tendrils had crumbled inside her mouth, she reached inside and began scooping out the debris. She then rolled the young woman over, trying to get her to expel plant material on her own. She hit Maura between the shoulder blades. Getting no response, she pummeled her again and again.

Other Books By Abigail Keam

Princess Maura Tales

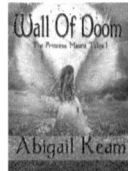 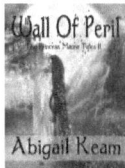   

Josiah Reynolds Mysteries

Last Chance For Love Series

CHECK OUT THE
JOSIAH REYNOLDS MYSTERIES!

"Abigail Keam writes with vision and
understanding."
Midwest Book Review

"We are introduced to a cast of characters and a
storyline that, like honey, is sweet and delicious."
Linda Hinchcliff, Chevy Chase Magazine

"Ms. Keam writes such that readers want to know
more of Josiah's life and the ending will not
disappoint their need to know."
Readers' Favorite

About The Author

Hello, my friend. I hope you are enjoying the Princess Maura Tales. I had such fun writing about Princess Maura and her adventures. If you like to read in other genres, I also write *The Josiah Reynolds Mystery Series* and *The Last Chance For Love Series*, a happily-ever-after sweet romance series. I would love to hear from you.
abigailkeam@windstream.net

If you like my stories, please leave a review and tell your friends about me.

www.abigailkeam.com

www.ingramcontent.com/pod-product-compliance
Lightning Source LLC
Chambersburg PA
CBHW051220120726
47905CB00004B/1200